# Triangle

Originally published in Japanese as *Tomoe* by SHINSHOKAN Co., Ltd., Tokyo

Copyright © 2001 by Hisaki Matsuura

Translation copyright © 2014 by David James Karashima

First edition, 2014

Library of Congress Cataloging-in-Publication Data

Matsuura, Hisaki.
    [Tomoe. English]
    Triangle/Hisaki Matsuura; Translated by David James Karashima. -- First Edition.

    pages cm
    "Originally published in Japanese as Tomoe by SHINSHOKAN Co., Ltd., Tokyo
    Copyright (c) 2001 by Hisaki Matsuura.
    ISBN 978-1-62897-026-5 (alk. paper)
    I. Karashima, David James, translator. II. Title.
    PL856.A8196T6613 2014
    895.63'5--dc23

                 2013049276

This publication was partially supported by the Illinois Arts Council, a state agency, and the University of Illinois (Urbana-Champaign).

ILLINOIS
ARTS
COUNCIL
AGENCY

This book has been selected by the Japanese Publishing Project (JLPP), an initiative of the Agency for Cultural Affairs of Japan

www.dalkeyarchive.com

Cover: design and composition by Mikhail Iliatov;
Printed on permanent/durable acid-free paper

# Triangle

## Hisaki Matsuura

*Translated by* David James Karashima

**DALKEY ARCHIVE PRESS**
Champaign / London / Dublin

*And this spider crawling slowly in the moonlight, and the moonlight itself, and I and you whispering in the gateway …*

—Friedrich Nietzsche, Autumn 1883

# 1
## HILL

WALKING ALONG A sparsely lit street at sunset, when the silhouettes of people and things are melting away, I'm sometimes overcome by the presence of spirits, or what I imagine to be spirits, even though I'm in the middle of Tokyo and not a barren field in the middle of nowhere.

This is exactly what happened to me when, under a violet evening sky, I turned off a street bustling with housewives hurrying home with the makings for supper and people getting off work onto a quiet lane with houses on both sides of the street. Suddenly, it seemed all human life had vanished. I felt like I'd wandered into a wholly different world, a world where spirits lurk. Smells of cooking drifted by, and yet I was convinced that the houses were abandoned, that pots were boiling unattended in bright kitchens, that I had been transported into an unfamiliar place and time. All I needed now was to have my childish fears rise to the surface and tell me something was hiding in the shadows behind the lamppost, its darkness accentuated by a patch of light in front of it, ready to reach out and touch my back. I didn't like it that dusk, known as *ōmagatoki*, "the time of evil encounters," was written with the ideographs for "great misfortune."

The heat of the summer's day had continued to bear down long after the sun had set. I was walking on Hongo Street, then turned into a narrow thoroughfare that ran adjacent to the Agriculture Faculty of the University of Tokyo, and it was exactly at this moment that I was struck by a sense of dread, as if I were standing on the edge of a cliff, looking down at a dark reef swirling with whitecaps. A shiver crawled up my spine, numbness spread through my hips, and I teetered at the edge of the abyss. The darkness grew more intense, but when I lifted my eyes to the sky, a calming blue radiated, making me forget where I was. I kept walking. After a while, I got the feeling something was following me; I smiled and told myself that it was all in my mind, but still I had to turn around to check. The fact that there was no one there did nothing to ease my anxiety. Now, the entire western sky grew tinged with a red that seemed purely sinister—a crimson that stretched like venom, grasping the plains above. What's going on? I asked myself.

I'd just put a woman in a cab, feeling relief that she'd finally left, and as a way of delaying going back to my place, I was taking this walk. She'd made a scene, didn't want to go home, wanted to stay the night, but there had never been any doubt that she really wanted to go home. She just had to have the drama. Of course, I had to participate in the drama, so by the time I managed to get her into a cab, I was exhausted. There was a time when the mere thought of saying goodbye to a lover would have been agony, but now that I was a jaded thirty-something, the best moments with a woman were not when she arrived at your door, or when you were undressing her, but when you watched her face disappear in the window of a cab as it drove off.

I knew that she wasn't seriously considering staying the night—the option didn't exist—but still she had to say it. The truth of the matter was, I was very close to coldly asking her to leave, but I held back and played along with her narcissistic little game by telling her I wanted to be with her longer, even if it was just a half hour. If bitter experience had taught me anything, it was to play along. Today, however, I might have *over*played along, as she fell into a mood as we parted. Once she'd gotten into the cab, she glanced back with a fleeting smile, then turned away; she didn't look back again. Maybe she was reveling in the disappointment of the departure; maybe she was just shifting gears, concocting a story for her husband at home.

But what if she never called again? Well, that would be fine. How long could this go on for anyway? I couldn't keep living my life as if I were wading through mud. Gritting my teeth to stifle my self-loathing, I tried to forget how seeing a woman off in a cab had become something of a ritual for me, tried not to think how worthless my life had become. No job, no money, and only the weakest grasp of another man's woman. This was a life built by picking up the pieces of one that had crumbled. Darkness was the only thing on my horizon, and I knew no way to come back out into the light.

So what was I supposed to do? Place my life in the hands of fate? Leave all decisions to others and fritter my life away—like I always did? Yes, I told myself, that's what I should do, and then I thought how, for a change, I could call her. I could call her and sob pitifully. I could do that much for her. I let these thoughts roll around in my head as I continued walking, then I came to an intersection where five paths met, turned a corner, and kept going, slapping my feet on the ground as I stepped into the further darkness of the night. That was when I felt it again, this shiver up my spine, this sense that something was waiting for me in the shadows. Or maybe this was nothing more than the low point that followed an afternoon of wrestling in the sweaty sheets and musty blankets of my clammy house. By now, I had reached the top of the hill that leads back down to Nezu Shrine, and for a moment, before I continued on this path, I considered turning back. But in the end, everything in this world is simply a matter of chance, isn't it? Anything can be decided by just a roll of the dice.

Halfway down the hill, a man with a shaved head, wearing a white undershirt and boxer shorts, was bending down then standing up, over and over again, with his back to me. The sinister glow of the sky had since faded into amethyst, and against this panorama the scene was not something I could ignore. The man oozed madness. It wasn't an evil madness as much as the kind of madness that might suddenly impel him to pull a knife on a passerby. The thought stopped me in my tracks. This wasn't one of those old areas of town where men cooled off on summer evenings sitting in their long cotton underwear, fanning themselves. No, here a man in shabby underwear doing bends and stretches in the middle of the street could only be described as peculiar. I wanted to keep as far away from him as possible, so I stuck to the opposite edge of the street. As I passed him, I noted, from a sideways glance, that he was wearing rubber beach sandals.

"Hey, Mr. Intellectual! What a pleasant surprise!" he called out to me.

"Oh, it's you," I said, recognizing the guy after all. He wasn't someone I was happy to bump into. He was exactly the kind of person who could go wild with a knife.

"Shun, the Intellectual!" he exclaimed again. "Been a while, hasn't it? What … three, four years?"

"Hmm, guess so."

"You look well. What are you doing? Working for a firm?"

"Yeah, you know, a bit of this, a bit of that, to make ends meet."

"Looks like you're doing pretty good," he said, pointing to the Armani logo on my shirt.

His forehead was narrow, and his eyes were set far apart, making him look like a fool, but the guy, I knew, was not stupid. He seemed to be waiting for me to volunteer information, but I wasn't about to tell him the shirt was a gift from a woman.

"Yeah, right," I said.

"Nice," he said. "Very nice."

His accent was strange; it was like he was singing. And the way he looked standing there—shaven head, undershirt, and boxers—that was really strange. His name, I remembered, was Sugimoto.

"So, are you still at that 'research institute'?" I asked.

"No, no. I quit. Quit that shady business. You were smart to leave when you did."

Sugimoto and I used to be colleagues in a small office with a sign outside that read ORIENTAL ECONOMIC RESEARCH INSTI-TUTE. It was in the backstreets of Okachimachi, near the edge of the bazaar-like Ameyoko, and aside from the chubby, evil-eyed middle-aged man who called himself the director of the institute, Sugimoto and I were the only staff. I stayed for six months, spending almost every day with this guy, teaming up with him to do things that I couldn't tell other people. It was a period in my life that I want to forget.

"I stayed for a year after you quit. Then Shimizu, you know, the so-called director, gradually stopped showing up. The money stopped too, and then yakuza started showing up, so I thought I better get outta here. In the end, they cheated me out of a month's pay."

I guessed that meant that I was lucky for the pittance of a sever-ance I got. But in that kind of job, you expected more.

"What are you doing now?" I asked.

"You know, a bit of this, a bit of that, to make ends meet," he said, snickering. I couldn't tell if he was mocking himself or me.

"Is that right?" I said, as the guy was starting to get on my nerves.

"Well, see you around." Next thing I knew, his expression turned serious, and he spoke to me in an entirely different tone.

"Shun. Excuse me, I mean *Mr.* Otsuki. Are you in a hurry right now?"

"Am I in a hurry? Yes, I suppose I am."

"Well it's actually really fortunate that I bumped into you here. If I remember correctly, you can speak French, can't you?"

"No, I can't. Not at all."

"But you used to be able to speak it fluently."

"I was just pretending."

Sugimoto was referring to my role at the Oriental Economic Research Institute. We'd find some French guy who was strapped for cash, hire him for a day, rent him a suit, and then he'd sit in a hotel lobby chatting with me in French about some professional-looking diagram in front of us. I'd hardly gone to any of my language classes at the university, but I could still string together snippets of basic grammar, which I dressed up with a shameless nasal accent and what I imagined were Gallic gestures. In other words, I was doing my best to create an illusion of being French—Parisian even. All the French guy had to do was time his responses, and to a casual observer, we looked like we were having a proper conversation. Shimizu would then bring over the client, who'd see us having this "consultation," and he'd start telling the guy about the project the Oriental Economic Research Institute was launching in France. It never ceased to amaze me how these jewelers and sweatshop owners in Okachimachi fell for it, and I guess the most important thing this job taught me those six months was that there are plenty of people in the world just asking to be taken for a ride.

"No, no," Sugimoto went on. "You're quite an intellectual. I know you are. Hey, can you come with me for a second? There's somebody I want you to meet."

"Who is it?"

"Um, I suppose you could say he's my sensei …"

"Your sensei?"

"Well, what I mean is, I'm working for this guy at the moment. At that house over there."

I looked where he was pointing, and I had to admit it made me curious. The wooden house would probably be octagonal if you could see it from above, and it was one of the best examples of the old Western-style architecture. I had long admired it. The property was enclosed by a low cast-iron fence, with a gate set a ways in from the street. There was a large garden, which seemed to stretch along the sides of the house to the back, and then there was the octagonal structure covered with ivy. Of course, at this time of the evening, all I could see was the imposing dark shadow it cast. Although the house didn't conjure up such stereotypical images as a young lady playing the piano by the bay window, it did make me want to poke my head in to see what kind of people lived there.

"Apparently he's got something he needs translated into French and he told me to find someone to do it. I thought of you, but I didn't know how to find you."

"You know I've never done any translating."

"Well, it doesn't have to be a professional job. Just a little bit here and there when you have time."

"Translation, huh … ?"

I'd barely passed the French classes I'd taken by cramming the night before the test, and that was years ago. But I remembered that I hadn't minded studying French and that I'd even found pleasure looking up words in the dictionary and slowly making sense of sentences. And it wasn't as if I had anything better to do with my time, which was wasting away like a slug in the sun.

"The pay shouldn't be bad. Come on, just stop by and meet the sensei. Just for a bit."

"Right now? But I have plans. And anyway who is this sensei guy?"

"The sensei? He's a great man." Sugimoto sounded sincere as he stood in front of me with awe in his eyes that seemed to leech the resistance out of me. Now, the Sugimoto I knew never said anything without there being a joke in it. But as I began to piece together his rambling explanation, it seemed that Sugimoto had somehow been rescued by this so-called sensei and was now acting as something like his secretary. Apparently, this sensei was not well known among the "general public"—Sugimoto actually used this word—but in the world of politics and business he was revered. Sugimoto didn't, however, know exactly what the man did, but as far as he could see, the sensei spent every day working on his calligraphy and never went out.

"Calligraphy as in, like, painting words?"

Sugimoto didn't seem to appreciate my response, and to my surprise, his tone turned prickly. "It's not as simple as that. It's calligraphy. I thought you were an intellectual."

"So what are you doing out here in the street in your undershirt and boxer shorts anyway?"

"Yeah, well, I just finished some tasks around the house. There are no other men around, so I have a lot to do. Come on, all you have to do is listen to him for a little. As a favor to me—your old friend?"

Half turning, he beckoned to me as he squeezed through the iron gate, then disappeared into the garden. I owed him nothing— in fact, if anything, he owed me—and as I stood there hesitating, I heard him call out, "Hey, Mr. Otsuki," which irritated me. But in the end, I followed after him. Maybe it had something to do with wanting to move on from the drama with that woman; more likely, it was my desire to see inside that octagonal house. So I slid past the gatepost and past a nameplate with a two-ideograph name I wasn't sure how to read.

I don't know how long I had chatted with Sugimoto on the street, but not a soul had gone by in all that time, and it was now dark. I followed a gravel path that went around a landscaped mound, between bushes, and across the lawn, stepping cautiously because the only illumination was from a patch of light spilling out from a door cracked open ahead. I walked to the light, found the doorknob, and pulled the door open.

I stepped into a dimly lit entrance hall that led to a dark hallway, in front of which stood a woman. For a moment, I was taken aback. I thought it was Hiroko, the woman I'd put into the cab, and that she'd somehow reappeared in a kimono. But then I realized it was a narrow-eyed, middle-aged woman who looked nothing like Hiroko. When her eyes met mine, there was not the slightest change in her mask-like expression. Something about this woman—in a silver-gray kimono with a pale yellow obi that seemed too expensive to wear around the house—was hypnotic. She stood as still as a mannequin, staring into my eyes, leaving me lost for words and with nothing else to do but stare back. I wondered why I had seen Hiroko in the woman when I had never seen Hiroko in a kimono.

It was then that I noticed, standing right behind the woman, a large older gentleman with prominent features and wild white hair, scrutinizing me with cold, reptilian eyes. I was completely unnerved. Had he been there all along? How could I have not seen him right off? Or had he just now materialized? The air stirred with a dustiness, which tickled my nose, followed by a fishy smell. Sugimoto was nowhere to be seen.

"I'm here about a French speaker …" I began. This brought on no response, so I tried again: "I was told you were looking for someone who knew French." Again, no response. When the gentleman finally opened his mouth to speak, it looked as if he considered it a great act of charity. Before long, I would realize that this was how it seemed whenever he spoke.

"Is that what Sugimoto told you?" he said in a deep, clear voice. "Well, my name is Koyama. The screening will start soon, so this way, please." With this, he turned his back to me and started down the hall with a movement that suggested gliding more than walking.

# 2
## TIME

"WHAT IS YOUR concept of time?"

Koyama's monologue started without warning. His face was hidden in shadows, so I could only guess at his expression, but what I could make out was an intense, piercing glare in his eyes as he looked directly at me.

"Throughout ages and throughout cultures, man has had different concepts of time. Prominent among these are the concept of time as something that moves forward in a straight line and as something that comes back around in a loop. But in our everyday lives we use both of these concepts out of convenience. On the one hand, we see time as something that loops around and starts again, like when we talk about how tomorrow is another day, or how the sun will rise again, or how things start anew at the beginning of spring. But on the other hand, we cannot escape the sense that we are simply strolling down a one-way street to life's end. In other words, these circular units such as 'days' or 'years' and these linear units that trace a direct link from birth to death merely present us with different views of time. Personally, however, I don't believe the passage of time can be explained in either of these ways."

As Koyama spoke, his glare did not waver; it was almost mocking.

"Take this example. One winter about ten years ago, in early December, I was walking along the streets of a small town in northern Italy in the middle of the night. It must have been 1983, perhaps 1984. At any rate, it was before the Japanese bubble economy, the bubble that has since burst. Things were on the up back then, and the whole of Japan was full of frivolousness. I didn't like it, so I was spending most of the year abroad. The town in northern Italy was called … Actually, I think I'll keep that information to myself. Suffice to say, it was a hazy, cold night. I was in the old part of town, which had been preserved from the Middle Ages and had labyrinthine paths that were difficult to navigate your way through on a fine day and impossible on that foggy night. I made right after left after right in the hope of finding my hotel, but I soon realized I had completely lost my way. It was past midnight, and although there were streetlights, it was pitch black in the stretches between them. This fog was really very heavy, the kind that made you feel like you were submerged in milk without any sense of direction. I couldn't even read the street names, not that it would have helped without a map. Of course, you imagine I could have asked somebody the way, but by then, the stores and restaurants were closed, and as this town wasn't a particularly popular tourist destination, there was not another soul on the streets. Just a gathering of cats around a dumpster."

This story seemed to be going nowhere, and I was about to speak out of irritation when he gently raised his index and middle fingers to quiet me. His gaze then shifted, as if he was listening to a sound in the distance. I waited, and moments later, a glass door opened with a creak and the woman in the kimono walked in carrying a tray. She placed two steaming cups of tea on the table between Koyama and me, then left without in any way acknowledging my presence.

We seemed to be sitting in a large glass-walled room, like a conservatory, but since tropical plants were everywhere, weaving and tangling themselves into monstrosities, the glass itself could scarcely be seen.

I had followed Koyama from the entrance hall through the house's unfathomable layout, going down the hallway, immediately turning right, walking for a bit, turning left, and emerging into a corridor with glass walls on both sides, beyond which I could see only darkness. We'd continued down the corridor, then Koyama opened a glass door on the left and stepped outside without a word. I was taken aback by his certainty that I would follow, but follow I did, in my stocking feet, and found myself in an open space with marble flooring. I looked up. The night sky, framed by the edges of the roof, glimmered with a scattering of stars, and gentle breezes, with the scent of the trees, caressed my cheeks. A path to the side seemed to lead to the lawn that I'd cut across earlier to get to the front door. From the street, I'd never guessed there was all this land back here. In the middle of the garden was a low fountain filled with water with an abstract metal sculpture in its center. Ten meters beyond was this glass conservatory.

The door had been left ajar, and I'd followed Koyama in. I was immediately overwhelmed by the thick, nauseating perfume of tropical trees. Above a large space of about twenty tatami mats was a glass dome. Koyama turned around, walked past me to close the door, then switched on the lights. But with vines strangling each fixture and leaves smothering every bulb, any illumination was yellow and faint.

Koyama and I had sat down in garden chairs facing each other, looking into one another's faces, as if trying to read the other's mind. I don't know whether it was the psychological effect of being inside this conservatory, but the humidity seemed to rise sharply, and I found myself sweating, even as the marble flooring under my socks seemed cool and comfortable all the while. Not feeling obligated to pay him any compliments, I'd sat there in silence until he said, with a blank expression, "I've heard a lot about you from Sugimoto. I hear you have a lot of women friends."

"That's nonsense," I said, brushing aside his comment. But there was something paralyzing about his composure, something that made you feel like he could see right through you, like there was no point in trying to make excuses.

"Well, that's not important anyway. It's a good thing to be popular with women. I think women are like food. There are some that taste good, some that don't … How can I put it … They're nourishment that a man needs to maintain his health. That is, of course, only if you choose the classy ones and take them in moderation. But if you choose poorly, then you'll suffer from poisoning." His body shuddered, but his face remained expressionless, and it was only a moment or two later that I realized he was laughing.

"They can be a bit like blowfish," I said.

"That's right, they can make you swell up."

"Which can be an interesting experience in its own way."

"I suppose that's a matter of preference. But then there's the question of whether you can get away with just a little swelling. You're a handsome man, Mr. Otsuki, but your jaw line is perhaps a little … soft. Maybe you're attracted to poisonous things." His body shuddered again, and then he added, "I'm sorry, that was unnecessary."

"Okay, I've gone along this far without asking questions," I began. "I think it may be time to move on from ... physiognomy. I don't have all the time in the world, so what's this job Mr. Sugimoto was talking about?"

"You are absolutely right," Koyama said. "There's this film, you see. But before we get into that ..."

And that was when he'd begun his discussion of the concept of time.

"Please drink your tea. It's got a strong mint flavor. I'm not sure if it will suit your taste, but it's my favorite tea."

I could see the bottom of the cup was thick with green leaves. I took a sip of the steaming liquid, and immediately the powerful aroma spread from my mouth to my nostrils and I almost choked. But once I swallowed, the aftertaste of the mint mixed with the bitter notes of the tea pleasantly. I felt my limbs relax and my fatigue melt away.

"This is delicious," I couldn't help remarking.

"Isn't it?" The corners of Koyama's mouth traced the faintest of smiles. And with the same expression on his face, he picked up his story of being lost in a town in Italy in the middle of the night.

"It was a town full of cats. Towns in the Italian countryside are always full of stray cats. Not so in France or Germany. But this particular town had a lot of cats even by Italian standards. There were cats absolutely everywhere, so many that I wondered if there was a law in place to protect them. There were, I suppose you could say, gatherings of cats. It's eerie when you see a dozen or so cats gathered under streetlights together, sitting and lying about, facing in whichever direction they please. And it isn't just in one place. You find these gatherings all over town ... At any rate, I was walking from street to street in a state of confusion when suddenly a human shadow cut across my path on the right. I quickened my pace, approaching it, but there was nobody there. So I continued on my way, a bit perplexed, when suddenly a shadow cut across my path again. I ran toward it, but again there was nobody there. This happened several times. I felt certain my eyes weren't playing tricks on me. Whenever the air stirred and wherever the fog thinned, the shadowy back of a figure in a gray raincoat would appear. I couldn't figure out what was going on."

Koyama spoke captivatingly. Every time I tried to get a word in, he raised the index and middle fingers of his right hand to silence me. Before long, I began to feel as if I was in that Italian town too, walking the maze-like streets alongside Koyama in thick fog. The thick humidity in this conservatory turned into Italian fog condensing on my skin, a cool clarity flowing from the mint tea into my mind.

"Walking through the old town was supposed to bring me to an area with new buildings from where I could easily find the main road back to the train station. But the maze of paths seemed to wind around and around the same old stone buildings, and I felt as if I was going in circles. I couldn't see further than a few meters and I was bumping into the stone walls that rose up in front of me, tripping over abandoned bicycles and stumbling on cracks between the paving stones. Yet every time the fog cleared, even just the slightest bit, the human silhouette would pass in front of me. After some time, I realized the figure always appeared on my right. Never on the left. And every time I sped up after it, the street curved to the left. Strange. Then I caught a glimpse of gray hair above the raincoat, and it dawned on me: I was seeing myself."

As I sat there, I heard water starting to drip. Or maybe it had been dripping all this time and I was only noticing it now. I supposed it could be the water overflowing from the fountain outside the conservatory and running into a narrow channel and into the interior garden where we were sitting.

Koyama started talking in a rather similar way. "I was looking at my own back, you see. You know the term 'now.' People often use it like 'I'm walking now' or 'I like the woman I'm seeing now.' But in reality, the concept of 'now' isn't so simple. What is 'now'? You probably aren't aware of this, but there isn't one 'now.' There are many 'nows.' Or more accurately, there are infinite 'nows.' I don't mean that there are many 'nows' lined up along a linear time line and that people live their lives jumping from one 'now' to the next. Time doesn't work like that. In reality, all the other 'nows' exist within each 'now.' Everything is already contained within it. Infinite 'nows' encapsulate each other and are encapsulated *by* each other in an infinitely over-lapping structure. Encapsulated in every 'now' are the infinite other 'nows' … Listen, this is the important part. We aren't moving forward toward the final destination of death. We go back. We go back to a different 'now.' It doesn't matter if it's a past 'now' or a future one. The past and the future are the same thing. We just make a loop and slip inside a different 'now.' That winter night, the silhouette that appeared, disappeared, and reappeared always on the right—it was me in a different 'now.' Whether it was the 'me' from a second earlier or a few moments later is something I don't know, and it ulti-mately doesn't matter. I was moving back toward it. I wasn't walking forward to a completely different destination. Neither was I making a circle back to where I started. I had gone around and entered a 'now,' but a *different* 'now.' I'd slipped right into a different me …"

"I'm afraid I don't know what I'm supposed to do with these ideas," I interrupted, irritated with the meandering, unbalanced monologue. "You say you just slipped right into a different 'now,' but really, weren't your eyes just playing tricks on you? In the middle of the night, in a thick fog, in an unfamiliar town, it'd be easy to mis-take what you see. You could mistake a dog for a wolf, or a cat for a tiger. There were probably other people who were lost and roaming around the streets at the same time. You could simply have come across someone as he stepped out of an alley. To link it to some con-cept of time seems like a stretch."

Koyama kept his gaze on the ground. His body shuddered, which must have been in amusement, as it was soon followed by laughter.

"You're quite right. I can see why Sugimoto called you Mr. Intel-lectual. 'That man is a walking library,' he said, 'but I don't like the way he looks down on me!' I can see you have a sharp mind—unlike Sugimoto."

If Koyama was trying to appease me, it didn't work; he came off more like a sensei coaxing a poor pupil into studying harder.

"I appreciate your words of praise," I said pointedly.

"Please don't be annoyed. I'm truly pleased to meet you. I—"

"What else did Sugimoto tell you about me?"

"He hasn't told me anything, really. As you said, the conditions in Italy were such that the shadow could have easily been an illusion. But it is at least possible to think of it this other way too. It was as if I'd been wrapped in thick, opaque material—a white darkness or a pitch-black whiteness—and been cut off from the rest of the world. In other words, I was in a state of solitude. The concept of solitude had taken a tangible form and had begun to press down on me. And within such a state of solitude, a truth surfaced, one of those that occur under such conditions. That night, I was able to catch a glimpse of the true form of this world—a glimpse unavailable to us in our everyday lives. You think this is all a joke, don't you? Well, laugh all you like. It seems you have no interest in the 'true form of this world.' And that is unfortunate. But, well …"

Looking slightly hurt, Koyama took a sip of tea, which must have gone cold already, and sat in silence. I likewise sat in silence, slightly embarrassed at my failing to suppress a grin.

Eventually, Koyama began talking in an exhausted voice. "I suppose I might as well finish. As I was saying, the silhouette would appear in front of me on my right. This happened a number of times, and each time it seemed to get closer. Eventually, the silhouette passed so close that I could have reached out and touched it. And that's exactly what I tried to do. I stretched out my right arm and took a big step toward it. As I did, I lost my balance and found myself toppling forward. Perhaps I'd tripped on something, I don't know. But the next thing I knew, the white hair and gray raincoat were right in front of me, and I stumbled … overlapping with the gray silhouette. Overlapped it and became one with it. That's when I returned to my 'now.' I suppose you could say that the 'me' on the other side came back to the 'now' on this side. It's the same thing anyway. Because in every 'now' is every other 'now.' So I returned. To a different 'now' from the one I was in. This is something that very few people have realized, but this is the way in which time flows. By the way, are you fond of money?"

"Well, yes …" I was caught off guard by his sudden change of topic.

"I'm quite sure there isn't anyone who isn't. But the Oriental Economic Research Institute?" His body shook to the rhythm of his snickers. "You said earlier that you had let yourself get dragged into this meeting with me, but I'm sure you won't regret it. There's something I'd like you to lend a hand with ... You were born in Tokyo, Mr. Otsuki? ... Excellent. You see, the task requires that you have some knowledge of Tokyo. But first things first."

Koyama shifted his gaze, which had until then been piercing, raised two fingers on his right hand in a way that seemed to be something of a habit and signaled to someone behind me. I turned and looked into the darkness to see Sugimoto, still dressed in his undershirt and boxers as he emerged from the shadows of an ivy plant. I hadn't noticed him come in at all. Nodding to Koyama, he pulled out a trolley with a film projector on it and began plugging in cables and threading film onto the reel. Then he walked to the other end of the room and pulled down a small screen.

Koyama stood up abruptly and switched off the light. A sliver of light from the main part of the house could be seen through the glass walls of the conservatory, but it was more than dark enough to see a film.

"Shall we begin then?" Koyama said, sounding discouraged.

I turned to him, and he was hunched over in his chair like a shriveled old man. Earlier, when he was rambling on, he'd exuded such energy and vitality that I thought he was in his early sixties, or even fifties, but now he looked aged, maybe in his seventies, maybe late seventies.

"I hope you enjoy this," he said, the film already having begun.

# FILM SCREENING

AT FIRST GLANCE, it looked like nothing but a pile of leaves being buffeted by the breeze. But looking closely, I noticed one leaf moving a little differently to all the others. The camera, as if acknowledging my point of interest, then zoomed in on that very spot as the suspicious leaf began to rock back and forth and to turn slowly around. The next moment, this leaf seemed, like a paper fan, to close itself, becoming gradually thinner until it resembled a stick. Before I could question what I'd seen, another tiny would-be leaf emerged out of the shadow of other leaves. It was then that I could make out two tentacles and two eyes—suggesting that this was an insect. Then, under its body, there was the movement of its tiny legs. Such a bizarre sight, this creature that looked just like a leaf. A leaf insect—a phasmid, I think that's what they're called. The insect spread its green secondary wings, displaying a pattern like the veins of a leaf, and then crawled back among the leaves it resembled so closely.

"What is this? A nature show? An entomology thing on—"

"A little patience, please," said Koyama, quieting me.

The image of this peculiar insect filled an entire screen as wide as two tatami mats, a few meters in front of me, and though I didn't find it uninteresting, it was grotesque, like a freak show, leaving me feeling rather uncomfortable. Then, suddenly, the insect's wings began to melt away into a green patch, and by some kind of trick photography, this patch began to expand and morph until it became like human skin or, to be more precise, the skin of a man and woman in the explicit throes of sex. White skin and dark skin tangled in sweaty desperation, but the scene was less the erotic act of lovemaking than a close-up of genitals having intercourse. Now, I'm not a prude, but to be pulled off the street at dusk and made to sit through tasteless pornography with a creepy old man wasn't my idea of enjoyment. And what made it even worse was Koyama shaking with laughter. I wanted to get up and leave.

Yet I sat there, watching the glistening cock pumping in and out of those pink lips, over and over and over again. This cock looked a lot thicker than mine—but was it really thicker or did it look thicker because of the angle of the camera? Well, I'd seen enough, I was getting fed up with this business, but then the man pulled the woman up and she straddled him, and I got a look at her face for the first time. She was young and beautiful, which took me by surprise. She had a perfectly oval face, with a thin nose and a striking, full upper lip that turned up slightly at the corners. Her hair was long, falling to the middle of her back, and she kept wiping it away from her face. Between sharp cries of pleasure, her breathing was heavy, and if not for the support of the man's hand, she looked like she might collapse. It was at this point that their individual voices began to be heard, gradually growing louder and louder.

The girl was drenched in sweat, from her face to her breasts as well as down her back, where her jet-black hair was pasted to her porcelain skin. Her eyes were closed, her lashes long. Every so often, tears formed into droplets that trembled on her lashes, before rolling down her face. But what surprised me most was how young the girl was. The swell of her breasts suggested that they had just begun to blossom, and the size of her nipples standing pertly led me to think she couldn't have been older than her mid-teens—perhaps even younger. What was going on?! This young girl, whose shoulders and hips had yet to fill in, was crying out in ecstasy in the arms of this muscular, sweaty, dark-skinned hulk of a man!

In the next moment, the image began to melt into a swirl of colors, which then dissolved into a dark ocher. But the image soon shifted to a close-up of a hornworm with a blue vein that ran the length of its body, squirming its way through dirt of the same dark ocher. The camera followed the progress of the hornworm, which began to swell and pulsate, almost violently, around its middle. The next thing I knew, the hornworm's body erupted, and out tumbled some white thing, which the camera closed in on, bringing it into sharp focus. It was a maggot, and its head filled the entire screen. The mouth was large and ferocious, with sharp teeth that seemed still to be chomping at bits of the worm. The maggot lingered for only a few seconds, then crawled back into the hornworm, having hatched from eggs that the hornworm was unwittingly carrying. Now this parasite maggot was going to grow into adulthood by feasting on its host. In its weakened state, the hornworm continued to twitch and squirm.

It occurred to me that I'd once read about a bee that had this disgusting practice. The bee stings its host with just enough poison to stop it from moving, then lays the eggs. The poison's not enough to kill the worm because if it were to die, then the flesh would rot and the larvae would be left without a source of fresh food. The mere thought of this was paralyzing.

Again, the image on the screen changed. The twitching hornworm melded in the ocher earth, which faded into the man and the girl having sex, tiny bubbles oozing out at the edge of her mouth. This time, the girl's cries made me quiver, and I got the distinct feeling that the thick sweet smell permeating the conservatory was not from the tropical plants but from the sweat of this girl, who was clutching the man's head to her chest as her delicate body trembled.

The scene changed again—this time to a close-up of a purple butterfly laying eggs on the back of a leaf. Glistening, gelatinous eggs filled the screen, which then dissolved into the skin of the girl having sex. From this point, I cannot remember the exact order of the scenes. Next may have been a praying mantis clasping a stoic smaller mantis in its pincers, ripping its head apart with her teeth. That is, I assumed it was female, post-coitus, from the savagery. She did not stop until she had consumed all but the hind legs of her mate, which she abandoned on the ground. Backing up the action, the camera focused on one eye of the male, looking out from a half-eaten head as the female tore into him—it showed not a hint of expression. The compound eye slowly filled the screen. The image then faded, and when the camera zoomed out again, I was looking into the beautiful brown eyes of the girl, who stared straight out at me and betrayed no trace of emotion.

The structure of the film was simple—scenes showing the habits of various insects inter-spliced with scenes of explicit pornography. The combination was grotesque, and as I watched, time and space began slowly to twist in my mind. The transitions from insect to girl and from girl to insect were so smooth, the images blurring and changing in a way that my own responses and desires blurred and changed.

Ants swarmed over a dead beetle. A semi-transparent crane fly emerged from its pupa. The rainbow wings of a tropical butterfly revealed a large eye-like pattern; on the brown wings of a moth it was a spiral pattern. In between each, the man and the young girl went at it, and at one point, the ecstatic cries of the girl were reverberating at a deafening volume, regardless of the image on the screen. Was ecstasy akin to gut-wrenching revulsion and fear akin to ecstasy so sweet it could melt the entire body? I could feel my nerves desensitizing, growing numb, and I no longer felt sure about what I was looking at. My perspective expanded and contracted erratically—endlessly large one moment, infinitesimally small the next—and I couldn't tell if I was looking at the screen or whether the butterfly's and girl's eyes were staring at me.

I'm not sure how much longer the film went on. Perhaps an hour, perhaps two. Apparently towards the end I was dozing, or more accurately, I was staring at the screen in a half-conscious state. I had the feeling that, besides insects, there was a goldfish with glittering scales making its way across the screen, that a giant salamander covered in warts was blowing bubbles underwater, but I couldn't be sure of that either. When I came to my senses, the movie projector had stopped and the screen was blank. Koyama and Sugimoto were sitting in silence, the lights off, as if waiting for a word from me. Or perhaps they were looking at each other and laughing at how I'd fallen asleep.

I sat up and said, stupidly, "I see." I wondered how much time had passed since the film had ended. Before, when I'd had to listen to Koyama's long-winded monologue about "time," I'd had the illusion that my mind was getting clearer and more alert. Now, my mind felt heavy and swollen. Was this another effect of the mint tea?

"I see," I repeated myself. "It was ... interesting ..." I was having trouble finding words.

"So you liked it then?" said Koyama.

Sugimoto remained quiet in the chair behind the projector. In fact, he hadn't made a peep since stepping into the conservatory.

"Yes, it was interesting," I said.

"Is that right?" said Koyama. "Well, if that's the case, you may be interested in the job."

Without turning the lights on, Koyama began to talk about the job in a way that was very vague, yet very detailed at the parts where detail seemed completely unnecessary. So, overall, I wasn't clear on anything. What he did seem to be saying was that the film was not complete, that further filming and editing were needed, that completion of the project would take several months, and that he wanted me to help with the "task."

"The director, or the guy making this film, is a young, talented guy," said Koyama. "I think you'll get along with him."

"I'm not exactly sure what you want me to do."

"We can discuss that gradually."

"But something like this, even if we finish it, it's not something that can be shown in Japan."

"We're thinking mainly of the European market. That's where your French will come in handy," Koyama said in the dark.

"My French really isn't good enough to be of any use," I said.

"Let's not worry about that. But to be honest with you, the whole idea of public screenings or commercial considerations is of secondary importance. The important thing is to produce a good piece of work."

"Well, there really is no way you'd be able to show this in public. Maybe you could sell it as an illegal porn video …"

The old man fell silent. Several moments passed this way. Uneasy, I was ready to open my mouth when Koyama muttered, "You have no idea." He said this in a voice that could barely be heard, but the tone was angry enough to freeze the atmosphere of the room. "An illegal porn film? This isn't anything of the kind. This is a work of art. I thought you would understand. I must have been wrong about you."

"No, I understand, of course," I found myself saying, as if to please him. "It gave me a strange feeling."

Apparently Koyama didn't like that comment either, and he shut up for what seemed a long time. Then: "A strange feeling? Fine."

Once again, silence in the room. Perhaps he was trying to control his temper. Then he took a deep breath and said, "So, how about it? Will you lend us a hand?"

I was hesitant. I had the time, and I had images of the girl's brown eyes, delicate limbs, and sparse pubic hair burned into my mind. But dealing with the old man was like being face-to-face with an enormous bug. He gave me the creeps. Still, I was curious. Not about his flow-of-time nonsense but about the whole funny business, about his ulterior motive.

"Let me think about it," I said. My mind was dull and hazy, and I was in no state to make a decision. I was thinking that I should go home and that if I didn't, I would collapse at any moment.

"Fine," said Koyama, "but I'd appreciate it if you'd make arrangements with Sugimoto to get in touch with you. That's all for today." He then stood up with the abruptness of a man used to ending conversations whenever he liked. It left me dissatisfied, but I had no say in the matter and I stood up myself. Without any words of leave-taking, Koyama walked toward the door of the conservatory, pausing to point nonchalantly into the darkness beyond the fountain. "You can leave from over there," he said. "If you go straight a little bit and turn left you'll come to the garden in front of the house." Then, shifting his gaze to the side of me, he added in a different tone of voice, "Get the gentleman his shoes."

I turned around. Sugimoto was holding the shoes I'd kicked off at the front door. With a serious expression on his face, he set them down before me. As I slipped them on, I tried to catch his eye, wanting to shoot him a look that said, "Hey, what's going on here?" But Sugimoto didn't look at me and didn't say a word. He was hunched over, and I got the feeling that he was cowering; I knew him too well to think it was an act.

Once, when we worked together at the Oriental Economic Research Institute, we'd been given the task of going out to collect on bills. Sugimoto never raised his voice during these visits, but his threats were no less intimidating than if he were a real yakuza. His intensity suggested a suppressed viciousness that made you fear that he'd kill you if you pissed him off, and it sent shivers down my spine even as I stood by his side trying to imitate him. So to observe him now in this pathetic state—cowering like a dog, ears drooping, tail between his legs, trying to please his master while fearing the whip—it was hard to believe, but you didn't doubt it.

My attention turned to the full moon that had appeared between the clouds, illuminating the surroundings and myself with a blue ray that made me feel like I was back in my dream. The daytime heat had cooled, and a slight breeze was drifting through the darkness. I wasn't wearing a watch, and I had no idea of the time, but it couldn't have been midnight. I stretched my back and suddenly felt overwhelmed with fatigue, and for a second, I thought my legs were going to give way from below me.

"You okay?" Koyama asked with a hint of what I thought was mockery. My brain burned with anger and shame. I was about to walk off when Koyama spoke in a completely different voice: "So you're back then?"

I turned around to see him addressing the slim figure of a girl at the end of the corridor that led to the conservatory. Because of the lighting, I couldn't see her face, although she seemed to be looking in my direction.

"Ah, Mr. Otsuki," said Koyama, who hadn't left the room yet, "this is my granddaughter. You may have the impression that this isn't the first time you've met." As he spoke, his body shuddered with laughter.

That was when it dawned on me: this girl, in a white T-shirt and jeans, with her belly button peeping out from bared midriff, was the girl having sex with the man in the film.

"Her name is Tomoe. She's a good girl. I'm sure she's pleased to make your acquaintance."

# 4
## Morning Glory

When I look at a morning glory blooming in the moist air of a summer dawn, I think that there can be no flower more beautiful. The bud begins to open at midnight, and the flower reaches full bloom at around four in the morning. It stays this way for several hours, but by nine o'clock the flower is beginning to wilt.

Since it was normal for me to sleep past noon, it wasn't often that I got to see the flowers in bloom. But on days when my bladder got me out of bed in the early morning and I caught sight of the dozen or so morning glories in full bloom, then their vivid red and deep purple made me forget momentarily the down-and-out feeling that has dogged me for the past several years. Sometimes I think I should use this as a way to motivate me into leading a regular life again—one where I get up in the morning, cook a pot of rice, prepare miso soup, and make a decent start to the day. But, as I stand admiring the large petals and breathing the clean summer-morning air, I start to feel that everything is unbearably bright, even though the sun isn't even completely out yet, and I retreat to the darkness of my room, with its closed shutters and stale smell of cigarettes, and crawl back under the covers.

I could have easily forgotten the evening I spent at that big house next to Nezu Shrine, pushed it out of memory as a strange onetime experience. But deep within me, there was an itching sense of expectation, combined with repulsion, and for days I couldn't get old man Koyama and the sixteen-millimeter film out of my mind. You might think this was because I had too much time on my hands. It's true that I was squandering my time, doing no work at all, but I was in the middle of a long recovery period. Of course, to describe this time as recovery makes it sound like things were getting better. In reality, I just couldn't shake the nagging feeling that I would be stuck in this rut for good, rotting away to nothing.

Two years had passed since I'd gotten myself out of my drug-drenched days. I was no longer wandering around Kabukicho in a scrawny body with glaring eyes and feeling like I was walking on mush with every step. But the feeling that somebody was following me hadn't disappeared—it was an anxiety that occasionally peaked in a sudden fit of restlessness even when I was sitting at home, leaving me desperate. I'd tell myself I could go back to a normal life if I could just put my mind to it, but then even the simplest thing, like talking on the phone, was more than I could handle. The inorganic, characterless voice that came through the receiver would, when the first words entered my ear, unnerve me inexplicably and I'd start to wonder if the person on the other end of the line was smirking, making fun of me, lying to me. Sometimes I'd wonder whether the other person even existed, or if the line was split so that an evil third person could listen in, and if that person was the guy who owned the print shop next door who was always giving me nasty looks. These thoughts would eat me up, I'd spiral out of control, and I'd be unable to utter a single word into the phone.

The side street that extends from the botanical gardens of University of Tokyo in Koishikawa was lined with print shops and small factories, and on days when it rained heavily, the smell of sewage would drift into the area and mingle with the ever-present smell of ink. It wasn't exactly a high-class area, but there was something about it that had always appealed to me. It was calming to stroll though the narrow streets where you could hear the *clunk-clunk* of the printing presses. After leaving the hospital, I'd moved in with relatives in Nakano. But sponging off them grew uncomfortable after a while, and I thought it best to get my own apartment. I dragged myself to the subway and found myself heading for this neighborhood, probably because of fond memories. I walked into a realtor's office, and the first place they showed me was an old house on the backstreets. I don't think I found it particularly appealing, but I was already getting worn down by the whole ordeal, so I decided to take the place then and there. It was a two-story house, but the rent was no more than for a cheap apartment, so the real estate agent's hackneyed pitch that this was "a great deal you rarely come across" wasn't completely unfounded. But it wasn't all that great either. It was located at the end of an alley and, because the southern exposure faced a gulley, it only got sunlight in the one six-mat room on the second floor, and even then only for several hours in the morning. There must have been seepage too, because the walls sprouted mold even when it wasn't the rainy season. I learned all of this only after I'd moved in, of course.

There was no garden either, but there was a small patch of earth next to the lattice gate in front of the house, and it was there I planted the morning glory seeds I'd bought for a hundred yen. Considering the daily struggle to get out of bed, it was surprising that I never tired of taking care of them. I built a bamboo trellis for the vines to wrap around, and I watered the plants regularly. In turn, it seemed, the plants responded to my attention.

In truth, I wasn't really worried about rotting away; instead, I was engaged in a kind of fantasy to see how far I could let myself go, how deep a hole I could wallow in, before reaching nothing. Or maybe what I was really afraid of was the gradual loss of the sensibilities that let me entertain the notion of sliding into oblivion. These were, after all, long and listless days. I'd be struck, every so often, by the feeling that I could no longer stand living like a parasite, but it was a minor irritation that never lasted long and soon enough I'd be overwhelmed by the feeling that rotting away suited me just fine.

About a week after that evening in Nezu, Hiroko came over to my house and stayed the entire afternoon. On days like that, the noise from the printing press next door was welcome, and, as I also had the shutters closed, I was pretty certain the sounds of our lovemaking wouldn't be heard outside. But as I was walking back home after seeing Hiroko off, I passed the old man who was my neighbor, and he gave me a disapproving stare.

When I told Hiroko about it the next week when I saw her, she said I was imagining it. When I persisted, she gave me a dismissive look and told me I was too timid. But she couldn't care less about what the neighbors thought of me. She didn't have to live here.

"So you're saying Koyama was getting his kicks by forcing his granddaughter to do sick stuff while he videotaped it?"

"It was a film, not a video. A sixteen-millimeter film. But yeah, that's the gist of it."

"So he's a pervert."

"Yeah, I guess."

"Of course he is. And this guy Sugimoto. He's the guy you used to work with in Okachimachi, right? You were telling me he was completely out of his mind."

"Yeah, he's crazy. Insane. His eyes were always wandering, and I could never tell what he was looking at. He was freaky."

"Is she pretty?"

"She? Oh, the girl. Um … yes, she did have kind of a cute face. But she was a child." This would have been a good moment for some nauseating flattery, like, "Well maybe, but nowhere near as beautiful as you." But my mind was blurred by exhaustion, and it wouldn't have been flattery anyway because Hiroko really was a rare beauty.

"But she was really doing it, this child."

"She was. And really going at it. Her face was red. I mean, what the hell was that all about?"

"How would I know?"

Hiroko wasn't in a very good mood. Two or three days ago, a couple of guys from an appliance store had showed up to install air conditioners in my house. Immediately, I knew Hiroko had sent them, but I didn't like it that she did it without telling me. Why couldn't she just say she wanted the place nice and cool so we could go at it without soaking ourselves in sweat? That was her point, wasn't it? I made it clear that I was annoyed, which put her in a foul mood, so the rendezvous ended up being pretty disappointing. Nonetheless, when she left, she placed a wad of money on the table and told me I should put it toward my rent. I accepted it gratefully; any ability to feel shame about such things had long been worn away.

As I was telling Hiroko about the night with Koyama and Sugimoto, I suddenly remembered how, while I was in something of a hypnotic state, at the exact moment that there was a close-up of the moon on the screen, outside the glass conservatory the clouds parted to reveal a real full moon. I got the eerie feeling that what was happening in the film dictated what was happening in the real world. But because I found it difficult to put this strange experience into words, I decided not to say anything about it. I put out my cigarette and began to make love to her again so as to fill in the absence of conversation, but that dark sky with its twin moons hovered. I even imagined that the two moons overlapped and became one, just as I experienced a long, intense ejaculation—smelling Hiroko's slightly sour breath in my face.

The vision left me feeling stifled, guilty, but I didn't understand why. As soon as I'd sent Hiroko on her way again, another close-up vision of the moon came to mind, except this time the moon was reflected on the surface of a lake. It was an image from the final scene of the film, which had then faded into nothing. It brought with it a frightening vertigo—a feeling of falling, flailing, into the void. But there was no way I could know whether this fragment of memory was real or not, and the irritation of this uncertainty burned inside me.

That night when I lay down to sleep, I was overcome by the desire to watch the film one more time—not to look at the naked Tomoe having sex, but to take a closer look at the final image of the moon. It was a desire that wouldn't leave me, that kept sleep at bay as I tossed and turned into the night.

The next evening, I stepped out of my front door, locked the front gate, and was about to start walking toward the main street, when Sugimoto happened to come around the corner. I say happened to, but I doubt it was a coincidence.

"So, here it is. Your place is hard to find," he said, grinning and talking like we were the best of friends.

He was wearing jeans, a collared shirt, and a red baseball cap—a relatively conventional outfit compared to what he'd been wearing the last time we met. When he removed the cap, revealing his shaven head, and began to fan himself with it, he still looked like an oddball, though.

"Yeah, I guess it is a little hard to find," I said. "Ah ... I'm just on my way out ..."

I was debating whether I should invite him in, but I didn't want him to see what a dump the place was. Sugimoto picked up my hesitation and said, "Don't mind me. I just came by with a message. It's about that thing the other night. The sensei is really counting on you to take the job on, Mr. Otsuki."

"He's counting on me? What was that all about anyway?"

"You heard the sensei's explanation. Well, that's all there is to it."

"Explanation? I couldn't understand a thing. One minute he's going on about 'time,' then suddenly he shows me this porn—"

"Don't call it porn," Sugimoto said, cutting me off sharply. "You'll upset the sensei. You heard what he had to say. He'd like your help." Then Sugimoto brought up money—a surprisingly large amount of money.

"I'm not sure I understand what he wants me to do for that kind of money."

"First, come to where the filming is taking place. You'll be told the details then." He handed me a piece of paper with a phone number and an address in Nihon-zutsumi, Taito ward.

I stared at the piece of paper for a while, wondering what to do. This gave Sugimoto the chance to start making small talk.

"The heat's been deadly these past weeks. Tokyo summers haven't always been like this, or have they? I walked all the way here, but as I went downhill from Hakusan-ue, it felt like it was getting hotter and hotter. Must be this area; it's like a basin, I guess, doesn't get any breeze ..."

As he went on, I thought of old man Koyama, how someone living in a mansion like that could probably be expected to make good on the money. But there was still so much I was unclear about, and I wasn't sure I wanted to have anything to do with an old man who could be extremely forceful and yet affable to the point where you felt he was reading your mind.

In the end, I said, "I'm sorry." It was probably the first time in years that I'd decided to go against the wishes of others, as demonstrated by the relationship with Hiroko that I had let drag on. "I'm sorry," I said again, "I've got a lot on my plate at the moment. But thank you for the offer."

"Come on, don't say that, Shun," Sugimoto said, suddenly acting a lot more familiar. "You've got to do it. For me! Come on, please!"

"I don't know."

"The sensei says he has the feeling he's known you for a long time. He says he really likes you."

"I didn't ask to be liked."

We carried on in this way for several minutes, with me saying "I'm sorry" and him saying "come on" back and forth. Gradually his tone changed from earnest pleading to direct request to threat. I had, of course, expected this, and though his threatening did nothing to change my mind, his sheer persistence made my resolve start to cave in.

"All right then, let me think about it a little more," I said with the half-hearted conviction of a person in recovery.

Sugimoto wasn't satisfied with that response, but maybe he was tired of sweating and arguing in the heat. "All right then, think about it," he said. "I'll contact you again." Then he turned around and left.

I watched him walk away, dread building within me as he tugged repeatedly on his cap.

The next day I woke after noon, as usual, and slipped on my sandals thinking to go out and put some cold noodles in my stomach. I opened the front gate and turned to admire the collage of bright colors of my morning glories on the vine. But to my horror, each precious flower had been ripped off and thrown to the ground and stamped on! The red and purple blossoms were torn and crushed and smeared in dirt. It was like someone had stomped on *me*!

I backtracked into the house, sat down on the edge of the entrance, closed my eyes, and pressed my fingers against my eyelids. I couldn't breathe. My heart pounded. I couldn't get the vision of the crushed morning glories out of my mind. I hurt. I was in terrible pain. My healing wound had been ripped open.

"The bastard," I muttered to myself. I wasn't feeling anger; I was feeling fear—a fear that turned my legs to jelly.

*A glimpse of the true form of this world!*

My lazy days spent soaking in sweet decadence in the sun—had they ended?

*She's a good girl.*

"The bastard," I muttered again. "The bastard!" And I sat there trying not to shiver.

# 5
## FLASK

I TOYED WITH the thought that the entire world was contained in a thin, fragile flask glowing in a room somewhere. And as such absurd thoughts flickered through my mind, I stuck one leg in front of the other in persistent rhythm until, before I knew it, I'd climbed the pedestrian bridge over the Yamanote train tracks and could see the sky around me fading into night. To my left was the greenery of Yanaka cemetery, which meant I was between Uguisudani and Nippori. Another day had gone by just like that. Only then did it occur to me that I hadn't eaten a thing all day, and a cold, hollow feeling moaned inside me. It was a yearning more than a hunger that rose from the pit of my stomach.

So there's the whole world, you see, and it's contained in a small flask made of glass so fine you could hear it tinkle if you ever touched it; and this flask is sitting on a dust-covered desk in the low-ceilinged attic of a long-forgotten house. In one corner of this work surface are various odds and ends, like a headless model of the human body, rusty scissors, a bent screw, broken machine parts, an enormous leather book stuffed with stained pages of numerical equations and indecipherable diagrams. And among these objects is the small flask emitting a dim glow and a faint buzz. One of these days, in an instant, without warning, that light could extinguish and that buzz could fall silent, bringing total silent darkness to the flask. But that instant could be the equivalent of billions of years in our world.

As I'm about to fall asleep, bizarre thoughts like this sometimes creep beneath my closed eyelids and help me to relax. But, really, isn't it my subconscious trying to stir into my being some encouragement?

I was walking along the pedestrian bridge, when I was hit by a wave of sheer exhaustion that made me reach—no, cling—to the iron handrail as I tried to catch my breath. What the hell was I doing here anyway? After the encounter in front of my house, Sugimoto had called many times and paid several more visits—or rather, he'd appeared out of nowhere several times, wearing that same red base-ball cap and grin on his face, when I'd just happened to be going out—until finally I gave in and promised to be at the address in Nihon-zutsumi at a specified time.

In the library, it didn't take me long to find out that Masamichi Koyama was in fact a renowned calligrapher. He was born in Tokyo in the twelfth year of the Taisho era, 1924, which made him a little over seventy. After being awarded the top prize at various calligraphy exhibitions, he'd served as president of the Japan Calligraphers Association from 1984 to 1988, when he was awarded the Order of the Rising Sun, Gold Rays with Rosette. In the biographical encyclopedia, his work was described as "combining a bold architectural beauty with gentle musicality" and "melting the surge of traditional energy into a formal modern experiment"—words that sounded like the ramblings of a sleep-talker to me. In short, he was a respected person. Certainly not the kind of person you'd expect to be mixed up in this kind of business.

It had been a gray, gloomy day, with constant streams of cars pumping thick exhaust fumes into the humidity. As I leaned my head over the railing, trains roared by, and the thought occurred to me that I might feel better if I threw up on them. I had been feeling terrible all day, and getting worse, but nothing came up.

As far as I remembered, the pedestrian bridge over the Yamanote tracks was part of Kototoi Street, which would take me to Kototoi Bridge over the Sumida River. My plan had been to walk to Asakusa, but when I was overcome by exhaustion, I wasn't able to continue. I turned and looked toward Ueno, catching the end of a dark-red sunset that gradually dissolved into darkness.

*Becoming tainted.*

*To have become tainted.*

*Becoming more tainted.*

These words found their way to the corners of my mouth, and I was filled with dread that a dark, heavy weight would come crushing down on the delicate, shiny flask.

*To become tainted.*

*To become more and more tainted.*

Wasn't that the most terrifying thing that could happen to this world? Since my morning glories were ripped from their vines, that fear—the stifling fear that had plagued my junk withdrawal—had come back to stay twenty-four hours a day. It was a constant reminder that something that was not me could invade my body anytime, anywhere. Suddenly, the wall I'd built between myself and the world was punctured with holes, battered until thin, until it no longer served any real purpose, allowing evil spirits to come and go as they pleased, eating away at my insides. When Sugimoto appeared after the mutilation of the flowers, he didn't so much as glance at the vines on the trellis and not once did he mention them in conversation. But I got the message. And there was no doubt he knew I'd gotten the message.

The idea of me worrying about *becoming tainted* when I'd already fallen so far brought a self-derisive sneer to my lips. Snapping myself out of this state, I started to move my legs again, walked to the other end of the pedestrian bridge, down toward Uguisudani, then turning off Kototoi Street and continuing on through the area divided into Shitaya, Iriya, and Ryusen, making left and right turns onto narrow roads. The streets in this far-from-spectacular district ran like the grid on a chessboard, with one boring two- or three-story building after the next, wholesale stores, homes, and small shops without signage where discussions could be seen taking place, but you had no way of knowing what kind of trade it was. This wasn't the kind of friendly, tightly knit community that people imagine when they think of old *shitamachi* neighborhoods, nor was it a vibrant area with new apartment and office buildings shooting up out of the ruins of old houses. But I guess everywhere in Tokyo had lost a little buzz since the bubble economy. Then again, even back when the price of land was skyrocketing all over Tokyo and I'd been busy living off the skim of the bubble as a so-called office worker nearby, this little area was stagnant.

I walked down from Kokusai Street, past the red-light district Yoshiwara, across Doté Street and into a part of Nihon-zutsumi where the atmosphere changed abruptly. This was Sanya—an area that would shock most Japanese. Here, day laborers who hadn't been selected for work hung out in their belly bands and tabi socks and, with beer in hand, stared at each passerby.

But I knew the area like the back of my hand, and the men lying on the sides of the road—their filthy torsos bared as they slopped down drink—didn't faze me. I walked down a shopping arcade that seemed to be frozen in the years just after the war, but with no vitality. At the open counter of an eatery where a pot of pig-intestine stew simmered, a man blabbered on incoherently; slumped against the sake vending machine was another poor soul, clutching an empty glass.

This was where Koyama had his film production studio?

At the police box, another laborless laborer was trying to engage the cop in conversation, waving his cup of sake around. "Killings, y'know? Murders ... lot of them these days. A few too many, don' ya think? There are, right? I'm right, ain't I? Huh? You watch TV and you'll see. One day there's a murder, another day there's another murder. People getting their heads cut off. Their arms and legs cut off. Japan ... at this rate ... is really, I think, really goin' ..." The bored cop humored the drunk, nodding a "yes" or an "is that so?" politely.

By the time I reached the other end of the shopping arcade, which led to the most rundown part of Sanya, it was night. I was exhausted from the long walk, but when your body gets that tired, you don't have the energy to focus on your inner struggles. The exhaustion was refreshing, and my anxieties seemed to dry up.

Before long, I spotted the Takabatake store with its rust-covered shutters, just as Sugimoto had described it on the phone. Above the store was a flaking sign that read: "We Buy Furniture for Best Prices—Year Round Bargains—Everything 100 Yen!" I walked around the corner, passed a cinder-block wall, and came to a wooden gate. The gate slid open with ease but loudly enough, apparently, for someone to have heard it. "Over this way!" I thought I heard a deep male voice beckon from the back of the building. I couldn't see an entrance anywhere, and as the only option was the dark, narrow space that stretched between the building and the wall, I squeezed in and made my way down the passageway.

The building was much larger than it appeared from the street.

As I approached what seemed to be a turn to the left, I heard footsteps, then a white shape came running towards me, and the next thing I knew, this white blur bumped into me. Astonishingly beautiful eyes, brimming with tears, peered up at me. One cheek was swollen, and her lip was bleeding. She was wearing a white T-shirt. Sobbing, she muttered a rush of words, then pushed me away, ran, and dashed into the street, leaving the gate wide open. I hadn't been able to say a word.

I wasn't sure, but I think she said, "Please." Did she mean, "Please get out of the way"? Or "Please let me go"? She might have also said "don't" between sobs, I couldn't be sure. And I couldn't tell if she remembered me from our strange meeting in the conservatory of Koyama's mansion several weeks before. But if she wasn't asking me to let her escape, then what was she saying? What was going on? I paused for a moment and considered the situation, but instead of following the trail of the sweet scent of the girl's hair, I continued on my way.

I turned the corner and found a path that extended straight between the store and the neighboring building. There was even less light, and I was unsure of my footing, but eventually I came out into a rather large open space. Huh? A garden hidden in the middle of a shopping arcade in this section of town? A tall, well-built man emerged and stood before me, looming, large, and imposing. He seemed to be about forty years old, but with his expressionless, unshaven face I couldn't be sure. He looked me in the eyes, rather disturbingly, before glancing away; I wondered if he was the one who'd said, "Over this way!" Abruptly, he turned around and walked noisily into the shadows of the building; he was wearing wooden sandals. Next, a man descended the stairs from the porch of the main building, making his way to me over stepping stones. It was Masamichi Koyama himself. He held his gaze with an unblinking, reptilian glare and seemed in no hurry to say anything. I kept my mouth shut, too. He finally spoke after a few more seconds, not bothering with a single word of greeting, "Did you bump into Tomoe?"

"Yes, she was crying."

"We had a little misunderstanding. You know girls that age … can never tell what they're thinking."

Silence again, this time for quite a long while as if each of us was waiting for something to interject. I heard purring and turned to see a big, black cat on a low garden table, its tail pointing straight up, rubbing against an abstract metal sculpture of spheres and spirals. Where had I seen this sculpture before? I couldn't be sure, but quite possibly it was a reproduction of the metal sculpture in the garden of Koyama's mansion. And the stone base it stood on looked just like the base of the fountain in the center of Koyama's garden, except that, whereas the fountain in his garden was overflowing with water, this one was dry and seemed to have been appropriated by the cat.

That was when the full picture started to dawn on me. Why hadn't I figured it out earlier? I suppose I could blame the darkness and the shadows and the shrubs planted at the perimeter, presumably for privacy, but on the other side of the sculpture there stood a dome-topped glass conservatory, which was, believe it or not, identical to the one at Koyama's house in Nezu. I realized just how much I wasn't paying attention when I looked down at my feet: The entire outdoor space was laid with blackish, irregular-patterned marble. In other words, this was, with little variation, a replica of Koyama's inner garden at his mansion in Nezu. Same sculpture, same fountain, same area, same layout of the house, which was sort of like a crescent.

"This ... this garden ..."

I don't know if he heard the words that slipped past my lips, but his response was to mumble, as if to himself, "Moon isn't out tonight."

Out of reflex, I turned to look up at the sky, too. He was right—wasn't out tonight. "Well, here I am, just as I was told," I said.

The old man had no reaction.

"So what should I do? You want me to write a letter in French pitching the film? If you want something that will get the message across ..."

Still nothing.

"But here of all places. What's this Takabatake store? Is it run by relatives?"

Pause. Then, again seeming to address the comment to himself, he began: "The guy who was making the film, or directing it, or whatever, for some reason he's indicated he wants to pull out. Something to do with his health. So we want you to take over and finish the movie. As director." His way of talking to me felt a little too familiar. "Of course, we will renegotiate your remuneration. Consider the amount Sugimoto told you as an advance."

This was unexpected, to say the least. "You want me to finish the film? As director? That's, I mean, ... I did dabble in something like that when I was a student ... But my skills in that area are even more rusty than my French ... And besides, that kind of thing is ... special. You need a cameraman, and lots of staff ... I wouldn't know where to begin."

As I rambled on, I recalled vividly the soft, slender body of the girl who had bumped into me just a few moments earlier. The warmth from her body that seemed to engulf me. The sweet smell of her sweat, her breath. The intense red that dripped from the corner of her lip.

# 6
## PUNCHED

KOYAMA WAITED until my babbling trailed off, then signaled, with a jerk of his head, that I should follow him. He started toward the main house, again as if there was no doubt that I'd follow. Was I really going to let this happen again? Was I really pathetic enough to go along with this, despite my rising déjà vu irritation?

Unlike the grand mansion in Nezu, this was a shabby old house. We walked up onto the veranda and into a bare six-mat room, where the man who'd first appeared before me in the garden was lying on the floor, his eyes, like a dead fish's, staring at us, startling me. His thick fingers were stroking the belly of the big black cat. I wondered if he was really looking at me or staring into the darkness behind me or exchanging looks with a spirit that hung by my head.

"This is Takabatake. He's a relative, and he owns this place," Koyama said over his shoulder, making no attempt to introduce us. He then waved his hand, as if gesturing to a dog, as if to say, "Haven't you got anything?"

"There's sake."

This was the first time I'd heard Takabatake speak, and his shrill voice made him seem unstable.

"Sake is fine. Go get it."

Takabatake rose up heavily and left the room, while Koyama plopped down on the well-worn tatami floor, pulling himself up to a low table. I followed suit and sat down facing him, crossing my legs. The room was bare, apart from the table and a single unadorned, dim lightbulb that hung from the ceiling. There was a single window. Although there was nothing to look at, I glanced around to avoid meeting Koyama's eyes. After a few minutes, Takabatake returned with a two-liter bottle of sake in one hand and a stack of three glasses in the other. He placed these on the table and began to sit down with us. Immediately, this small, low-ceilinged room, with the sour smell of liquor on Takabatake's breath, made me feel claustrophobic.

He poured three generous glasses. I picked up my glass and took a few sips—noting its vaguely industrial taste and feeling my all-too-familiar sense of futility creeping back in. As Koyama and Takabatake sipped in silence, this sense of futility took on a sweet taste and I caressed this feeling the way one keeps running a tongue over a tooth that was aching. This made me feel more positive, and I started to wonder if this strange-sounding job could turn out to be the break that had eluded me for the past few years. It was a thought that permeated my mind like a rose-colored haze; it was a thought I almost allowed myself to believe.

Koyama cleared his throat and began to speak. "I don't know if Sugimoto told you, but I'm actually a calligrapher."

This struck me as comical, the way he'd started the conversation like that.

"You know, letters, characters, words, they're strange things. Basically, all they are is just a set of rules. For example, the Chinese character for bird is written like this." Holding an imaginary brush in his right hand, thumb, index, and middle fingers extended together, he began to write the *kanji* in the air, rather rhythmically. His fingers, like Takabatake's, were long and thick. But they also seemed indecent to me, obscene, like five fat worms.

Completing the *kanji* with the four dots at its base, he went on, "Bird. They say this character was originally drawn to look like a bird. And it probably was. But in the end, it's become merely a rule, an agreement if you will. At some point it was decided that there would be one rule for crow and another for sparrow and so forth. Because as human beings, we need common agreement. More constant elements to allow for greater communication—to avoid miscommunication. So now, this *kanji* means 'bird,' by formal agreement, and as long as this agreement is shared between everybody, that's all that matters. All you need is the pronunciation for 'bird.' And characters and sounds that can distinguish a 'bird' from a 'horse' or a 'rabbit.' In that sense, words can be written in basic *kanji* or even in the scribbles of a child. Up to this point, calligraphy has no role to play. But—"

"Ah, cold sake! I love my sake cold!" exclaimed Takabatake, out of the blue, interrupting Koyama's little discourse. He downed his glassful and exhaled loudly. Maybe he'd been oblivious to the intimidation Koyama had been slowly building, or maybe he'd interrupted purely to provoke him. Whatever, it was difficult to ignore the blackened soles of his feet, which showed themselves to me with his crossed legs. A filth every bit as repugnant as Koyama's fat, pale fingers. Even Takabatake's shoulders and upper arms were grotesque, as if they would rip open his shabby shirt at any moment.

Until he started to speak, Koyama had looked like any old man who was tired of life, pouring down his sake and resting his elbows on the table, but the moment he'd sat up straight, focused his eyes on a space in front of him, and begun to paint brush strokes in the air, I sensed an animal energy desperate to escape his body. *That* was intimidating. Could Takabatake, his so-called relative, not have felt anything?

Koyama frowned at the interruption but didn't bother to glance over at Takabatake, who was opening and shutting his mouth repeatedly, for no reason I could figure out.

"When we dip a brush into the ink," Koyama continued, "and run it across paper like this, we're tracing out the formal agreement that is the *kanji* itself in this pleasant-scented substance we call ink. And when we do this, the *kanji* for the bird can suddenly come alive, break into beautiful song, spread its wings, and prepare to fly away. This kind of thing can really happen—although not more than once in a hundred or a thousand efforts; no, in tens of thousands of efforts. It is such a rare occurrence, but when it happens, the whole artificial agreement collapses without warning. It really can happen."

"I must say I had no knowledge of the sort about calligraphy."

"Tell me, have you ever seen the calligraphy of Taneomi Soejima?"

"No."

"That's a shame. In the same way they say a picture is worth a thousand words, you look at something like his brushwork, and immediately you see the tremendous forces at play in Meiji-era Japan."

"You mean Taneomi Soejima, the politician?"

"He was a politician in the Meiji government, but more importantly, he was a calligrapher. The greatest calligrapher in modern Japan. Throughout history, most people known as calligraphers, or cultivators of the written word, have been mediocre men who were simply obsessed with their hobby. They locked themselves away with empty theories of aesthetics, all doing the same work, with nothing else going for them but their handiness with a brush. But Soejima's calligraphy? That was completely different. You can see his life in his work. But not that alone. His work reveals the turbulence of the historical period itself. Japan was a country with a closed border in the Edo era, leading a quiet, secluded existence with modest levels of happiness and sadness. But if you really want to know what life was like then, the best thing to do is to look at the calligraphy and paintings of Buson Yosa. That self-containment collapsed with the arrival of the Black Ships. Just like that. Suddenly, Japan was forced open by Western civilization and forced to face modernity. All this shock and violence is evident in the calligraphy of Taneomi Soejima—as if the old ways were locking horns with foreign modernity …"

Koyama's flight of fancy was almost an echo of what I'd read about him, which led me to mumble, "A bold architectural beauty, perhaps."

Koyama blinked, then kicked his head back and laughed an exaggerated laugh. "So you've been reading up on me! I see you're not to be taken lightly."

"Yes, I did a little reading. You're a man of great achievement; you've been honored with the Order of the Rising Sun. But what I don't understand is why would such a man be sitting in a dark, dingy room, drinking cheap sake with the likes of us?"

"Well, I don't see why not. This room is comfortable enough, isn't it? Anyway, as I was saying," he continued, completely unfazed, "about the old ways and foreign modernity, Soejima's calligraphy gives witness to the battle between the two. His works are masterpieces. Taneomi Soejima, otherwise known as Sokai, born the second son of a samurai family in Saga prefecture. He led a mission to Beijing to exchange documents of ratification for the treaty between Japan and the Qing dynasty and became famous as the first foreigner to stand throughout his audience with the Qing emperor. This was in the days when it was normal practice to keep your head bowed and pressed against the ground in the presence of the emperor. Soejima simply gave a quick bow and remained standing. So, yes, I would say that the characters written by such a man were bold. And as free as Pegasus leaping across the sky. Some call his work pretentious, but it is nothing of the sort. I'd recommend you see an original if you can. Calligraphy can't be understood by looking at small photographs in books. You have to see the original and feel the grace and elegance in the strength of the brushstroke, in the shade of the ink."

"Grace and elegance?"

"Yes, some things can only be described as graceful and elegant."

"Right."

Koyama went quiet at this, and I wondered if I'd offended him with my cavalier response. I decided to pick up the conversation.

"If we could return to what we were saying earlier, why are you asking me to do this job? I mean, you met me for the first time a few weeks ago, and even that was a coincidence. This film is obviously very important to you; it's not the sort of thing you'd want to place in the hands of a stranger."

"I don't consider you a stranger at all. In fact, I do know a little about you. I know, for example, the eight-millimeter film that you made when you were at the university."

I couldn't believe he'd mentioned that amateurish effort as anything "in pursuit of beauty."

"You didn't actually watch that thing, did you?"

"I did indeed," he replied matter-of-factly. "It was quite interesting."

I wanted to remain nonchalant, but I'm sure the old man saw my face turn red with embarrassment. Just the title of it and the desperate way it was trying to sound poetic made me cringe. "Did it possess grace and elegance?" I asked, trying to turn the whole thing into a joke.

Koyama, surely out of mockery, pretended to take my words at face value and mull them over for a while before casually saying, "No, I didn't see much grace or elegance in it." There seemed to be a glimmer of malice in his eyes.

"So that must mean that I have no talent," I said, finding myself challenging him, then immediately regretting my cockiness, worrying that I'd fallen into a trap.

"No, no. That's not true at all," he said, as if to appease me. "Anyway, let's drink tonight. I don't get many opportunities to drink with young people … Is that rain I hear?"

Yes, it did sound like rain. I turned to look out the window at the garden, which was dark except for the slight glow of the sculpture.

Koyama stood up, slid open the window, and looked up to the sky.

"I can't see the moon tonight. Was it the eighteenth moon of the month tonight? Or the nineteenth?"

Takabatake had said nothing since his interruption. He'd just sat there pouring sake after sake and drinking it down. Now he lay on his side, with his eyes closed and his elbow as a pillow, oblivious to the rain that was now falling heavily. Giving up on the conversation, I reached for the bottle and filled my glass with sake. I took a large swig and then another and then, for some reason, found myself thinking about my mother.

It must have been because of the rain. I don't have many memories of her as she died before I started elementary school, but there is one vivid memory that I have of her. I was in the park, playing in the mud, when the sky suddenly turned dark. Big raindrops began to fall, and within seconds, it was a downpour. I was rooted to the spot, crouching down, tears streaming from my eyes, when out of nowhere my mother appeared. She picked me up in her arms, whispered comforting words in my ear, and carried me home.

When I describe the episode chronologically like that, I can't help but feel I'm distorting the real memory. What I remember most clearly, what's most deeply engraved in my mind, are fragments of sensations—the raindrops splashing on my mud-covered hands and knees, leaving large clean spots; the utter relief that seemed to drain all strength from my body at the moment my mother's brightly colored apron filled my field of vision; the damp warmth of my mother's arms around my neck; the familiar, wonderful scent of her neck, the raindrops that fell from my mother's hair onto my head as we made our way home. By piecing together these fragments, I'd arrived at the chronological version of events. But were they true? Couldn't I have strung together fragments of memories from several incidents to create this single, logical narrative?

I'd always lived my life in need of someone who would suddenly appear and sweep me up in her arms like my mother had. Maybe this was because I lost my mother before I'd had a chance to mature mentally and physically, maybe this was why the desire for a female guardian figure has always remained within me, lodged in the deepest core of my being, preventing me from ever becoming a true adult.

On the other hand, I hated my father. I hated him for the way he exchanged one woman for another after my mother died, and I allowed that hatred to force me into a corner. I hadn't spoken to him in more than ten years, but I had heard that he moved to Chiba prefecture, started a small company that did maintenance work for apartment buildings, and was doing pretty well. Yet, even when my life had spun completely out of control and I'd ravaged my body with drugs and hit rock bottom, never once did I think of going to that man for help.

Who was I to criticize, though? I was certainly no stranger to going through women. I was smart enough to know it didn't take talent to find a woman and live off her earnings like a parasite. It didn't matter so much that you were good-looking or knew how to treat a woman well. What was important was feeling comfortable with an idle lifestyle while maintaining a hatred for being a deadbeat. That was the key—being able to stand living with that contradiction. Take Hiroko, for example. I can't say I hate her, but at the same time—although it's irrational—I can't say I don't feel anger toward her for not being the sort of person who would come running if I was drenched and lost, sweep me up in her arms, and hold me tight all the way home. As long as I hold this anger within me, I'll never forgive Hiroko. Which means I'll never love Hiroko, and I won't feel shame if I'm cold toward her, throw my ego around with her, or toss her away like an old rag …

Sake can do this … make you think all this, dredge all this up. I needed to get out of here, go home, let whatever was going to happen,

happen. Then I heard Koyama mumble.

"Levitation."

"What did you say?"

"Levitation," he repeated, more clearly this time, as he turned around. "The rising of the body above the ground."

I felt like a large shadow had been cast on me. "I ... I ..." I stuttered, not knowing what to say.

"It's like a deadly disease. Do you remember how Tomoe was crying?"

"Yes, I saw her. She came running into me."

"That poor thing's suffering. I really do feel sorry for her."

"I don't understand. I mean, your granddaughter ... She is your granddaughter, right? She's just a child. And yet you make her do that ... stuff."

"And by *that stuff* you mean?"

"You know, *that stuff* in the film."

"Oh, in the film. You mean making a guy like this have sex with her?"

I was stunned. I couldn't believe how slow I was. The film had avoided the man's face, so on that count, no way I could have known. But the connection I had missed—and now saw clearly—was not any physical resemblance, but his vulgarity and the vulgar way he devoured pleasure from the girl. That hired stud in the film was Takabatake! No one had tried to hide this from me, true. Nonetheless, for Koyama to admit blithely to "making a guy like this have sex with her" was hideous! "Making," forcing, coercing, ... My blood was boiling.

"I thought she was still a child also," Koyama continued dispassionately, "but actually she was quite impressive."

My hands grasped the table. I pulled myself up, head hitting the lightbulb and causing it to swing wildly. I leaned in close to Koyama's face, and spat out: "You perverted fucker! Aren't you ashamed? You sick fucking bastard!"

In that one stroke, I washed away any claim to the nickname of "Mr. Intellectual." I heard something surface in my voice that hadn't shown itself since scuffles with Kabukicho thugs in days gone by.

Unshaken, smug even, Koyama let out a derisive laugh. "Are you seriously telling me you didn't know that the guy doing Tomoe was this half-wit here?"

That did it. I lost control and flung myself at him. But something intervened in this dramatic act, something that slammed down onto my back. It took my breath away, and I stumbled into the wall and slipped to the floor. Through eyelids crinkling with pain I saw the flickering light and shadow of the swinging lightbulb, and from the chemical stink, I realized I'd been hit with the sake bottle. I couldn't move and could barely breathe. But the high-pitched, throaty laugh behind me was perfectly clear.

# 7
## BREASTS

I PRESSED MY face into the creamy pale skin of Hiroko's back as she lay on her stomach, drifting off to sleep. I was enjoying the warmth of her body through closed eyes, allowing myself to be drawn to the verge of slumber before raising my head to drag myself back into the waking world. Drinking in her fragrance, I open my eyes to see her paleness extend mercilessly. It is all I see, and I am engulfed. Her velvety smooth skin moist with perspiration seems to go on forever, at once imprisoning and protecting me.

As that stifling feeling transforms into an immense pleasure that relaxes me from the tips of my fingers and toes to every part of my body, I am overcome by the feeling that this is the kind of thing— no, that this is the *one thing*—that I live for. I am being bathed from outside and in, my body is soaked, more deeply and more sweetly drenched with every passing moment. Hiroko transforms from being herself, or anyone else, to being the essence of woman, and I give myself to her paleness, to be carried away by a silent stream, bumping along with the current ... Then again, I bury my face in her back and I surrender to the gentle ebb and flow that is the rhythm of her breath. From the window, dusk is already seeping into the room, and the paleness of this body next to me and the jet-blackness of her hair that teased its way across the pillows begin to melt into darkness.

I bare my teeth and gently bite her shoulder. I enjoy the way it resists my teeth, and I bite with a little more pressure. I feel my saliva drip onto her skin. She lets out a sound that's not quite a moan, rolls onto her back, and tells me with eyes half-open and forehead slightly furrowed, "You're heavy."

I smile and press my face into her stomach.

"You're like a child," she says, running her slender fingers through my hair. "So, do you?" she whispers.

"Do I what?"

"Come on ..." Her fingers wrap their way around a tuft of my hair, giving it a playful tug. "So, do you or don't you?"

Again, I don't answer, so she pulls my hair harder, enough to hurt.

"Do you love me?"

"Yes, I do." I press my lips to her navel. I love Hiroko's navel. A beautiful horizontal indentation, like a dimple that shows itself when her body relaxes and smiles.

"You could sound more convincing," she says. "I fell asleep. What time is it? Oh, is it five thirty already? What were you doing while I slept?"

"Just spacing out."

"Spacing out? What kind of answer is that?"

She shut her eyes and stayed still for a few moments, then raised her head a little and wound her hair around behind her head. I thought she was going to tie it up, but she just held it like that, twisted into a bun. I dropped my head, turned toward her, pulled her body up to me, and buried my head in her hair. She responded by burying her face in mine, and we searched through our tangled manes to find each other's lips—me biting down on the hair that fell between mine, breathing in its sweet scent, getting it wet in my mouth.

"Come on, stop it. I don't have time to wash my hair," she mutters, pushing me, rolling me over, getting on top.

"Ow."

A pain shoots through my back where Takabatake hit me with the sake bottle. Hiroko lets out a sympathetic gasp and tries to shift her body. But then she changes her mind and decides to lean forward on me and press a breast to my mouth. I shift my head; her breast follows my mouth. When I turn the other way, she presses her other breast to my mouth. I move away again, and still her breast chases after me. I push my arms through hers and around her back, and I pull her to me and hold her tight. She looks so beautiful as she closes her eyes and brushes her hair back to reveal a hint of a smile from our little game of cat and mouse. When she closes her eyes like this, you can't really tell, but her eyes are very slightly uneven, and this unevenness is accentuated by a beauty mark under her left eye. In the middle of sex, when she looks up at nothing in particular from flushed and swollen eyes, this unevenness sometimes seems obscene. Ignoring the pain, I awkwardly stretch my neck out to her and kiss her on the chin. Then we roll onto our sides and lie there with our lips touching until sleep starts to close in.

"Now," she says. And with that word uttered distinctively coolly, she moved her mouth away from mine, leaving a trace of her kiss on my lips that quickly turned cold. I watched her pale, naked body stand up in the dark and hurry off to the bathroom. I caught sight of the dirty soles of her feet as she disappeared into the other side of the door, and the image burned itself onto my mind. Though I did own a vacuum cleaner, I'd used it only a handful of times since moving in. And just like all my other electrical appliances, she'd bought it for me with her credit card—although she wasn't the kind of woman who'd actually do the vacuuming for me.

While Hiroko showered and hurriedly dressed, I lay stomach-down on the futon, smoking.

"I need to clean this place," I mumbled.

"You should. There's dust everywhere," she replied, without taking her eyes off her hand mirror. She was sitting on the tatami, applying eye shadow.

"Yeah, maybe I'll clean today."

"You should."

"Yeah … I suppose so."

"You're so lazy. What do you do every day? You've got plenty of time, don't you?"

"Yeah, I know. But my back hurts."

"Have you been to see a doctor?"

"No way."

In her skirt and stockings and only a bra on top, she ignored my last comment and concentrated on putting on her makeup, which made me feel lonely, like I wasn't important to her, and it made me go quiet.

Then, after a while, she said, "But it worked out well in the end."

Hearing that, I realized she had been listening after all. She meant that it was good that the whole film thing had come to an end before I got too deeply involved. "Yeah, I suppose. The whole thing was just unbelievable," I replied.

I was lucky the incident that night hadn't escalated into a full-blown fight. I waited until I caught my breath, got up and brushed Koyama aside, dashed out into the garden, grabbed my shoes, and ran down the passageway and into the street. I thought they might come after me, but for whatever reason, they didn't bother.

I continued barefoot until I reached the shopping arcade, and when the police box came into view I began to breathe easier. I stopped under a streetlight to put on my shoes, but as I leaned over, a sharp pain shot through my back and I had to sit down on the ground. It was then that my fear turned to anger. I consoled myself by thinking I was smart not to hit the guy back, because this brute wielding a two-liter bottle could do serious damage to me. That may also have been the first thing to cross my mind after I was slugged, prompting me to run off, but to be honest I was deceiving myself into thinking I'd acted prudently. The fact was, this animal with the high-pitched laugh terrified me.

I started off along to Doté Street, stopping occasionally to catch my breath, then hailed the first cab I saw. As I sat in the back seat, I asked myself the question that then echoed in my head for the next few days as I lay bedridden—what is this *other* fear, and where is it coming from? It wasn't the threat of his ogre-like muscles, and it wasn't the shock of the bottle striking my back. It was something else. Like maybe it was connected to the film I was shown.

"The whole thing is just so creepy," Hiroko was saying. "A perverted old man making his granddaughter strip naked and do those things."

"Yeah, you're right."

"You know, I told you to keep out of it. But you go show your face anyway and then get beaten up. How stupid is that?"

I hadn't told Hiroko why things had turned violent. Nor that the guy who hit me was also the guy in the film.

"I think a couple of ribs might be fractured."

"You're an idiot."

"And how do you feel about idiots?" I said, putting my arms

around her from behind as she continued with her makeup.

"Hey … I'm trying to put on my lipstick."

She wasn't really irritated, but she had no interest in fooling around, so she removed herself from my grasp and stood up. "Now my skirt's all dirty! Really, you need to clean this place up. If you don't, you'll be sick *and* injured."

"All right, all right."

She stood up and started to gather her things.

"So when next?" I asked

"I'll give you a call. You better clean this place up."

I acknowledged her request with a grunt, which was generous, and watched her as she made her way to the door. That was when she mumbled, "Such a coward."

I don't know if it was meant for me to hear or not, but I wasn't going to pretend I hadn't heard it. I raised my head as well as my voice, "What was that?"

It was no use. She was putting on her shoes, ignoring me.

So what if she gave me pocket money every now and then; what was worse was she wasn't even thirty. In fact she was a good five years younger than me, so her treating me like that irritated me like a swarm of insects crawling inside my chest. I fought off my sluggishness and went up to her. "Say that again."

For a moment, I stood facing her on my narrow patch of earth by the gate. While she dusted her skirt, she gave me a look that I'd never seen on her before. It was one of ridicule, which was not surprising from such a strong-minded woman. But underneath it was a pity bordering on indifference that made me recoil. She was looking at me like a pathetic puppy abandoned on the street!

The pity seemed to take the edge off the aggression in her eyes, however, and though I'd seen many sides of her over the past year and a half, I realized this was the first time I'd seen anything approaching compassion.

"What a waste," she said, before her tone turned prickly. "Such a pretty girl …" As her sentence trailed off, she glanced away and she slipped through the gate and disappeared.

Assuming she was talking about Tomoe, how could she say "such a pretty girl" when she'd never even laid eyes on her? And what was that look of pity all about? I was at a loss, and I missed the opportunity to go after her to ask. My slow reactions could have been the result of years of drug addiction, but in the end all I did, after standing there for several moments, was to go back into the house and slide the front door shut.

Exactly what was such a "waste"? I'd like to know.

I did know that I didn't want to go anywhere near that guy Takabatake again. Sugimoto had always been weird, although something must have happened to him in the few years since we worked together. First of all, his loyalty to old man Koyama didn't seem to be an act, but with his rambling half-truths, threats, and flattery, I at least had some idea of what he was capable of. But Takabatake was a whole other breed. The way he sat slouched in his filthy clothes, quietly downing glass after glass of sake, he was like a hulking beast hiding its claws and fangs while surveying its surroundings, ready to pounce at any moment. It was this unpredictability that had me on edge all evening.

He had, of course, bared his fangs in the end and sunk them into me. But it wasn't his violence that had scared me. No, what scared me and still terrifies me was the fact that he was the beast that forced those cries out of young Tomoe. Those cries that numbed my brain and ripped through my thoughts.

I remembered the way her eyes wandered as she sobbed—and the torment it was for me to sit there, forced to watch. I remembered the shiver of fear that ran through me when the beast first appeared in front of me in the garden in Sanya. I remembered how I'd screamed in Koyama's face but avoided looking at Takabatake. And I couldn't forget how I'd pathetically lost my nerve after being hit just once.

Still, again, the fear that festered in me was not from the blow that left me in pain for days afterward; that was nothing compared to the fear of listening to Tomoe's cries. They were like an endless, dripping, sweet liquid that was sex. Even when I'd hit the wall and collapsed to the floor, surrounded by the stink of cheap sake and rancid tatami, Tomoe's syrupy cries of sex reverberated in the back of my mind.

I lay down on my disheveled futon, which still smelled of Hiroko.

The summer heat was stiflingly humid, and the cooler droned on. I wasn't kidding when I'd told Hiroko about my ribs aching; for the first few days I'd barely been able to sleep. But after a week the pain subsided and the swelling went down, but the dark blue bruise showed no sign of fading. Still, I didn't feel like going to a doctor. I didn't want to have to step into that place again, its air thick with disinfectant, unless it was absolutely necessary.

The last time I'd been to hospital was at the height of my drug addiction. I'd been rushed there with an inflamed liver. Supposedly, I hovered between life and death for over a week. After going through that, I spent an agonizing year going in and out of hospital, and only now was that memory starting to fade.

I'd hit rock bottom, which manifests itself in all kinds of ways. If I happened to see the dead, rotting body of an animal like a cat or a crow or a sparrow or a mouse twice in the same day, my mind would tell me that it wasn't a coincidence. It would tell me that these tiny corpses with their guts hanging out were actually appearing in front of me around every corner I turned. Once, in order to dispel the illusion, I bent down and fingered the slimy innards of a dead cat to make sure it was real. This sent a couple of middle-aged women who were walking by scurrying in horror. But of course I hadn't noticed the two human beings; I only saw the dead cat.

I didn't want to be reminded of that.

I'd survived the last year's unusually cold winter by curling up into a ball and hibernating like an animal throughout February and March. Only after the cherry blossoms came into bloom did I regain a semblance of calm. I remember the desire to rebuild my life growing gradually inside me and that my uncle, whom I wasn't especially close to, called to tell me about an office job opening at a small company. I didn't do anything about it, but the fact that I had a chance in the working world made me feel more optimistic about things. But if I was really honest with myself, I had to admit that, despite her selfishness, meeting Hiroko a year and a half ago was what had helped me crawl my way out of the abyss.

I wrapped a bath towel around my waist and got up slowly, as always. I walked into the bathroom and gazed at my reflection in the mirror. I couldn't be sure if it was because of the dim lighting in this sunless room, but I was looking older. Not just because of the wrinkles around my eyes or the sagging of my neck. There was something else. I didn't look thirty-four. As the words "middle age" popped uninvited into my head, I smiled at this older, more mature man looking back at me.

I glanced down as I washed my hands and suddenly noticed that Hiroko's collection of cosmetics around the sink was gone. That's when it hit me. Those pitying eyes. Hiroko had no intention of ever seeing me again. At first, it shocked me. But within moments, it had become a firm conviction.

# 8
## FLIES FOR FISHING AND A SWORD

THE FIRST TYPHOON of the summer was approaching, and already the weather was unsettled. Warm winds were blowing in every direction, and the heavy atmosphere made it feel as if an unseen hand was pressing down on my head. I'd woken early in the morning and had been unable to get back to sleep. So instead, I passed the time making flies for smelt fishing—wrapping feathers around a hook, tying knots in the line where small lacquer balls would be attached, and finishing each of them off with a touch of gold foil. That was all there was to it, although to succeed in getting the fish to bite, everything had to be in the right proportion. I had to choose the right type and color of feathers that I snatched from cages at the zoo, which wasn't as easy as it might sound. I had spent many hours trying out various combinations, and some fishermen swore they could never go back to other flies after having used mine. One trick I'd learned in making them was to use dried shark intestine from my local fishmonger. Once I'd made enough flies, I'd take them over to a fishing supply shop over in Kameido, which was run by an old guy who sold them on to his own personal network of discerning fishermen. According to him, they sold quickly and for a good price, and the old man used to joke that I'd make a decent living at it if only I had the ambition and concentration to make more of them.

These flies were an improved version of the ones my grandfather taught me to make when I used to spend summer vacations at my father's parents' home in Tosa. Back then, I'd go fishing every day with Grandfather, and my memories of that time are some of the happiest of my life. I later learned that those Tosa flies were a specialty of the region that dated back to the Edo period. Of course, I also learned about the best material for flies—one theory swore by dried catfish skin, another swore by dried cat skin. But if you ask me, it all comes down to the skill of the fisherman—whether he knows the right spot on the riverbank, whether he has the right touch to make the fly dance realistically on the surface of the water, or whether he is using the right kind of fly for the right fish. I believe the flies I make with shark intestine work like lucky charms, though, of course, the quality of the fly isn't irrelevant.

But it had been a long time since I'd last gone fishing. My grandfather, who was a wonderful, taciturn, rather small man who moved with great composure, died when I was in junior high, and I didn't attend his funeral. When he died, he took with him those long, lazy afternoons spent on the riverbank, moving between feelings of anticipation and relaxation and a sense of being one with the steady babble of the river. Now my only amusement consisted of imagining a smelt napping behind moss-covered rocks in a cold river while I prepared flies that would tempt it into biting.

That afternoon, with the typhoon in the air, the temperature suddenly dropped and rain began to fall—lightly at first, then harder and with stronger winds as the night wore on. My shabby house in the backstreets was sheltered from the high winds, which was fortunate because its rotting foundations wouldn't have the strength to hold it up otherwise. Even so, the walls still creaked, the lightbulb swung, and the sounds of rainwater running down the cliff behind the house made me anxious. Bit by bit, my headache got worse until it was impossible to concentrate on my fly-making, so instead I opened a book about river fishing and traced my fingers along the words, until the phone rang. Uncharacteristically, I rushed to pick it up in the hope that it might be Hiroko, but no such luck.

"I heard there was a bit of trouble," said Sugimoto, stifling laughter.

"Yeah, there was. The shit I let you get me into. Koyama is such a piece of work. What's up with that freak relative of his anyway?"

"Well, let's just say he's a little odd."

"A little? I'm just glad he's not the kind of nutcase who goes around with a knife."

"Actually, he does, kind of," Sugimoto said, pausing. "I mean, he's got one of those traditional swords."

"You're kidding me, right?" A shiver went down my spine.

"He's a college graduate too. Well, a college dropout anyway. Not so different to you. Though his university wasn't as good as yours."

"A college dropout turned porn star?"

"Why not? There are college dropouts turned drug addicts, too."

It shouldn't have surprised me that they'd know about that part of my life. After all, not only had they learned about the eight-millimeter film I made in college for fun, but they'd also managed to get their hands on a copy of it. I didn't know how to respond and said nothing.

"Don't worry. I'm just kidding!" said Sugimoto. "I didn't mean anything by it. I'm sorry. Takabatake was into kendo at college. Got pretty far in the Tokyo championships. Apparently he used to turn up at tournaments late, stinking of booze. Then he got into trouble for an attempted sexual assault on a cheerleader. At least they called it an attempt. That's when they kicked him off the team, and then he dropped out. After that, well, he just bummed around doing nothing."

"How old is he anyway?"

"A little over thirty, I'd say."

"Looks a little over forty to me."

"No, he's about the same age as you. Maybe you just look young. Maybe you've had an easy life …"

"Yeah, right. So what's the story with that store?"

"The jumble shop in Nihon-zutsumi? The guy lived there with his father for a long time, but the old man dropped dead last year, so Jin's the owner now."

"His name's Jin?"

"Yeah, Jin. The *kanji* for god."

"You've got to be kidding."

"Nope. He's actually quite intimidating when he's taking practice swings with his bamboo sword. Jin, the divine!" Sugimoto laughed. "But other than practicing kendo on his own, all he does is lie around drinking and watching TV. I have no idea how that store makes any money. He opens it up when he feels like it, every once in a while, but he doesn't bother replenishing any stock. It's all cluttered and dusty. Who would want to go near it? Even if a customer did walk in, I bet he'd ignore them."

"He should have sold the place in the bubble years."

"You're right. Shimizu would have jumped at an opportunity like that."

As part of our work at the Oriental Economic Research Institute, Sugimoto and I were supposed to keep an eye out for land for development. Back then, if the director learned about a family-owned shop run by an old man and his mentally slow son, he wouldn't have wasted any time moving in for the kill.

"But then again, that location …" Sugimoto went on. "The area's a bit, you know, on the low end. Anyway, the bubble burst, the old man died, and now Jin does whatever he wants, swinging his bamboo sword around. Well, wouldn't be so bad if it was *just* a bamboo sword, but he stole a real one from the sensei's place."

"That's crazy."

"Well, the sensei's to blame too."

"How's that?"

"Apparently they're related, and the sensei looks out for him. But he's too easy on him."

Was I detecting a little jealousy here?

"It was a real expensive sword. The real thing. And pretty dangerous, if you think about it. Like in that proverb—'Putting a sword in a madman's hand.'" Sugimoto was really getting worked up. "You know, I once saw Jin cut a straw figure in half with that sword. Talk about scary. I mean, this loose cannon was all concentration—all spirit and energy. But swords can kill. They're not like a large knife or a cleaver or something. They're in a different class. They're amazing, really."

"Oh yeah?"

"Yeah, really. I mean, you know it's coming down on a straw figure, but somehow you imagine it spurting blood and—"

"None of this stuff seems to bother you, though, does it?" Sugimoto was beginning to irritate the hell out of me.

"You're right there. I'm an easygoing guy. Best way to be. Nothing good ever comes out of taking life too seriously."

"You didn't used to be so easygoing. In fact, you used to be pretty intense; you used to scare people just with your eyes. Even Shimizu was a little afraid of you."

"That's not true. I've always been easygoing. I take life as it comes, always have."

"Yeah well, I'm sure this is all very interesting for you, but this Jin guy whacked me from behind. I don't particularly want to chat about how impressive he is with a sword," I said. "Anyway, Sugimoto, I'm glad the whole thing fell through. Give Mr. Koyama my regards. Tell him Mr. Otsuki says hi—in-between moans from the pain of fractured ribs."

"*Fractured* ribs? Was it that bad?" Sugimoto was humming a different tune.

"Yes, it was *that* bad. And it's your fault. You played me for a fool. Thank you very much. See you around. And by the way, don't forget to thank the sensei for such a *fun* experience!"

"Wait a second!" Sugimoto yelled.

I didn't wait at all. I hung up, then I pulled the phone jack out of the wall. But I was agitated. Sugimoto's stupid, annoying voice kept ringing in my ears. I sat, I stood up, I sat, I got up and paced. It was an irritation like having something stuck in the back of my throat. So, in the end, I decided to distract myself by cleaning the house.

I didn't care if it was unusual to be running a vacuum cleaner in the middle of the night; at least the sound of the pouring rain would keep the neighbors from hearing it. I figured it wouldn't take long anyway. After all, this wasn't a real house—just a six-mat room for a first floor and a four-and-a-half-mat room for an upstairs. I put the futon away in the closet, piled my scattered books and magazines into one corner, and vacuumed. Easy, really. So much so, I wished I'd done it sooner.

But it also made me realize that Hiroko had cleared out all her belongings—cosmetics, toiletries, clothes, whatever—without me noticing. Everything had disappeared without a trace.

I was in no position to blame her. I knew that I would have been quick to cut her out of my life if she ever became a nuisance. But when I thought of the sweetness and intimacy of the afternoon before, after we had made love, I felt a dull pounding in my stomach. All the while I was pressing my lips to hers, I'd felt like my skin was melting away and everything inside me pouring out. And all the while her soft lips and tongue were caressing mine, she'd been thinking this was the last time she'd ever have to see me.

I had her home phone number. But even though it crossed my mind to call her up and use my real name, instead of the code name we'd agreed on, or even to show up at her door, I knew I wasn't going to do anything of the sort. It wasn't because I was gutless—a coward, like she said—though perhaps she'd only said that to make me not want to have anything to do with her. It was because my attachment to her just wasn't strong enough to make me go that far. All I really felt was that the breakup was a bit of a loss and that it was a sneaky way for her to go about it.

I wasn't entirely without emotion. Somewhere deep in my heart, I felt shut out again by a cold wall. The wall never came down—not with any woman I'd known since getting badly burned in my early twenties, certainly not with Hiroko. But maybe it was the right time for it to end with Hiroko anyway; maybe it was becoming a little bit monotonous after all. Forget her, I told myself as I downed half a glass of whisky. Or at least try not to think of her. In my unusually clean room, I pulled out my futon and curled up on it, promising myself I'd air out the mattress when the rain stopped.

I am in a dim, dusty space, gripping the handle of a gleaming, unsheathed sword as I prepare to walk down a narrow staircase descending into the abyss. I am angry but not sure at what or whom. With tears in their eyes, my wife and daughter are trying to pull me back, begging me not to go, pleading with me to change my mind. That's right: I have a wife and daughter. I also have a respectable job. How, I ask myself, could I have been so stupid as to risk throwing it all away?

"I'll never do it again!" I tell them. "I'm sorry. Please forgive your father." And as I speak, it sounds like I've said these words before. Feeling embarrassment at having been so dramatic and referring to myself as "father," I turn around to look at my wife and daughter, and for some reason I bring the blade of my sword down on them. I look at them—lying on the ground in silence, not having had a chance to scream—and I know I should be shocked, horrified. But instead, I find myself bringing the sword down again and again onto their two faceless, kimono-clad bodies. I can't stand still; it's like I'm floating on a buoy at sea. I'm drunk on my own brutal excitement, and it comes to me how angry I am at this woman, how much I have always been wanting to do this.

When I look down again, there is only one woman on the ground, face down, I don't know if it's my wife or my daughter, but the belt is undone and her kimono is undone to reveal the paleness of her back. I drink in the aesthetic ecstasy of the sight before me, and I see the excitement tint my vision red as I bring down my sword on her body over and over again. I can feel the blade slicing into her flesh, and I expect blood to be splattering out of her, but instead her back stays perfectly smooth and pale and it glows in the light of a full moon. I look down at my feet and see I am not standing on an unstable buoy but sinking into the sticky water that the buoy is floating on. Suddenly, she's on top of me, covering my nose and mouth with her breasts, smothering me. I cannot breathe, and she's asking me, "Do you love me?" "Do you?" "Do you?" "Do you love me?" But I cannot speak, I cannot reply, and the word "Coward!" "Coward!" over and over again, pierces my body, and I sink deeper and deeper into the depths of this thick liquid.

My lips, swollen from Hiroko's tender bite, are sliced open by a fishing fly I've swallowed. Its hooks gouge into the flesh of my cheeks, and I'm pulled from left to right, dragged along with such horrifying force that I squirm and writhe in agony as the taste of my blood fills my mouth. Why is this happening to me? Why? Why? I wanted to live a quiet life in the shadow of a rock, safe among the tasty moss, caressed gently by the current of the stream. But I am ripped from the water with such force that chunks of flesh from the inside of my mouth are torn away and the burning air rushes in. I am dangling in the air, suspended, powerless prey before the face of a woman. Is she Hiroko? The face seems to belong to another, someone older, someone middle-aged. Do I know her? Is it the woman in the silver-gray kimono from Koyama's mansion? Or is it Hiroko ten or twenty years older, having become more beautiful and more ruthless? She is smiling, and I cannot bear to look at her. "They're amazing things," Sugimoto's voice intones, irritating, taunting. "They're amazing things."

That did it. I awoke, screaming silently. My heart was pounding, my body soaked in sweat. Like the night before, I'd woken hours before the dawn with the wind and rain raging outside. I rolled off the futon onto the tatami floor, feeling its coolness against my skin as I gasped for breath. When I managed to calm down, I got up, walked upstairs, and opened the creaking windows to stare out into the darkness and feel the spray of the rain on my face. Neighboring buildings were too close to allow me much of a view, but I could focus on the electric wires that stretched from pole to pole and on houses with the faint mercury glow of the streetlights, until gradually my suffocating panic dispersed. There'd been a time when nightmares and sleepless nights plagued me for months on end. In fact, they were part of the reason I turned to drugs, which brought a nightmare of their own, and the thought that it might happen again terrified me.

I stayed looking out, agonizing, until the sky was bright enough for me to make out individual raindrops in the morning light. Then I waited a few hours more until I could call my uncle and inquire about the job he'd told me about. He seemed surprised to hear from me. We exchanged the briefest of greetings, talked about the position, then arranged for me to go in for an interview. When I put the phone down, I was able to breathe.

I watched the heavy rain fall through the rest of the morning. Then, shortly after noon, the rain stopped, the wind died down, and the clouds dispersed to reveal a sky so clear and blue it was almost surreal. Then, in a matter of minutes, before the leaves on the trees had a chance to dry, a chorus of cicadas filled the air. It was as if they'd been waiting for that moment forever.

# 9
## TINY CHRYSANTHEMUMS

As the evening drew on, I wandered through the narrow streets between Hakusan-ue and Nishi-katamachi like an animal trying to find its way out of an elaborate maze. It was a ward of Tokyo that had assumed the stylish name Bunkyo, meaning something like "culture capital," as a shiny façade of respectability, but on those late summer evenings when the first hints of autumn swirled in the air, you could smell carnality in the breeze, brushing against your cheek. In days gone by, the area had courtesan and geisha districts to the east in Nezu and to the west in Hakusan-shita. The *ryotei* restaurant district had flourished in Hakusan-shita as a result and survived to this day. The glamour and seduction were gone, but the stagnant air in the basins lingered—charged with the allure of sex, tainted by the suffering of the women, and rising like smoke every so often.

I grew up in Koishikawa, a section even lower than those basins, so as I roamed these higher grounds, I felt like something of an outcast. I was also feeling something like pain from the arrogant, heartless way this community treated the meek, forcing them down to Shinobazu Street in the east and Hakusan Street in the west, leaving them to struggle while they lived in luxury. Nowhere was this arrogance and heartlessness more evident than at the University of Tokyo, and even though I often found myself strolling through Nishikata and Mukogaoka, I stayed away from front gates of that wretched place. More than ten years earlier, for a brief period of time, I'd been a student there myself. Now all that remained of those days was a sour taste in my mouth that made me want to gag.

I stood at the top of the hill and watched the sun set, thinking how, deep inside, I'd always gotten perverse pleasure from my self-destruction. But at the same time, my body had accrued a fatigue over the weeks, months, and whole ten years of my demise. Was I ever going to find a steady job, start a family, and claim my place in society? Or was I going to let myself rot away? Perhaps change started with small steps toward a more orderly and comfortable life. But had I let things go too far, allowed my life to shatter into too many pieces for it ever to be put back together?

In the aftermath of the typhoon, the afternoon sky was a brilliant blue that turned gradually into deeper shades and the air was so fresh that it was the first time in a while that my back hadn't been sticky with sweat. But as I walked the narrow, winding paths, I was so preoccupied with trying to find a way out of my sad state that I was incapable of enjoying the weather. Would the job my uncle offered to introduce me to be the thing to do? Then again, the job Koyama offered, weird as he is, could be quite interesting, no? I weighed the pros and cons and kept walking with a heavy nervousness bearing down on me, eventually finding myself at the top of the hill on the street that led down to Nezu Shrine. I wondered whether I'd been lured near to Koyama's mansion by a grotesque, subconscious will.

Although I can't say that an image of Sugimoto popped into my head, I did get the feeling that somebody was following me. But when I turned around to check, there was no one there, and nothing but the glaring crimson of the western sky—just like the last critical time I'd passed this way. Was this déjà vu? Again, I felt as if all human life had vanished, that I'd wandered into a wholly different world where spirits lurk. And even as the smells of cooking drifted by, I was convinced that the houses were abandoned, that pots were boiling away unattended in brightly lit kitchens, that I was in an unfamiliar place and time. My childish fears rose to the surface, telling me something was hiding behind the lamppost, ready to reach out and lay a hand on my back. I'm overwhelmed with the desire to turn around and head for home, but instead, I continue walking timidly down the hill, sinking further into the sunset. I tell myself that life is like a roll of the dice. That when it comes down to it, everything is no more than a simple matter of chance.

"We go back …" I could almost hear old man Koyama's voice say. "We go back to a different 'now' … We just make a loop and slip inside a different 'now' … Encapsulated in every 'now' are infinite other 'nows' …"

Words that had sounded like nonsense were reverberating in my mind. Unnerved, I shook my head in a pointless attempt to silence them.

No one was in front of Koyama's house—not even a guy in an undershirt and boxer shorts. I felt a shudder of relief, and then anticlimax. I continued with faint-hearted footsteps. Soon, I was at the low iron fence and then the front gate. I looked at the lawn and the mansion behind it. I said to myself, "Well, you've come this far ..."

Before taking the actual step forward, I turned to look around and was jolted to see a girl leaning on a lamppost. It was Tomoe! But I'd just come that way. How ... where did she come from all of a sudden? She was in a half-crouch, half-slouch, like she'd been waiting there for hours, then lost strength in her legs and was holding on to keep from collapsing. She was wearing a white T-shirt and jeans, just as she'd worn the last two times I'd seen her. Part of her T-shirt was enveloped in shadow, which made me realize it was late enough for the streetlights to be on.

I could have, of course, pretended I hadn't seen her. I could have passed on by. But instead, I found myself approaching her. She had an anguished look on her face; her eyes were tightly shut. "Are you all right?" I asked quietly. This seemed to surprise her. She opened her eyes wide and tried to get away, but immediately lost her balance and fell to the ground.

"Tomoe," I said, crouching down to her.

She seemed to recognize me. "I felt a little ... dizzy," she said, in a delicate, high-pitched, clear voice.

Grasping her elbow, I pulled her up, as pain rippled through my back and heat spread through my body. She stood on her own and exhaled. She seemed feminine, youthful.

"I'm anemic," she said. "This happens sometimes ..."

In the film, she'd hardly looked fifteen; she was so small. But now, in person and up close, she seemed taller. She came up to my nose, and she seemed more mature, like, say, a seventeen- or eighteen-year-old, maybe even a twenty-year-old. Her eyes wandering, she continued to sway a little, so I held her elbow. She seemed ... unearthly, or was it just her wandering eyes?

"Can you walk?" I asked. She nodded. So, holding her arm, I walked her to the gate of Koyama's house. "Thank you," she said. "I can manage from here ... Thank you very much ... " her words trailing off.

"Are you sure you're all right?"

She nodded yes.

I didn't want her to leave, so I said off the top of my head, "That film..."

Her eyes found their focus on mine in an instant. She nodded a couple of times, then, slowly, her eyes began to fill with tears.

"Listen," I said, not quite sure how to continue. "You know that I've been asked to ... well ... I don't know what I ... you know what kind of film this is. I just wanted to be sure you're okay with it."

For a moment, she didn't say anything. Then, in a barely audible voice, she said, "I'm fine with it."

"But are you sure?"

"Yes."

"But—"

"I'm fine with it," she said again. Then she dropped her gaze.

I couldn't think of anything more to say. It wasn't as if I was inexperienced at talking to women. It's just that they had all been about Hiroko's age, and it had been years since I'd spoken to anyone as young as Tomoe.

While I racked my brain for words, she slowly came closer to me, pushing against me, part leaning on me, part embracing me. My first thought was she'd become lightheaded again, but when I looked into her face, her teary eyes were looking up at mine.

"I'm fine with it," she said again, then her delicate pink eyelids slowly closed.

In retrospect, I guess I was the one who brought my face close to hers, but at the same time, I didn't have a choice. The law of nature was in effect, and free will had nothing to do with it. As if I was a piece of iron attracted by her magnetism. I savored the soft moistness of her lips; I inhaled the sweetness of her breath, which tickled my nose and made me imagine I was learning over to smell a tiny chrysanthemum. Then, all too quickly, it was over. She freed herself from my arms, turned away, opened the iron gate, and hurried along the gravel path that crossed the lawn to the house. The narrow-eyed woman, wearing the same silver-gray kimono, stood at the front door ready to receive her. Her eyes were fixed on Tomoe, which gave me time to step behind the gatepost. Had the woman seen our embrace? Or had the gatepost hidden us from her sight? How long had she been standing there? Was she waiting for Tomoe to return? It seemed these people made it a practice to creep up on you when you least expected it, appearing out of nowhere!

As I made my way home in the darkness, past Hongosakana-machi and down Hakusan-zaka, it occurred to me the film might have made Tomoe look younger than she actually was, by framing her in contrast with the rough masculinity of Takabatake. But as I continued down from Hakusan-shita crossing to the corner of the herbarium of the University of Tokyo, it also occurred to me that she'd been wearing makeup today, which might have made her look older than she actually was. I traced my lips with my tongue, enjoying the lingering taste of her lipstick, then I remembered how I'd glimpsed her face under the streetlamp as she came running into my chest from the house in Nihon-zutsumi, with blood running from those same precious lips. Later that night, I'd been hit so hard that I could still feel it now. Was it possible that she'd been hit hard enough to still need makeup to hide it? As I played with these thoughts in my head, I almost felt as if I could taste that blood on her lips. I started to feel more alert, and an idea came to me that I hadn't entertained before: Could it be that the person who'd struck me on the back with a two-liter bottle had been the same person to strike this young girl across the face?

On arriving home, my front door, which I was pretty sure I'd locked when I left, was slightly ajar and the light was on inside. I hesitated for a moment with my hand on the door, then slid it open and, as expected, was greeted by Sugimoto, who smiled as he turned to me, cross-legged on the floor at the low table, smoking. He hadn't bothered to take off his red baseball cap, which he was wearing back-to-front.

"Sorry about this," he said, without a hint of sincerity. "The door wasn't locked, so I thought I'd wait inside. You should be more careful about locking up."

I didn't say a word. Was it going to make a difference if I did? This was a guy who knew no boundaries. Once, I'd gone with him to collect on a debt. We rang the doorbell, and nobody answered, so Sugimoto casually pulled out a set of screwdrivers and wires, like it was part of the job, and picked the lock. He said he was wondering if the guy was just pretending to be out. It didn't faze him in the least that we were breaking the law.

I took off my shoes and stepped into my house. I sat on the floor opposite him, crossed my legs, and pointed to his cigarettes. He slid the pack to me; I lit up and took a long drag. I was hoping Sugimoto wouldn't notice my hand trembling, but I knew he wasn't one to miss that kind of thing.

"So, what do you want?" I said, my voice more calm than I'd expected. "Why are you here?"

"'s about the film."

"Right, the film. But that ape that hit me, you know, I don't want to see him ever again."

"Yeah, about that, Jin feels bad. He was very apologetic. Says he got drunk and overreacted. The sensei says he feels terrible about it too. He asked me to give you this as a small token of apology."

Sugimoto took off his baseball cap, removed a thick brown envelope from it, and slid the envelope to me. There had to be a wad of cash. But seeing as the envelope was puffy and wet from Sugimoto's sweat, I let it sit. This was such bad timing. Having been abandoned by Hiroko, I didn't really have the luxury of telling him to stuff it.

"I'm going to start at a new job soon," I said.

"Well, well. What kind of job?"

"Doesn't really concern you guys, does it?"

"You're right, it doesn't. When do you start?"

"Just leave me alone."

"You've got a week or so before this job starts, right? And even after becoming a salaryman, you'll still be free on the weekends. I mean, it's not like you have a family to keep happy."

I'd only taken a couple of drags of the cigarette, but I stubbed it out. "I just saw that girl," I said. "Tomoe."

Sugimoto looked genuinely surprised. So while I had the upper hand, I dropped a few crumbs. I told him how I just happened to run into her. Of course, I didn't say anything about the kiss. And I got him to talk.

"Yeah, she's anemic … I don't know a lot about her. It's a complicated story. She was born in Hong Kong, where her father was sent for work. Her mother died of pneumonia while she was a baby. Her father—the sensei's son—was a newspaperman, I think. He never remarried. After Hong Kong, he was stationed in London, taking her with him, then Rome, and then, right when he was appointed bureau chief in New York, he had a heart attack and died. That was two years ago, and that's when Tomoe came to live with the sensei. You figure he should have left her with relatives when he was doing all that traveling, but on the other hand, maybe he really cared for her and wanted her with him. Not so surprising since he was already getting on in years, but that meant she spent a lot of time with maids and secretaries. I don't know if she was a bad kid or anything; you can never know what she's thinking, she hardly speaks. But that may be a function of moving to a different country every few years before she picked up the language of the last one."

"Well, she does give off this unusual vibe. And she has those eyes—"

"Her mother was half-Italian. Which I guess makes her a quarter Italian …"

Sugimoto knew a lot more about her than he'd said, and the more he went on, the more my blood boiled. "But she's still a kid," I said. "What the hell is the old man doing, forcing his own granddaughter into porn?"

"I'm sure the sensei will explain that to you in due course. If you'll come to the house tomorrow—"

"Not interested."

"That new job of yours … I take it they know about your drug addiction?"

"If you've got a threat to make, then make it, you bastard!"

"No, forget it. I apologize. Didn't mean to say that. I'm always saying things I don't mean. Just come to the house in Nezu tomorrow, please. Is three o'clock okay?"

Everything in my being was telling me to throw him out. But the deck was stacked against me: I couldn't get Tomoe out of my mind. And Sugimoto, seizing the opportunity, got to his feet and said, "See you then!"

With a swift, snakelike movement he made his exit, smoothly closing the sliding doors behind him.

I stayed at the table, chain-smoking the cigarettes he'd left behind. I tried to think, but I couldn't think clearly. I couldn't get past the feel of her lips, the scent of her breath. I crushed another cigarette into the ashtray and remembered the envelope of cash. I pulled its contents out onto the table. It was a pile of crisp, new ten-thousand yen notes. Thirty, to be exact.

# 10
## SHINJUKU STATION

I STUCK AT my new job for four weeks. But on the Monday morning of my fifth week, as I stepped off the local train at Shinjuku station to transfer to the express, my legs suddenly froze up, exhaustion filled my chest like a torrent of dirty water, and I knew then and there that I wouldn't be able to keep doing this. Using all my efforts to drag my feet down the stairs, I shuffled through the exit and headed for a coffee shop. Perched on a stool at the counter, I closed my eyes and did my best to white out the sounds of people rustling their newspapers as they stuffed toast and donuts down their throats.

It was the end of October, a windy, rainy morning, and as I'd stood on the platform of the station near my house, waiting for the Chuo-line local that'd take me to Shinjuku, I was struck by the chilly premonition that here was the monotonous rest of my life laid out before me.

The small pharmaceutical company my uncle had introduced me to was in Hachioji, which meant a long train ride out into the boonies. Its only saving grace was that it was an opposite commute, which meant I could get a seat on the express. The Chuo local pulled up to the platform, and I got on with my eyes fixed on the neck of the person in front of me, propelled forward by the shuffling nudges of the person behind me. There's an art to this: You've got to be careful not to push the person in front of you, but at the same time there shouldn't be a gap between you. Whatever you do, you mustn't step out of line or get in the way of the people behind you. You've got to let yourself be sandwiched between strangers, make yourself transparent as air, stay out of anybody's way, try not to draw attention to yourself. The same recipe for success, come to think of it, as holding down a dull job, spending every waking hour doing only what you're told. But this was what I'd asked for. A life where I moved forward like livestock, trying to match the steps of the animal in front, the animal behind, keeping my head down, trying not to stand out, trying not to fall out of step, trying to be like everybody else.

The first thing I'd been asked to do on the job was to manage inventory. They said it might be boring but it needed to be done, and they promised there'd be something a little more interesting in time. I wasn't in any position to complain. Not surprisingly, the task of sitting in front of a computer typing in number after number was every bit as boring as they'd said, but for the first couple of weeks, I was able to tell myself that the boredom was proof of a proper job. Also, there was the fulfillment I experienced, a kind of childish delight, in being given a health insurance card for the first time in my life.

By the third week, however, that feeling had begun to subside, and by the fourth I was fully aware of my growing impatience and anxiety as I spent hours staring into the computer screen, visualizing Tomoe's armpit as she raised her arm above her head. A part of me hoped that somebody would say stop slacking off. But nobody seemed to care and that, ironically, seemed to take the wind out of my sails.

One day, while staring at the rows of numbers on the computer screen, I started to snicker out loud to myself, which led someone to check if I was all right. Sure, it's entirely possible that simple administrative tasks like this eventually become worth living for if you stick at it long enough. It wouldn't really be such a bad life, would it? Going drinking with colleagues after work, killing time on the weekends at the race track or pachinko parlor, eventually finding a girl who was right for me, having a child to carry on my shoulders at the zoo, growing older each year with a firm grasp on my insurance card and bankbook, and slowly finding happiness in my own ignorance, like a stupid but faithful dog.

I'd thought I could get used to this—the life I'd been leading was hardly to be preferred. I could learn the skills to put up with it. But could I *do* it? Realistically? Well, there wasn't much choice in the matter. Either grit my teeth and carry on, or fall out of step with the pack and end up living in a cardboard box in the plaza of a train station.

That is the conversation I'd been having with myself. But as I boarded the local that Monday morning, I just couldn't shake the picture of me doing this day after day, with nothing to look forward to but my measly half-yearly bonuses and minimal retirement allowance. Throughout the ride to Shinjuku, I kept telling myself that if I could manage to get through this week, then I could probably manage it for the rest of my life. There might be a change of jobs, there were bound to be unexpected events to break the monotony. All the while, I'd be able to continue marching forward, hanging on to a shred of self-respect by occasional well-timed self-derision.

But no, I couldn't do it. I got out of line, walked off the platform, and ended up hiding out in the coffee shop. Typical. Typically irresponsible. Story of my life: think about things ad nauseum, then make the final decision on impulse, without thinking about the consequences. But even after a couple of hours nursing a cold cup of coffee, I felt I was better off here than in front of the computer in that linoleum-floored office. I had just enough etiquette to call and say I had a fever and was going to take the day off, although my etiquette didn't go so far as to try to sound convincing.

I was exhausted. The four weeks had exhausted me. Of course, a part of me had known this would happen all along, so I didn't really feel the need to reproach myself.

The truth of the matter was, before I started the job, I'd spent a week in September in the garden behind the Takabatake store filming Tomoe from every angle possible as she floated in a tank of water. And I have to say, it wasn't a terrible experience—far from it. I got to shoot with a sixteen-millimeter camera, and when we finished shooting and Sugimoto placed a hand on my shoulder and said, "Well done," I was sorry that the shoot was over. I started my job at the pharmaceutical company two days later, on the first of October, with a fair amount of enthusiasm. But in comparison with the intense pleasure of filming the delicate, beautiful Tomoe, molding her appearance on film as if she were a piece of clay, that enthusiasm didn't have a chance.

We set up the glass tank in the garden, erecting scaffolding to suspend it in the air and constructing an apparatus to create the effect of a waterfall. I designed the lighting and the sound—all with the purpose of doing justice to Tomoe's young sensual beauty. I'd spent a week thinking through all kinds of ideas, and it was exhilarating. I'd also been surprised by Sugimoto's resourcefulness. Not only did he manage to get hold of every material and device I requested, but he also located items on his own that proved to be quite useful.

"Film Tomoe's hair." That was Koyama's instruction. Not just to film her hair, but to capture it in ways that emphasized its particular beauty. Footage didn't need to be solely of her hair—her face, her body could be included as well—but the point was that her hair should be the focus. I was free to do the shooting anywhere, against any background. All necessary equipment and materials would be supplied. And, finally, Tomoe would cooperate fully and do anything I asked.

"Do you mean that? I might want to have her get naked again."

"Please do as you will." Koyama was saying very little, and his arrogance was absent.

"I can do what you ask. But what do you plan to do with what I shoot?"

"I'll incorporate the footage into the piece I showed you earlier."

"That piece? The stuff you didn't want me to call pornography? You want to incorporate footage of her hair into that? I don't understand how it's supposed to fit together. Does the film have a story? Or is it an *art film* that's basically a string of images?" I couldn't suppress a certain sarcasm when I said that, but Koyama was unperturbed.

"I'm sorry, I can't give you an answer to that right now," he responded straightforwardly. "I'm going to ask you to leave it to me to decide what I do with your footage. I basically want you, Mr. Otsuki, to direct this scene and film her hair. That's all. Considering your compensation, I don't think that's too much to ask."

He was right about that. It would have taken me a year in that dead-end job to earn as much as this was going to rake in for me. And that was on top of the three hundred thousand yen I'd already pocketed.

"Fair enough. I understand what you want," I said. "I'd like to see that piece you showed me earlier once again then, please."

"You've seen it once. That should be enough."

This came as a surprise. "To be really honest," I began, "I'm afraid I was nodding off a little that time. I didn't look carefully. Especially the second half of it. I couldn't tell what was—"

"That's fine. That is *that*, this is *this*. It's best that you don't get hung up on that. I want you to film according to your own ideas."

"But how can I film this scene if I don't understand the overall concept?"

"That's why I'm telling you to do as you like. I trust you."

"I appreciate that. But I'm afraid it doesn't really help me. I mean I have no idea how to proceed. You want me to just film her hair? That's pretty vague."

"Let me put it this way. There's something magical about the hair of a young woman that's difficult to describe. Especially in the case of Tomoe … There's a mystery about her. Why don't you take some time and talk with her? She's a very quiet girl. But when she looks at me with those eyes, I feel like I'm being sucked into them. Maybe because she kept moving from country to country while she was growing up. She's my granddaughter, but I hardly met her until she came to live with me last year. It's hard for me to believe we're related. She says very little, and I never quite know what she's thinking. But her sensuality and vitality … That's what I want you to express."

"One other thing, then. You mentioned something the other day … something about levitation."

"Ah yes. Levitation. The body rising in air," Koyama replied, a smirk escaping from the corners of his mouth. "She says it happens to her. That she sometimes awakes in the middle of the night to find herself floating five to ten centimeters above her bed."

"She must have been dreaming."

"I thought so too. But she's very insistent. When I teased her about it, she got quite upset and became very quiet. For some reason she's very persistent about this one thing. She'll bring it up again and insist it isn't a dream. Perhaps she's a saint." Koyama smiled. "So basically I want you to film the hair of a saint."

An underground film about a saint's hair? This was truly weird.

"If you want to talk with Tomoe, use the winter garden," Koyama said.

"The winter garden?"

"That's what we call the conservatory. The place where we showed you the film."

I waited for Tomoe in the conservatory. Eventually she appeared, carrying a tray with two steaming cups of tea—the same mint tea I'd been served on my first visit. That visit was, of course, when I'd been shown the film of Tomoe in all kinds of indecent positions, and the thought flustered me. We sat down and sipped our tea.

The shade of her brown eyes made me remember the Italian blood in her veins, but her hair was very Japanese, with each strand swept up in a ponytail—beautiful, thick, jet-black hair, like that of an Ichimatsu doll. It made me think of her pubic hair, which made me feel self-conscious, and I didn't know where to direct my eyes. She was dressed simply today, with white pants and a plain pink T-shirt. I wondered if it was really okay to ask her to take off her clothes, so I asked her how old she was.

"I'm seventeen," she replied in a barely audible voice.

What transpired then wasn't what you could call a conversation— all she did was mutter a "yes" or a "right," or shake her head sideways while looking straight into my eyes. I became gradually more uncomfortable and resorted to asking her silly questions like, did she like music and did she like films? Frustrated, I cut the conversation short and went home.

I spent the last week of September, after the water tank was suspended, filming Tomoe from every angle imaginable. I filmed her as she hung upside down, by the crook of her knees, swinging trapeze-like as her hair trailed through the water. I filmed her as her face very slowly emerged from under the water. I know this may all sound silly, but the last thing I wanted was to create something resembling a shampoo commercial. As I mulled over various ideas before the shoot, I decided to show Tomoe as a woman of the water. The image of Ophelia floating down the river after she was rejected by Hamlet had crossed my mind, I confess, but I was aiming for vitality, not death.

Koyama didn't visit the set, not once. I had no idea how he would respond to what I'd given him.

One thing I was especially happy for was my attempt to create something that evoked the luminance of moonlight reflected on water. I'd ordered all kinds of bulbs and filters and spent hours adjusting the reflector until I got it right. The idea for this may have come from the image of the moon depicted in the film I was shown that first night; for as much as I was awake for, it had been rather unsettling, and it stuck with me. In fact, when Hiroko came to my house a week later, the image of that moon kept popping into my head while I was trying to make love to her, and I climaxed with it hanging there in my mind, like a luminous ovary belonging not to Hiroko, but to a faceless woman.

Who knows how such ideas happen. I decided that I was going to transform Tomoe into both a woman of the water and woman of the moon.

Basically, this, without the flourishes, is the film I made. It begins with a shot of Tomoe completely buried under a blanket of red and yellow leaves. Then, we see her eyes, which are closed, her nose, cheeks, and mouth slowly break through the surface of the leaves, which sends ripples through the water—the first clue that the leaves are floating on water. Drops of water seem to bounce off of Tomoe's smooth complexion and roll down her cheeks, chin, and neck. A tiny crimson maple leaf sticks above an eye. She opens her eyes very slowly, so that it feels like an eternity passes between the first flicker of an eyelash and the eyes opening completely. The camera closes in on one eye, going to an extreme close- up, then seeming to close in further still until her brown iris fills the entire screen. Her eye sees nothing. It isn't focused on anything. Then the eye begins to close, like the eclipse of a moon, and she ceases to see as the screen darkens. The camera then zooms out gradually, as the light changes so the brightness of moonlight floods in. The moonlight absorbs all colors, turning them into a transparent glow that reflects off the water's surface, blinding the viewer to the leaves that covered it, so that all that is seen is Tomoe's hair spread out, covering the water. The moonlight illuminates each strand of hair, and the viewer is left suddenly wondering if she's dead, and as each strand of hair is shown undulating, each is animated by its own independent being.

Question is, *how* the hell did Sugimoto score those maple leaves at that time of year?

I smiled to myself. I was still in the coffee shop. I paid my bill, then walked over to the same payphone I'd used to call in sick. I dialed Hiroko's home number.

A woman who I assumed to be the maid picked up. "My name is Kinoshita, from Sumitomo Securities," I said. This was our code, though I'd never had occasion to use it. After asking me to wait a moment, the woman returned to say, nervously, "I'm sorry, but Madame is out." It was a response I'd been half-expecting, so I put the phone down without making a fuss.

I then flipped through my datebook and called the number of a woman much younger than Hiroko. She worked in an office, so it was no surprise that she wasn't there; I hung up without leaving a message.

I stood there, unsure. I picked up the phone, held the receiver to my ear, hesitating. I took a breath, and then I dialed the number to Koyama's house. As I waited for the phone to ring, my nerves began to jangle.

# 11
## ENCOUNTER AT NIGHT

THE PHONE MUST have rung ten times, as I stood there in a daze, the receiver pressed against my ear. I just let it ring. On about the twentieth ring, somebody picked up and in a quiet, flat voice said, "Hello."

"Um ..." I began, uncertain how to continue. Suddenly, my mind conjured up an image of the shadows under Tomoe's arms, which made my heart beat faster. What was I doing?

Whoever was on the other end waited in silence.

"Um ... this is Otsuki," I said timidly.

After a further moment of silence, the toneless voice replied "yes," and a ridiculous idea popped into my mind. I tried to push this crazy notion away, but the coarse breathing that tickled my eardrums started to make this thought not so ridiculous after all. "Hiroko?" I heard myself ask, bewildered, incredulous.

There was a long pause, followed eventually by a snicker.

"*Hiroko*?!" I gasped. "What are you doing there?"

Again, a long pause, teasing me, and then in an inappropriately casual voice, this person said, "It's been a while. How have you been?"

It was Hiroko all right, acting completely blasé.

"It's been a *while*? How can you say that? Do you know how many times I called you and you never picked up? How self-centered can you be? In fact, I just called your house a minute ago—"

"You called *my house*?"

"Of course ... How was I to know you'd be at Koyama's house! ... What are you doing there anyway?"

"You called *my house*?" she said again. "Did you say you were calling from Sumitomo Securities?"

"Yeah."

"That's not good. You know, my husband thinks I'm at your house."

"Why would he think that? ... Have you run off ... ?"

"Something like that ..." Her voice trailed off, then there was a distant rustling, followed by the sound of a kettle whistling in the background. She probably had her hand over the receiver. Then she came back on. "Hello, are you still there?" she said, unruffled, relaxed, as if everything was ordinary but maybe suppressing any excitement.

"What's going on with you?" I said. "How do you know Koyama, and what are you doing there?"

"You actually called my place and asked for me? What did my husband say?" she giggled, ignoring my questions.

"That you weren't home. I talked to the maid. So she was actually telling the truth."

"Yes. And now he'll think this guy Kinoshita from Sumitomo Securities is to blame."

"To blame? For what?"

"Well, I took some money with me when I left."

"What are you talking about?"

"Well, I feel a little guilty about it, especially since I told him I was going to move in with you. But then, you seemed to be having a lot of fun recently, bathing a young girl and that sort of thing, so maybe I shouldn't feel so bad after all. Since when have you been into that sort of thing anyway?"

"Oh, that," I said. "I'd been given orders to create a piece of 'art.'"

"You know, I …" she said, her voice calm, but louder, as if she'd brought the phone closer to her mouth. "I … really cared about you. You didn't know that, did you? Of course you didn't. You were never serious about us, were you? I knew you were seeing other women, too. Not that I think you were in it only for the money either."

I wanted to say "of course not," but I couldn't get a word in.

"Do you remember that scorching summer day? The last day we spent together? That was when it hit me. The fact that you're totally self-centered. You were just with me for the pleasure, nothing more. Like a grown man who wants to keep sucking on his mother's breast. That's all you are. It didn't have to be me. You'd have been happy with any woman who'd give you her tit. You never thought about how I felt. Never took any interest in my life. Maybe you said an occasional nice thing to me, but, you know, in hindsight they were just empty compliments. You never meant anything. You were really smart, weren't you? Careful never to say anything serious so it'd be easier to dump me and cut me out of your life as soon as you got tired of me. "

On and on she talked, without a pause, without a breath. She couldn't be stopped.

"You know, I think the really sly thing about you is the way you manage not to lie. You avoid it by saying nothing or rambling on about something nobody cares about. That's what you do to avoid lying, isn't it? Well, I may not be the brightest person, but that was pretty obvious to me. You know, I would have left everything to be with you, if you only had asked. I was waiting for you to ask me to move in. You never did."

"Well, I didn't think this was anything more than a fling for you," I said weakly. She didn't respond to that. Of course, this wasn't the first time I'd had a confrontation like this with a woman, so I'd become brazen, shrugging everything off inside with crocodile tears in my eyes. But this time was different, eerie. It wasn't the nature of Hiroko's complaints—they were nothing unusual—it was the way she was speaking, without tears, without a trace of anger, just matter-of-fact. I wondered if she'd rehearsed this? Unlikely. After all, I'd called Koyama's place not expecting to find her there. I was caught off-guard, bewildered, without any idea how to respond. So I interrupted her and cut to the chase.

"I want to know what's going on with you and old man Koyama," I said officiously.

I heard what sounded like a low moan, and for some reason, I was reminded of Hiroko's final words as she left that last day: "What a waste … Such a pretty girl …" Something about the way she'd said it, as if she knew Tomoe herself.

"Why should you care?" she said.

"Of course I should care. How could you act so innocent the whole time I was talking about him when you knew him all along?" My voice was rising.

"You're the one who was acting," she responded without a beat. "How many other women were you seeing when you were with me?"

"Why are you bringing that up now?" I didn't expect an answer, and the question was left hanging.

After a moment, she spoke again in an emotionless voice: "I'm going to be staying here a little while longer. Why don't you come here tonight?"

"You mean Nezu? What's going on there tonight?"

She didn't answer. And then the line went dead. When I redialed the number, nobody picked up.

Overcome by a sense of futility, I took the train home and spent an anxious afternoon unable to do anything.

I started thinking I'd be better off going to work. Nope. I brought out materials to make a few fishing flies—anything to distract myself, to kill time. Nope, not interested. No way I was going back to doing this sort of thing, holed up in a closed room. And, come to think of it, what was I doing, making flies for people when I didn't even fish myself? I tried calling Koyama's house. Nope, just endless, monotonous ringing. How come Sugimoto can be dispatched to stomp into my life at any time, but I can't get through on the phone to that household? I whiled away the rest of the day lying on the tatami floor, trying the phone every so often, feeling thwarted.

Once the sun had set and the evening had grown dark, I began to feel increasingly anxious about being shut up in my shabby little house. Eventually, my irritation took over, and I found myself getting into my sandals, sliding open the door, and stepping out into the night. My feet, of their own accord, pointed the way toward Koyama's house.

This was no good. *I* was no good. I couldn't stop thinking about the sound of Hiroko's breathing into the phone. Suddenly I felt desire, need, for her pale flesh. It was this baser instinct that was ruling the night. I could think of nothing else—certainly not the pitiful job in Hachioji.

After all the time it'd taken me to get oriented toward main street, I was hell-bent on taking back streets and side streets and slipping further and further into darkness, where the wind smelled foul and it was impossible to tell front from back or right from left. I felt a melancholy spread through me and then a wayward urge for the ecstasy of drug-fueled sex, for the euphoria of blood bubbling in my veins, taking me higher and higher until I was gasping for breath, like sucking in high-altitude air. I wanted that drive to keep devouring her body, but never having enough. I wanted to have sex for three days and three nights without sleep before reaching the pinnacle of pleasure and pumping out enough semen to fill a two-liter bottle ...*Hold on, hold on!* I felt my body shrinking away in fear. I needed to get a grip. But it was obvious: the prospect of getting Hiroko back and falling back into self-degradation had its appeal.

But what the hell was going on with her and Koyama?

A dozen black cars were parked outside Koyama's mansion, their drivers waiting, smoking through their open windows. As I passed them, I heard the sounds of what seemed to be a party in the back garden. I opened the iron gate and quietly made my way in.

The lawn, which I'd only seen in darkness, was brightly lit. Tables of food and drink had been set up, and several dozen men with drinks in their hands mingled, as waiters in black suits and heavily made-up women in kimonos circulated among them. There were a few men my age, but the majority appeared to be in their forties and fifties. Some could have been older, and all were dressed in elegantly tailored, expensive-looking suits, all brimming with confidence. A short, heavyset older man, whose salt-and-pepper hair was in a crew cut, seemed to be the center of attention, talking loudly and throwing his head back with laughter. From my distance, I couldn't be sure, but I thought I recognized him from newspapers and television appearances as a high-ranking member of the Liberal Democratic Party. This didn't seem like a political gathering, however. In fact, it seemed like a mix of people from different professions; there were even a few Caucasians present.

Self-conscious in jeans and sandals, I stood at the edge of the gravel path looking on. A waiter noticed me and came over. "Can I help you?" he asked politely, although the frown on his face betrayed his intention to shoo me away, as he would a dog scavenging for food.

For a second, I considered mumbling, "No, no, it seems I got lost," smiling and making my escape, but his condescending attitude hit a nerve. I was annoyed, furthermore, that Koyama hadn't had the decency to tell me what he thought of the film I'd gone to so much effort to make, so I found myself telling the waiter high-handedly, "Just get Mr. Koyama, will you?"

"And you are …?" he asked archly.

"A friend."

"Your name … ?"

"Just get him, will you!"

"I'm afraid he's not receiving visitors today."

"Tell him it's urgent."

"And could you elaborate on this urgent matter?"

"It's private. I'll tell him myself."

"May I at least have your name?"

"I could tell you, but it wouldn't mean anything to you."

"But, you see, today …"

This irritating exchange went on for far too long. When I couldn't take it any longer, I shouted, "Just shut up, you idiot!"

Immediately, several guests turned around with shocked expressions on their faces. Out of the crowd, one kimono-clad woman made her way over to where we were standing.

"Hiroko!" I exclaimed, putting on a smile that must have looked false and unnatural.

She reassured the guy in black that I wasn't a crasher and gestured that he go back to his duties. Then she fixed me with a cold stare. "So you came," she said.

"You asked me to come. What are you doing?"

"I felt bad just staying here and doing nothing, so I'm helping out."

"What's going on? Did you leave your husband?"

"Mr. Koyama was very kind."

"What's with the 'mister'? How do you know him anyway?"

"I know that, unlike you, he isn't scum."

This took me aback. "You don't have to call me scum."

"Oh, did I hurt your feelings?"

Smiling for the first time, she reached out to touch my cheek, which was something she'd always liked to do. But I turned away, avoiding her touch, and immediately regretted it. I had, in my own way, cared for this woman.

"I had no idea you'd look so good in a kimono," I offered in consolation.

Her smile broadened, and I let my eyes drink in her appearance. She was wearing a finely patterned amber kimono with a gray obi. Her hair was pulled up into a bun and kept in place with a small silver comb. The corners of her eyes were made-up to emphasize their slight slant, and the area below her eyes was a little swollen in a way that always made her seem lustful. This part of her face always blushed when I got her excited.

"I borrowed it from Masayo. This comb as well."

"Masayo?"

"You know, she's not exactly a maid. She's the lady in charge of running the house."

She must have been talking about that narrow-eyed woman who I'd suddenly found next to me, lifeless as a mannequin, the first time I came here. "So that's her name."

"Yes. Masayo is a very nice person."

"You ran away from home like a teenage delinquent, and now you're in the care of very nice people."

Her smile relaxed, and for some reason she reminded me of a cat purring after gobbling down a fish.

"You've got quite a gathering here tonight. That short old man there, the guy with the obnoxious laugh, is that the guy from the LDP? Don't tell me Koyama is planning to run for the Lower House."

But instead of responding, Hiroko stared into my eyes before suddenly grabbing my left hand and yanking it toward her. "Come with me. Over this way."

"What do you mean? What are you doing?"

"Over this way … Mr. Koyama is waiting."

Like a happy couple, we walked hand-in-hand along the gravel path around the lawn bustling with guests. We walked into the shadow of the house and turned onto a dark, narrow path where I tried to pull her into my arms and she gently pushed me away. We continued on, entering the space with the vaulted ceiling that I was by now familiar with. In complete contrast with the bright lighting of the garden party, this marble-floored inner garden was bathed in a dim light that barely painted silhouettes of the objects around us. There was the soft sound of water coming from the fountain. And there, sitting on the edge of the fountain, his face obscured by the walking stick his hands rested on, was Koyama. As we approached, he stood up with a grunt.

"Tonight really tired me out. What is the matter with those people? All they talk about is money, golf, and who's been appointed to what position..."

"It's been some time," I said, ruffling my hair with my hand as if to shake off the embarrassment of my inappropriate clothing.

"So, Mr. Otsuki, I hear you've begun a job. Congratulations."

I didn't say anything. Koyama didn't say anything either as he dangled his walking stick slightly above the ground.

"What happened to the film?" I asked.

"The film? Thanks to you, it's getting closer to completion."

"You're editing it now?"

"Well, yes."

"You know, I wouldn't mind helping with the editing."

"No, no, we won't need to trouble you any more than we already have. We can do a decent job with it ourselves..."

"Could you at least show me what you've done? I'm really curious how my scenes worked out."

"They came out just fine."

"What do you mean by just fine?"

"What does it matter?"

"It matters to me." I heard the pitch of my voice go up. "And what happened to the payment I was promised? I've only seen the small advance."

"That, of course, you'll see very soon. I leave those things to Sugimoto, but he's a little busy at the moment."

Talking to Koyama was like talking to a brick wall. Our conversation was going nowhere and my irritation was building, but I didn't know how to get an answer out of him. Stymied, I was quiet, and as if he had been waiting for that to happen, Koyama suddenly said, "You know I'm a calligrapher ..."

This completely threw me off.

"And because I'm a calligrapher, I think about my work, about words and *kanji*, all day long. And what I think is that humans are just like *kanji*. Writing, it is said, was invented by imitating the actual shapes of things. But it seems to me that it's the people who are imitating the *kanji*. The movement of the human body. A running man. A dancing woman. Aren't these kinds of characters, too? Written characters? Not just the body. The human mind and spirit are also composed of combinations of strokes—dots, flicks, flowing lines, bold lines, lines that fade away."

"Yeah, a bold architectural beauty," I mumbled.

Koyama kicked his head back and laughed, "Go easy on me with that, will you?"

He bent down in a slow, dignified manner, taking his seat again on the edge of the fountain, then beckoned to Hiroko with his stick. Immediately, she came over and took the stick from him before hurrying back to the edge of the room, where she stood in the shadows like a humble housemaid.

I was really perplexed. The two of them—these two individuals whom I'd always known separately, whom I'd never considered in the same frame. They seemed to understand each other and communicate without words.

"Take the example of Tomoe floating on water," Koyama began. "No. First, let's have a drink. Tonight let's you and I drink together." Again he made the most subtle of gestures to Hiroko, and my beauty in a kimono disappeared into the house.

# 12
## ROPE

I GRABBED THE bottle of scotch that Hiroko brought over. I poured myself a full glass and threw half of it down my throat in a single, greedy swig. A ball of fire blazed a path down to my stomach, and a moment later, I felt a mild heat spreading out to the tips of my fingers and toes. A weight was lifted from my chest, if only temporarily, the weight that I'd been carrying around all day since fleeing the train. At the same time, the question of what I would do next swirled through my mind, mixed with the alcohol.

"When Tomoe's hair spreads across the surface of the water," began Koyama, "that is also a written character. A glossy and graceful character. Or perhaps I could say the opposite—that the *kanji* I form on paper I wish to imbue with the same texture and scent as Tomoe's wet hair … Yes, that's what I want to say …"

He was going off on one of his rambling monologues again, and I couldn't stand to listen, so I nodded half-heartedly while staring at Hiroko's face as she stood framed against the backdrop of the night. A waiter brought over a small table, and Koyama and I sat facing each other while Hiroko was perched alone at the edge of the fountain, sitting forward with an attentiveness that actually seemed genuine. Although I didn't like seeing her enthusiasm and although I was annoyed by her show of reverence, I was at least granted the freedom to drink in her sweet profile.

As she sat on the edge of the fountain with her hair held up by a comb, my eyes wandered to the pale nape of her neck above the collar of her kimono. A few strands of hair had strayed there, and I wanted so badly to press my lips there. To feel her, to touch her. "She's my woman," I said to myself. This woman who'd lain beneath me countless times, the woman I'd made cry out in ecstasy. She'd changed over the last two months—lost weight, become almost emaciated, but somehow this only enhanced her beauty. Suddenly, I was overwhelmed by the conviction that she embodied everything I wanted in a woman and how could I possibly have been so blind? There was the memory of us lying together in a post-coital fog as she gently touched my face—my cheeks, my eyelids, my lips—humming a familiar tune. I opened my eyes and asked her what it was. A Beatles' song, she said shyly. But she could be haughty too. She could treat you like you were less than human, but then, in the midst of it, a glimpse of the same shyness would cross her face, and in moments like that I'd feel such tenderness for her.

In this state of mind, I convinced myself that we could go back to the way things were. After all, she did say that she'd have left her husband for me if only I'd asked. With her by my side, I might even be able to go back to my job. It wasn't too late—I'd only missed one day. We could find a big apartment in the suburbs to begin our life together. We could have a child, start a family—something I'd never dreamed of before. I'd stop catching my sperm in a condom, wrapping the thing in a tissue, and throwing it in the trash. My sperm would unite with her egg, and we'd create an entirely new life. I'd say good-bye to my sad little games built solely around pleasure. That had been my life until now, hadn't it?

But with the next sip of my whiskey, I told myself that was the end of that life.

"According to the Hindu story of creation," Koyama droned on, "first, there was Shiva, the supreme deity. The origin of everything, the embryo of existence, the seed of thought. The source of latent creativity. And this deity keeps spiraling downward to lower levels of existence, buffeted by the vibrations of the cosmos on the way down. No, actually it's Shakti, the female deity, that keeps spiraling downward, but Shiva borrows Shakti's spiral shape and releases her energy to the outside world. And by doing so, Shakti takes a place in every human being—in other words, in the body of each and every one of us. She becomes a concentrated point of energy on the tip of this descending spiral, and this is often represented as a coiled-up snake holding its tail in its mouth. Are you familiar with it? It's wrapped three and a half times around an erect penis ..."

Koyama paused and let out a hearty laugh.

"It must seem so silly to you. But this snake, it's called Kundalini, and it may be hiding inside your body as well. Your spirit is completely dependent on the vitality of this small, long-bodied reptile. Shakti's feminine energy of life, Shiva's creative energy, and everything else is dependent on the vitality of the Kundalini …"

I glanced up at the moon, having lost track of the time. Hiroko was still sitting on the edge of the fountain, which had been in the shadow of the building but was now bathed in light. Her eyes were wide-open, expressionless, and fixed in my direction. I wondered if that meant I'd drunk too much. Or maybe it meant that Koyama had reached the end of his monologue. But when I focused, Koyama was still talking, and I still didn't understand what the hell he was getting at.

Frustrated, I turned to him and cut him off with words I had to squeeze through my lips: "What's going on with you and Hiroko?" At least, that had been what I wanted to say, but my speech was so slurred I could barely understand myself.

"Going on? There's nothing going on," Koyama mumbled, annoyed at my interruption. But in a moment, he seemed to regain his composure and added with a smirk, "This lady was not getting along with her husband, so she's a guest at our house. That's all there is to it. And from what I understand, you are the reason she wasn't getting along with her husband."

My eyes met Hiroko's, and she dropped her glance, pretending to examine the back of her hands. Koyama picked up his monologue again, his voice seeming to fade. I took a few sips of whiskey, then sat back and let my consciousness wander into a dark room, like descending into a waking dream, until I no longer had the energy to bring the glass of whiskey to my lips. But it wasn't entirely an alcohol-induced intoxication. There was also something of delirium, like the one I'd fallen into the first night here watching the film with its close-ups of insects and sex as I sipped mint tea. I was aware that a change had taken place, but my thought process had slowed so much that there was no panic or fear, and if anything, I felt calm. My mind was too clear for me to be drunk. The moonlight was exceptionally bright, and if I put my mind to it, I could hear voices, although they sounded like incomprehensible chants.

I did catch, I thought, Koyama talking to a waiter. "Time to call it a night," he was saying. "They'll find their way out. Just leave them be."

"But if you could just say a few words to them, Mr. Koyama."

"Don't be ridiculous."

Again, I lost track of time. The next thing I became aware of was a soft, pale arm wrapped around my neck from behind. My vision was disoriented, and I wondered if I'd collapsed onto the floor. I slowly raised my neck, my vision clarified, and I saw I was still sitting in the garden chair, only slouched forward sloppily. The half glass of scotch was still in my hand. Helpless, I watched as the glass tilted slowly, spilling the contents onto my jeans, the stain spreading across my thigh. I felt Hiroko's warm breath on my ear. In surprise, I jerked my leg forward, kicking the table and knocking over the bottle of scotch. It fell to the marble floor and shattered, amber shards and amber liquid spraying across the floor, then my glass followed the same route—slipping through my fingers and falling to the floor, shattering. Everything was unfolding in slow motion.

As Hiroko wrapped her fair arms around my neck, I felt the softness of her breasts on my back. She came around to face me, and I saw that she was naked. She came to me and mounted me, her warm breath in my face. The light shining behind her made it impossible for me to see her expression. I wanted so badly to wrap my arms tightly around her smooth, pale body, to kiss every part of her, but I couldn't raise a finger any more than I could keep myself from drooling out of the corner of my mouth. With her little finger, Hiroko wiped my lips, then wiped her hand on my shirt. And even as I loved her warm breath on every part of my face—my eyes, my nose, my mouth, my ears—it was painfully frustrating that she wouldn't touch me with her lips.

I must have lost consciousness. When I came to, I was dizzy. The light in the room was different, and I glanced over to see a chink of brightness coming from the wall of the smaller glass conservatory that Koyama referred to as the winter garden. As my eyes began to focus, I could see a dark-skinned, well-built man having sex with Hiroko on the floor of the conservatory. As the buzzing left my ears, I could hear the cries of her ravishment—the same cries she'd made in bed with me—and I experienced an explosion of heat in my head. I tried to scream, but my mouth was dry and not even a whimper could escape my lips. I tried to move my hands, but lifting them was agony. I rubbed my chin and neck, and they hurt, then I touched my face, and it was covered in blood.

My vision blurred, then came back into focus, and I realized I was lying on the floor, amid shards of whiskey-bottle glass. I must have fallen, I must have cut my neck on the glass when I fell. I tried to gather my senses, but my consciousness was reverberating with Hiroko's high-pitched cries of ecstasy. At first she was under him, then they changed positions and she was on top. A horrific sense of déjà vu washed over me. It was Takabatake! Doing to Hiroko what he'd done to Tomoe in the film. But of course, this wasn't a film, this was happening before my eyes, with only a slim pane of glass between us: Takabatake was slamming his body, without care, without consideration, into the soft, petite body of *my* woman.

Takabatake was doing as he pleased with her—pushing her down, turning her over, twisting her, opening her up, stretching her, grinding into her. Like a savage. Like the parasitic bee that chews its way through the body of a caterpillar. Like the female praying mantis that chews the head off the male. Like all those things I'd seen, then pushed to the back of my mind in the hope I'd forget them all. The savagery, the degradation, the malaise, the amorality, the brutality, the loss of one's way. And all of it was here again, entwined with Hiroko's cries, ripping through my brain.

I tried to raise my head. But all I could do was lay it back down on the floor. The slightest movement sent a jolt through my jaw and neck where glass had cut through my flesh. I lay there with my knees up against my chest, unable to do anything but watch the sickening sex act in the conservatory. I was the caterpillar now. With a maggot eating me alive from inside.

I was pretty sure Hiroko didn't enjoy this kid of rough sex, and I was almost certain I could hear hatred and pain in her cries. But at the same time, I couldn't stop wondering if this hatred and pain added intensity to her ecstasy. The hideousness of the thought pierced me like a stake. I could not bear to see her losing herself in such twisted pleasure that she'd never shared with me, and I refused to believe that it was a part of her character, this dimension within her that I'd never known existed. Was this how she had wanted to be treated? Had her cries of ecstasy with me been faked, when all along she'd been craving something more?

Out of nowhere came the voice of Koyama, muffled and distant.

"A lot of people died here once …"

His words seemed to be coming to me through a thick layer of film. I struggled to make sense of them.

"During the Great Ansei Earthquake of 1855, fires raged over Edo, and much of the city was enveloped in fire. Hundreds who tried to escape to the safety of Nezu Shrine never made it. They were caught by the fire and perished. Tomoe says she can actually see those people scratching their throats as they die. Mothers crouched down, wrapping their bodies around their babies. Even those who pushed children and the elderly out of their way in an effort to save themselves succumbed. 'It's hot! It's hot!' they screamed, as their skin burned and their lungs choked. 'It's hot! It's hot!' Tomoe screams."

I'm confused, not sure I'm hearing correctly. But are those screams like the screams in the film—the cries of ecstasy? They would never be like Hiroko's screams—the screams of a woman at the peak of her femininity, screams with a richness, a range of high and low tones, and a sweet persistence and thickness. How many women who died in this very location 150 years ago died with cries like that?

My neck felt as if it was bleeding from several places where the shards of glass had dug in, and I could feel a sticky wetness spread from my ears to my chin. My entire body felt heavily swollen, and were it not for the creeping cold from the marble floor, I would have thought I'd lost all feeling. As my hands and feet gradually became colder and the pain in my neck more acute, I fantasized about stretching out on a soft, warm bed.

But my eyes kept being drawn to the action in the conservatory.

Takabatake pulled himself out of Hiroko, pushing her body away before getting up and disappearing from sight. When he returned with a length of rope, I knew that everything I'd been forced to witness was nothing compared to what would follow. Takabatake was trying to violate much more than Hiroko's body; he was trying to violate everything inside her as well—her pride, self-respect, tenderness, modesty. Perhaps I had been guilty of using women in my life, but even when I'd played mercilessly with their hearts and bodies, I'd never dreamed of such brutality, such humiliation. But as I lay transfixed watching their reptilian mating, my ears burned with the sounds of her ecstasy, which grew louder and louder yet.

Twisted, contorted, Hiroko stopped crying out suddenly—not only because her mouth was overflowing with the jet stream of Takabatake's piss, but also because her moans and cries had left her hoarse. Now her panting sounded like hiccups. The deepest depths of her being were being revealed for all to see. Unable to witness this any longer, I closed my eyes.

"Can't stand it, can you?" It was Koyama. "But you really should watch. This is what they're all like, you know. Women. There are some that taste good and some that don't."

I'd heard these words somewhere before.

"How can I put it ..." he went on. "They're nourishment that a man needs to maintain his health. That is, of course, only if you choose the classy ones and take them in moderation. But if you choose poorly, then you'll suffer from poisoning ..."

Here, where I lay, was where I'd first seen Tomoe in person. She was wearing jeans and a white T-shirt, standing at the end of the corridor that led to the conservatory, with her face hidden from view by the light behind her. If I could stand up and turn to look at the same place, would she be there? So much had happened since that first meeting, but absurdly, no time at all had passed since that night. I'd been sitting here watching the film all along. I closed my eyes again, and Hiroko's panting from the other side of the glass echoed through my consciousness. She was a woman. As much a woman as any woman could hope to be. Compared to her, Tomoe wasn't even close to being a woman, not even in the moments when she'd been savagely violated by the beast Takabatake. The thought brought on a longing for Hiroko intertwined with a deep hatred. If I could ever move again, I promised myself I would strangle her.

Again, my mind went blank, as if something had burned out. I was awakened by the sensation of something trying to pry my eyes open. The first thing I saw was a slimy piece of meat and I did my best to pull back. Then I made out Takabatake looking down at me with a wide smirk on his face. As I took in the full scene slowly, I realized sickeningly that the wet piece of meat inches from my eyes was his erect penis.

"Here! Here!" he kept repeating like a lunatic, slapping me in the eyes with his reddish-black member in cadence with his words. I clamped my eyes shut as tightly as I could. But his penis kept digging into my eyes, sticky fluid dripping down my cheeks. I was desperate, wanting to get away from him, but my body was paralyzed and all I could do was alter the angle of my face. My eyes were on fire, tears streaming down my face. I lay there, utterly humiliated. The abyss of vulgarity. But then, no matter how far you've fallen, there's always further to fall. Vulgarity was a pit with no bottom.

"Why?" I tried to say, but my mouth was sticky and nothing emerged except rasping breath. I tried again. "Why … me?"

I didn't know if Takabatake heard me because I was slipping back into unconsciousness.

"It's give and take. That's what it is," I was sure I heard him say— before everything faded to darkness.

# 13
## NECK

WATER, GREEN water, spreading, in my eyes, washing, stinging, burning. Blue-green water, green water, thick with algae, choking; skanky, dead water, squeaky water, squeaking water, deep water, in my eyes, washing, choking, my body melting, mixing, diluting, spreading, endlessly, endlessly shrinking, endlessly smaller, endlessly younger, childhood, infancy, fetus, even smaller, and smaller, sperm, and egg, even smaller, and smaller, lukewarm, nothingness, to a place where neither I nor anyone exists, a place where I am not me nor anyone, and by this time the water has become colorless, neither green nor blue, neither light nor dark, no sound, no smell.

When I was a kid, I ripped wings off butterflies; yes, I remember well, I also tore wings off dragonflies and cicadas, and once I pulled legs off a locust and placed it in an ant nest, placed the live legless locust into a nest of ants, brown ants, and the sight of it squirming as the ants with their powerful jaws swarmed over it delighted me so much that I couldn't stop watching. Every day, I performed some such act, the veranda was covered with insect parts—legs, wings, torsos—and then, under the veranda, there was not a single ant to be seen, the ants had disappeared, the ant nest had disappeared, and …

… that's right, these skaters were gliding over the foggy, blue-green water of the pond …

… that's right, in elementary school, I was playing baseball and messed up a throw and the ball hit a girl in the head, I went pale and kept asking her if she was okay and carried her to the nurse's office, and learned later that the nurse said how kind-hearted I was, but she had no clue; I *meant* to hit the girl because I liked her, I liked her hair, always tied up with a yellow ribbon, I liked her big, round eyes, her thin body, and her unhappiness; I liked her so I wanted to tease her, and when I thought of the patches of sweat under her arms when she played volleyball, my little hairless dick got hard.

The snicker I heard sounded like Sugimoto. *You're always putting on airs, looking down on us like you're too good for stray dogs.* Did Sugimoto really say that, or did my soundless voice speak the words in my head? *I was waiting for an opportunity to teach you a lesson, to paint your proud face bright red, but then you took off before I got the chance. So what's so great about France anyway?* I open my eyes a sliver to find Sugimoto right in front of me, his murky irises staring at me with reptilian blankness. *I wasn't looking down on you, I was afraid of you, I was afraid of your cool, how you were always cool, calm, no matter what. That's why I put on a face and tried to act like that, so you wouldn't look down on me,* I said in a pathetic voice, but I wasn't sure if words were actually leaving my mouth, they could've been just ringing in my head. *Listen ... you and me... we're in the same boat. It's all downhill from here, everything, these wretched times, all we can do is shed any shame and enjoy the indolence, the emaciation, the degeneration, the degradation, as much as possible.* I hear the words, but I don't know if they're mine or his ...

I peek again. Sugimoto is still here, his stare not letting up. I'm feeling sick, a sickness in my stomach, my body shivering with chills, and the last thing I want is to see Sugimoto's bloodshot eyes. Something's wrong, everything's off-balance, the whole world's warped, totally. That's it! Now that I've figured it out, it's so obvious. Everything's strange because Sugimoto's face is upside down. His eyelashes go where they shouldn't, his nose stretches upward, and at the top is his mouth hanging open and his chin, unshaven. Because of that, I was feeling sick. Because, also, I couldn't move, not my head, not my body, sprawled on the floor or sitting in a chair, I didn't know. Because Sugimoto was staring into my face, his face upside down, making me feel queasy. Please get out of my face. Please don't stare into my eyes from so close. Just let me sleep. Let me sleep in peace. Let me return to my sweet dreams.

I did everything you guys told me to do. I filmed Tomoe's hair. I filmed a close-up of her face, upside down, like the way yours is now, half in water, gradually rising to the surface and emerging on screen. I followed that with her long, lustrous hair spreading across the surface. Real good stuff, right? And she was great—she did as she was told, did everything I asked. No matter what I said, she nodded yes,

yes, her eyes always looking down slightly, like a doll with no will, and though I was happy for it, to go along with it, I couldn't get that kiss we had in the shadows out of my mind. But never did she approach me like that again. I thought she was attracted to me, I know, ridiculous idea, it's my imagination, I know, but the outrageous notion of marrying her crossed my mind, I never ever thought of marriage at all before. I won't lie, marriage to a girl from a good family, like hers, was tempting, and I'd catch myself talking like I was trying to charm her, and worry if anyone had suspected, this inner conflict, and if I saw you smirking at me, my heart would miss a beat.

*You fool!* Sugimoto's cold laughter reverberates. *You can pretend all the sophistication you like, but you'll always be cadging and crawling even to get to the low point you're at now. The granddaughter of someone like Mr. Koyama—hah! You're not on the same planet!*

"I know, I know," I say, trying to put on a smile, but I can't even move the corners of my mouth, and I don't know where I am. But even though I've lost feeling in my body and cannot move a finger, my brain is clear, very clear. And everything is very clear to me now. The reason I dropped out of university after working so hard to get in is all those boys and girls from good families. I couldn't stand them. I tried to hide it, but it always came out in a twisted, phony smile. But if I became part of this family—the patriarch having received the Order of the Rising Sun!—maybe then I could fix this self-serving way of thinking. What would be so wrong with that? So you call me low, huh, Sugimoto? What does it mean to be low anyway? There's the lowness of a man who lives by sucking out the blood of women like a leech. Sure there's that. I won't deny it. But there's also the lowness you need to survive in this society. The kind of lowness that you can exhibit openly without shame—the same lowness shared by the well-bred boys and girls who can smile and talk casually to someone they meet for the first time without using stiff, polite language to make a good impression. The kind of lowness they were picking up when they were in nursery school. Wouldn't somebody like me, somebody who rejected that kind of lowness all my life, actually be less vulgar, more pure, more true to himself than those people, huh? What do you say?

*What a load of crap*, Sugimoto says, spitting out his words.

A load of crap? Yeah, of course it's a load of crap. But I've finally realized at this late stage that there's a lowness you have to acquire; the lowness you need to join in this game called society, the lowness that is the minimum requirement for becoming a player in the game. Basically, I lacked vitality. I worked hard at part-time jobs, worked hard at cram school, and finally got into the University of Tokyo on my third attempt, but the classes were boring and I didn't make any friends. About the only worthwhile thing I did there was an eight-millimeter film for a film club, but then I quit that too, and not having enough credits, I dropped out and started this dissipated existence, working a string of shady jobs.

Someone grabs my arm. I open my eyes slightly to see a man or a woman with a mask wrapping a rubber cuff around my left arm, above the elbow. The vein pushes its way to the surface, which he or she sticks a needle into. Immediately, I feel heat, my heart starts pumping, fast, for a moment, then slowing nicely, peaceful and quiet, and finally I'm happy.

I am caught in a sudden evening downpour and soaked to the skin. I'm crouching down, crying, too afraid to move, when out of nowhere my mom picks me up in her arms and carries me home, saying, *Now, now, don't worry. Everything is okay, you silly thing. You really are a silly little thing. Such a little crybaby.* That sweet smell, my mother's smell ...

Skaters glide across the water of the pond, *wheeeeee, wheeeeee, wheeeeee, wheeeeee!*

The ant colony under the veranda has disappeared and there is not a single ant. As if they've all been wiped out, leaving behind only dead, legless locusts and water, green water, skanky water, dead water that spreads, in my eyes, washing, choking, my body melts, mixes, dilutes, spreads endlessly, shrinks endlessly, becoming endlessly smaller, becoming sperm and egg, no, even smaller and smaller into lukewarm nothingness, to a place where neither I nor anyone exists, a place where I am not me nor anyone, a place with no color, shape, smell, or taste. That's right, I've ripped wings off butterflies, and I've placed a bright green caterpillar onto hot asphalt in the midsummer sun, watching it squirm and writhe; when I came back later, it had shriveled, become like rubber, and I stamped on it, over and over, but it didn't flatten, it was like rubber.

I assumed I'd been abandoned on the floor of the glass conservatory. The moonlight shining through the glass penetrated my eyelids. I opened my eyes to find Sugimoto's face still there, so I shut them quickly. I thought quietly about my childhood, and time passed very, very slowly. Or maybe it was passing at frightening speed. I couldn't tell ... slow ... fast ... it was the same. What were the criteria? And could I have cared less? I remained silent, smiling thinly, immersed in gentle, dark-blue water, becoming smaller and smaller, becoming diluted and diffused, more and more. Sugimoto's ugly mug was gone, and the moonlight was pouring in. A sprinkle of lights in a corner of open space, like a forest of fireflies aglow. Stars? A galaxy? Or iridescent plankton in the depths of the sea? This glass submarine descending into a trench so deep that it touches the core of the earth.

*Me, I take things easy. I go with the flow.* Sugimoto breaks the silence. I am annoyed to be pulled out of the depths of my sea, and it is excruciating to have to regain equilibrium so I do not flinch from his stare. *I'm just doing what I'm told, just going with the flow,* he says jokingly, but his eyes are cold and his mouth is stiff. *I do what I'm told. I leave the thinking to my sensei.*

*Is that right? You really are into that funny old man.*

Sugimoto turns red with anger. *What would you know, you fool! Before I met the sensei, I was a worthless piece of shit. But he let me prepare his ink, as he sat on his knees meditating. When he opened his eyes, he picked up his brush, dabbed it in ink, and in one motion, drew a line across the paper. My hair stood on end. I knew I had found what I was looking for—beauty in a single horizontal line ...*

*Didn't figure you for the type.*

Sugimoto doesn't rise to the bait, continues in an unusually sincere manner. *You think you're such an intellectual, Otsuki. But things of beauty, things of filth, they're all the same when you burrow down to the core. If you descend to the depths, you reach a place where everything becomes one, a place where total opposites melt into each other completely. Beauty and pollution, life and death, lowliness and nobility, penis and vagina.*

Sugimoto's face is close, far too close, but his rambling lips are not moving. They are a dull, sea-slug–like color, splotches covered with a filthy film, like he has ringworm. One eye has something wriggling in the corner. I realize it is a maggot that infests dead flesh. I try not to throw up.

I look at his upside-down head from bottom to top. I do everything to concentrate my tangled mind. On first gaze, I capture his closely cropped hair, by his narrow forehead, his thin, almost nonexistent eyebrows, his eyes (one with the maggot), his nose that points upward, his mouth half-open, then his prominent jaw, then his neck, then … nothing! Nothing after the neck! Just a severed head on the floor like a melon. I force my eyes to his stump of neck and squint to see the reddish-black flesh, a sharp edge of bone peeking out from its core, and wriggling maggots everywhere. His entire face, from his cheeks to his ears, to his forehead, is covered in dark dried blood, which makes the whites of his eyes shocking in contrast. Under his left ear was the baseball cap he was always wearing, red to begin with, but now overflowing with a thick, sticky crimson, overflowing across the floor as if reaching out to touch my ear. *You're starting to rot.* I must have spoken out loud.

*So are you*, replied Sugimoto.

So here I am, one sad severed head lying next to another. My brain already beginning to rot. Strangely calm, I consider how Sugimoto must be starting to stink; the fact that I can't smell him is proof of my own brain decomposing. My consciousness fades again, a rubber cuff is wrapped around my upper arm, and a needle slides into my vein, dispatching me off into a peaceful, half-conscious state.

I had so much fun back then; the wings I ripped off butterflies and dragonflies falling gently to the ground, the camisoles and brassieres that I ripped off women falling gently to the ground, the wingless, legless insects squirming as they sizzled, the stench of sitting water in a basin, a dense gathering of clouds, a swarm of mosquitoes, a large dahlia, the dull cries of late-summer cicadas . . .

An evening shower brings the temperature down sharply. I lie on my back on the veranda, pull down my shorts and underwear, and play semi-consciously with my hard penis until I'm pierced by an unexpected, intense pleasure and a thin, transparent fluid squirts out. I have no idea what has just happened. My sweat dries off, my body cools down, the dusk arrives, and I'm frightened by my own body. The distinct smell of the grass and the water in the sun. The smell of the rain from that beautiful midsummer afternoon. Now lost, forever.

# 14
## LEVITATION

"I'M SO TIRED. So very, very tired." The words trickle from the dry, ashen lips of Sugimoto's upside-down head, causing a single maggot to wriggle at the corner of his mouth. "Terrible things happened here," he says. "Things you can't begin to imagine."

"What kind of things?" says a voice that might belong to me, if spoken through a long tube.

"You know …" Sugimoto continues, free, in death, of the nauseating sweat and animal energy that dogged his rants, "awful things. Horrible things. I did as I was told. I've lost count of the people who died in my time here. The drugs, the equipment, the heart attacks, the deaths. They happened all the time. The men were big in politics, big in big business, and old, easy for overexcitement to kill. Wrinkled old perverts, tying up women, begging to be tied up themselves. No sorry from me when they croaked. We had to sneak them into a hospital where we had someone to take care of the mess."

"But the girls … some of them barely of age … some lost consciousness … they wouldn't wake up … the sensei said no doctor … Many things I'm not proud of, but that was the … In three years, two girls died. One was a runaway. We picked her up on Center Street in Shibuya, or maybe Takeshita Street in Harajuku, wherever. She's probably still registered as missing. I don't even want to know what they did with her, but I saw her lying there, still warm … and I saw the rope marks on her neck … That was when I first came to work here, before I knew anything …"

"Then there was the beautiful Filipino girl … I don't know what her story was, but when she got here she was really thin, just skin and bone. At first, she spent all her time curled up in bed. But slowly she started to come alive, and then she was like fresh grass sprouting in spring. She laughed, and I used to talk to her in my broken English. Once I was in the garden shaving my head, and she came over and took the razor out of my hand and shaved my head for me. She had small hands, like a child's, thin, delicate fingers. She was laughing the whole time. She was so sensitive and kind, she was genuinely good."

"Some girls can do it without getting totally polluted by the old men and their filthy perversions. But some girls get destroyed; it eats them up inside, even if they don't show it. The first time that Filipino girl went with a customer, she came back looking like a ghost, she just went to bed and wouldn't eat or drink. After a while, I thought maybe she was getting used to it, but one morning, we found her … she was … she hanged herself. It was on that incredibly hot day in August … or July … the day I bumped into you—first time in years—in front of the mansion. It happened that morning. I spent all afternoon digging a hole for her in the garden."

"He had her buried?" I couldn't believe it. "In the garden?"

"That's right. She's right there, decomposing in the dirt. Her flesh rotting and stinking while we eat our meals a few meters away. When it rains hard, I start to feel sick. Anyway, I was digging the hole all afternoon, and when I was done, I couldn't bear to go back in the house. So I stepped out onto the street, and that's when you walked by. I was feeling pretty down and …"

The more Sugimoto droned on, the more unbelievable his story sounded. He was never the type to care about "beauty," and he certainly wasn't the type to get sentimental over the loss of a "genuinely good" girl. He was cruel—*especially* when it came to women. This was a guy who thought nothing about kicking a pregnant woman. She was the wife of some lowlife who owed the company money, and she was giving us attitude, acting like she didn't have to tell us anything because she had this huge belly, but still. I had to drag Sugimoto away from her, and then he pushed me back with an icy glare. Come to think of it, he was no different from that monster Takabatake. One and the same. He says how the Filipino girl was so sensitive and kind, but he doesn't say anything about what he did to her. I bet he was the one who pushed her over the edge.

"… I try not to think about the things that went on here before me," he slurs. "It unhinges me. The only person who really knows what went on here is Masayo."

"The woman who always wears a kimono and has a face like a

Noh mask?"

"Yeah, her. She's been with the sensei since the beginning. The only one who's seen it all. She's terrifying …"

As Sugimoto's voice echoed and faded, a peaceful darkness began to spread around me, drawing me in deep, enveloping me as I got smaller and smaller. Then a completely different scene appeared before my eyes. I was watching Tomoe as she floated horizontally to the surface of a pool of water and then continued rising into the air. By now, any concept of time was lost on me, and I couldn't tell whether this was really happening or whether this was projected from my unconscious onto a screen in the darkness of my mind.

She was dressed in a thin, white garment. Water was streaming off her body and falling from her hair. She seemed to hover, remaining magically horizontal, her cascading hair just touching the surface of the water. At this point, I noticed that the pool of water was actually the fountain in the inner garden and that I was lying on the floor of the glass conservatory, looking out. After a while, I wasn't so sure I was lying on the floor, or whether I was standing, or whether I was sitting in a chair with my arms and legs tied together because all I really knew was that I couldn't move.

My eyes would only open a crack, I couldn't feel my hands or feet. Could I have been reduced to a severed head too? Perhaps we were just two bloody heads lying on the floor facing each other, pointing in different directions, mumbling nonsense. But when I opened my eyes again, Sugimoto's head was no longer there and the shadow of death had disappeared into darkness, as I myself and everything else pulled back into nothingness. Then, gradually, a barren, lifeless space spread out on the other side of the glass. The moon was reflected on the rippling surface of the fountain, which the twisted metal sculpture rose up from, with Tomoe floating in the air above, the pointed tip of the sculpture touching the small of her back. Then her garment slipped off, and her naked body sparkled in the moonlight. Such a spectacular scene. Such a spectacular, bewildering scene.

The inner gardens of Koyama's mansion in Nezu and Takabatake's house in Sanya, I was reminded, were identical, including the fountain, the sculpture, and overall layout, and now I was wondering which garden I was in.

"Quite a sight, don't you think?" It was Koyama's voice. "She is like a calligraphic stroke."

The last thing I wanted was to listen to another of Koyama's long-winded monologues, but in my situation, there was nothing I could do to avoid it.

"It is a grand receptacle. One that catches and embraces everything—beauty, evil, purity, impurity … That's what this seventeen-year-old girl is. That's why she is so precious to me. Her pale body creates a single white horizontal line against the darkness of night … Myself, I draw a single black line in ink across a piece of white paper … The black becomes white, and the white black. They are the exact opposites of each other. But it isn't enough. That single horizontal line isn't enough. It is a receptacle that catches falling things, takes them in, purifies them, and ultimately offers them salvation. It is a device that relieves sinking things of their own weight, allowing them to float back up to the surface. It is a sign that can represent anything and everything. How should I put this? In the end, to represent everything is to represent nothing. Everything is the equivalent of nothing."

"So what should one do? One needs to find another stroke to complement that single horizontal line—a curved line to complement the straight line. In other words, the sign has to couple with another sign. To copulate, to fertilize. That's why I had Takabatake have sex with her. But it didn't work. It didn't work with that barbarian, that walking dick. That's why I asked you, Mr. Otsuki, to do the filming. But I'm sorry to say that didn't work either. You weren't able to achieve the perfect character I was hoping for. It's so simple, you see. What I wanted to do was to turn Tomoe into a single, perfect *kanji* … I'll even go as far as to say that this is the ultimate objective of my life. And Mr. Otsuki, it may be something that only you can do. You do want Tomoe, don't you?"

I wanted to tell him to shut up, but I couldn't give voice to my thoughts. I was unable to talk. In fact, because I couldn't see his face, I had no idea where he was. He was everywhere at once, inside and outside me, blabbering on in his self-importance. Had I turned into Koyama? Was I speaking through him? Did I want Tomoe? Of course, I did.

She was, as Koyama said, like a *kanji* that represented everything and nothing. She was an abstract, neutral sign. And therefore I didn't want her or desire her as I did Hiroko. No way could she become the object of the same thirst I had for Hiroko. I wished I could say this to Koyama, although he had no interest in any response I might have anyway.

When I glanced toward the fountain again, Tomoe's floating body was no longer there. Koyama's sticky, persistent voice continued to come and go, however, before transforming into a colorless liquid that began to fill the space around me, lapping against my toes, gradually rising until it covered my head. Darker, darker, thicker. The liquid kept flowing, and I descended deeper into a silent darkness.

I was jolted awake by an icy coldness that was accompanied by colors like flames dancing on the inside of my eyelids, stinging, tears pouring. I strained to crack open my eyes. I was on a road. A fire was roaring a few meters away. Laborers huddled around the fire sipping sake from glass cups. I tried to get up and warm myself by the fire. I had regained feeling in my arms and legs, but I couldn't move them. I tried to focus but could manage no more than a twitch of a finger or a toe. I couldn't right myself, sit, or stand. The moment I realized this, all energy drained from my body and my face slumped back down onto the road, which was so cold I feared my cheek and ear might freeze to it, to be ripped off if I ever managed to lift my head.

But there was the knowledge that my senses were coming back into focus. Earlier, I'd been a powerless, unwilling audience to strange dreams and hallucinations, unclear whether I was hot or cold. But with the icy asphalt reality at my cheek, I knew this was real—the fire, the laborers huddled around it, the ash floating in the air like snowflakes. The reality remained full of pain and despair, but it was reality, and I was thankful that I had made my return to this world. Bit by bit, the pain crept its way across my arms, my legs, my torso, and though I could do nothing except lie there, I at least began to realize how my body was positioned.

"I'm going to live," I told myself. "Live and kill that old bastard!"

A loud honking. A car drives by, inches from my body. The smell of gasoline taints my nostrils. I open my eyes wide to see one of the laborers glancing at me, opening his mouth to reveal holes where teeth should be. I try to call to him, but I have no voice. Laughter erupts around the fire.

"I need an ambulance!" I try to shout, but can only gasp weakly. Within moments, my world begins to blur, and again I fall into darkness.

# 15
## HOSPITAL

I KNEW THAT I was in a hospital, but in my delirious state I didn't know much more. They told me I'd been talking in my sleep, muttering all night long. They told me I'd been asleep for a long time, drifting in and out of consciousness, though only enough to stare off into space and mutter. They told me I didn't respond to questions and that the only words they recognized were "I'll kill him, I'll kill him, I'll kill him."

I'd been brought in to the hospital with my collarbone and two ribs broken, my shoulder dislocated, and my body covered in cuts and bruises. But internal damage had been much worse, my heartbeat extremely slow and irregular, my liver on the verge of shutting down. For three days, they weren't sure I would make it, and for a week, I had to be fed intravenously. But slowly, gradually, my mind began to function and the world came back into focus.

They kept asking if I had family or anyone to contact, but I just stared at them blankly, and soon enough they gave up asking. Judging from the others in my hospital ward—shriveled old men and unshaven middle-aged soaks who stank of alcohol and bad hygiene—I supposed the staff was used to a lack of response. The hospital, located near Minami-Senju, was full of patients found lying on the street, so I imagined the staff thought my story was not a whole lot different: a laborer down on his luck who'd drunk himself to the point where he couldn't afford a flophouse, then somehow got into a fight or mugged, or both, and was left lying on the streets in his underwear. That was how a policeman had found me, in Sanya, in the early hours of the morning, in my undershirt and briefs. They threw away my underwear. The doctor had to add that my underwear stank—filthy with blood, urine, and feces—which was unnecessary and condescending.

"I'm very sorry," I said with a reflexively servile attitude. But I was numb to humiliation, which, given the situation, wasn't a bad thing.

"I don't suppose you found my wallet?" I asked.

"You didn't have one on you when you were found," the doctor replied curtly.

Once I'd recovered enough to force rice congee down my throat, I got around to looking at myself in the mirror. What I saw was a gaunt, ghost-like face staring back at me, which was shocking. It was this transformation that made me ask what date it was. Late November—so I'd been out of it for over ten days. Ten days! What had they done to me?

"You're on something, aren't you?" the doctor asked casually as he pushed open my eyelids with his large, disinfected thumb.

I refused to dignify his question with a response.

"You on drugs?" he asked again.

"No."

"Well, the urine test didn't show anything, so I guess you're telling the truth. But given the state you're in, you've got to be on something?"

"I'm not on anything."

"I'm just surprised your heart held out. But your kidneys and spleen are in a pretty bad state."

"I see."

"… So you'd better call somebody to take you home."

Again, I didn't respond.

"Shunichi Nakamura. Thirty-four years old."

The age was truthful, but the name I made up. The choice of Nakamura was so patently common that as soon as it came out of my mouth, I regretted it. Shunichi was real, though, so maybe the combination sounded believable.

"Where do you live? Do you have a criminal record?"

At this point, I was exhausted, feeling too weak to answer. When I said nothing and closed my eyes, the doctor walked away in irritation. After a few days, with a clearer head, I decided I'd keep my mouth shut for all questions, meeting them only with a vacant stare and a stupid smile.

By the hospital's not having any means to identify me, I could remain as just another homeless person, someone who didn't even make the official statistics. That was fine with me. Actually, it was better than fine. Of course, the easiest thing to do would have been to tell them who I was and ask them to call the police. After all, I had been the victim of a violent crime and my attackers should be made to pay for what they'd done—prosecuted for kidnapping and assault, and their asses sued. But I couldn't bring myself to involve the police, mostly because I had no idea how to explain what had happened. I wasn't sure myself what happened.

There were marks on my wrists and ankles that looked like rope burns, and the abrasions on my right wrist and ankle had been the worst, swollen and infected. The swelling had gone down, but I still had difficulty moving my fingers. I must have been tied up the whole time, given weird shit to drink, and beaten up over and over again. I wasn't sure about anything, though. It was like one long continuous nightmare. I wasn't conscious for a lot of it, and I didn't know who did what to me. Koyama was behind it all, but he probably didn't deign to dirty his hands. Could be that ape Takabatake, but I had no way of knowing.

It was far from sure that the police would act on such a bizarre story and go after a renowned calligrapher in his Bunkyo mansion. If Koyama simply denied everything, then it would be my word against his. If I were to say anything about him drugging me, my criminal record for possession of controlled substances would completely undermine me. I'd be treated as some lowlife junkie trying to swindle a rich man so I could go buy more drugs. What motive would a renowned calligrapher possibly have to kidnap and assault a former drug addict?

That, in fact, was what I'd been asking myself over and over.

"Why me?" I'd asked Koyama. Why choose me, of all people, to get sucked into this wild stuff. I could understand why he wanted me to do the filming, and I'm not sorry he did. But the excitement was a trap, and I was a fool to allow myself to be drawn into it. Still, why? Why would Koyama do this to me? If I didn't know, there was no way I'd be able to convince the authorities of anything.

I didn't want to ask for their help anyway. I didn't want to have anything to do with them. Fuck the law. Fuck the cops. That's always been my stance. I wasn't about to go to them like some obedient lapdog and expect them to help. If I had a problem, I had to take care of it myself.

After about a week, when I was able to get out of bed, I wandered off alone and tried to exercise to speed my recovery. My body was in the worst shape it'd ever been, but my will to live was stronger than it had been in years. It burned in me like fire—fanned by my hatred for the old bastard and by thoughts of Hiroko and Tomoe. I was determined to storm into that mansion in Nezu. I was going to free those women from his grasp. I was furious but then overcome by a despair that would leave me in tears. Over time, this volatility and these pathetic emotional outbursts began to fade and I went back to staring into space from my small but clean hospital bed.

After a couple of weeks, I'd recovered much of my strength, but I pretended to need to hold on to the wall when I was going to the hall bathroom. I wanted the safe haven of the hospital, but I wasn't sure how long I could stretch it. When the doctor indicated that I had improved so much that it was time for me to talk to an officer from the Ministry of Justice, I knew I needed to get out of there fast. Escaping from the hospital wouldn't be difficult; the problem was I had no clothes and no cash. I could steal clothes from one of the seven other guys in the ward, but they didn't look like they had money for the taking.

I practiced getting out of bed without a groan. I waited until the middle of the night when all was quiet and snuck into a room adjacent to the emergency exit. It was the staff lounge, where the staff members had their lockers. I was hoping for a wallet or a purse. But all the lockers were locked. I was afraid that any noise I'd make would attract attention, so I gave up and went back to bed.

The next day, I slept all afternoon to try to conserve my energy, then in the middle of the night, I snuck back into the staff lounge. Again, no luck. Boldly, I stepped out into the hall to look around. I walked carefully toward the nurse's station at the end of the hall and suddenly came face-to-face with my arrogant young doctor, who just happened to be standing there.

"Oh, hi," I said.

The doctor stood in silence for a few moments, staring at me from behind silver-framed glasses. "What are you doing out of bed in the middle of the night?" he asked in a tone that was uncharacteristically polite.

"Well, I … was going to the bathroom."

"The bathroom's in the opposite direction."

"Right." I turned around and started briskly back the other way.

"Hey, Nakamura!"

I turned around.

"I didn't know you could walk that well already."

I didn't reply.

"You know, I get the feeling there's something funny with you."

"Funny?"

"Judging by the wounds on your wrists and ankles, I'd say someone kept you tied up for a good while. At first, I thought you were beaten by a bunch of thugs. But then I started to wonder, are you …?" he asked, tracing a line across his cheek like that of the stereotypical yakuza scarface.

"No, I'm not."

"Well, I don't know what's going on with you, but it better not be drugs—"

"It's not."

The doctor said nothing more, although he continued to stare at me while I headed off back to my room.

Time was running out for me. I no longer had the option of hanging out in the hospital. I needed to find a way to get some cash.

I lay in bed, waiting until the dawn was breaking. Then, as the large old man in the neighboring bed slept soundly—he barely made a peep while awake—I stuck my hands around the curtains and grabbed his rolled-up shirt and pants. I went to the bathroom down the hall and locked myself in a stall. I pulled off my pajamas and slipped on the guy's dirty gray flannel shirt and light green pants. The shirt was a size too big for me and the pants were too long, but since my shoulders and chest were still wrapped in bandages, I was glad for the extra room. The pants I just rolled up.

Wearing plastic bathroom slippers, I stepped cautiously into the hall and made my way toward the steel doors of the emergency exit, glancing over my shoulder to see if there was anyone—there wasn't, fortunately—and I stepped outside. Immediately, I was hit with a blast of cold air. This shouldn't have been a surprise for someone wearing just a flannel shirt on a late November morning, but I was shocked by the stabbing pain in my chest—a little reminder of the doctor's saying my heartbeat was "extremely slow and irregular." But there was no turning back. Shivering, I hurried down the emergency stairs and across the parking lot next to the building. The hospital grounds were surrounded by a chain-link fence—the final obstacle. I exhausted myself trying to pull myself up and over, then tumbled onto the other side. I hadn't recovered so much as I thought.

The sky was getting steadily brighter, and the cold was beginning to penetrate my hollow cheeks. Not a soul was around. I stumbled to my feet and promised myself I would live. I put my plastic slippers on properly and headed off as fast as I could in search of a cab.

# 16
## Returning Home

I GAVE THE driver the address of an ex-girlfriend, then sat back and watched the darkness recede from the sky. When the cab arrived at Satomi's apartment in Higashi-Nakano, I had to wake her up to come down and pay the fare. It had been a while since I'd last seen her, and although she didn't bother to hide her annoyance at my sudden intrusion, she agreed to let me stay with her for a week.

She didn't ask any questions, not about how I came to appear at her place out of the blue with nothing in my pockets. When she first saw the cuts and bruises over my body, there was shock in her eyes but she never asked about those either. I guess she just didn't want to have anything to do with whatever it was I'd gotten myself mixed up in, but still she'd been willing to take in this scruffy dog from the street. I appreciated that. She kept a certain distance throughout my stay, but she took care of me, changed my bandages, bought me underwear and a set of clothes, and even stocked the fridge with prepared foods. On my last night, I tried pulling her to me in bed, but she gently pushed me away.

"I'm sorry to have troubled you," I said in the morning as I was leaving.

"I'm sorry that there's someone in my life right now."

"I know. I really am sorry. Thanks for everything."

She'd always been kind and warmhearted. The complete opposite, in many ways, of Hiroko, who was so thin and fragile that I was afraid I might accidentally break her. Satomi wasn't particularly tall or heavy, but she did give the impression of being solid. Well grounded too. She had common sense and took care of herself, which was probably why she ended it before we got serious. We managed to remain friendly—even meeting up occasionally in Shinjuku for drinks. Satomi had a good-paying administrative job with a foreign insurance company, but it hadn't ever occurred to me to milk her for her money. She was willing to lend me some, though, as I stepped out into the crisp December air.

"So here I am, back in Bunkyo ward again," I said aloud to myself as I made my way through a shopping arcade where cheesy Christmas music was being piped out of loudspeakers. I was walking slowly, in pain still. Grimacing, I made it to my front door before squatting down to catch my breath.

When I placed a hand on the sliding front door, I saw that it was unlocked. In a way, I wasn't surprised. The lock was a flimsy thing anyway, more for show than security, so anyone could have broken in by sticking a screwdriver into the keyhole and twisting it a little. But upon closer examination, the lock hadn't been forced at all.

If whoever took my wallet took my keys too, then they could have just let themselves in. But everything in the house appeared to be exactly as I'd left it. Admittedly, I didn't have much worth stealing, but nothing was touched. My bankbook—with what little money was in it—was in the top drawer alongside my official seal. Not one yen of my paltry savings was gone.

I pulled out the futon from the closet, which was ripe with mildew, laid it out on the floor, and crashed on it. In no time at all, I found myself wandering through an endless maze-like landscape, painted entirely in primary colors. I woke up exhausted and nauseated. I took a few deep breaths to try to relieve the sickness, then sat in silence. Total silence. A silence so complete that I wondered if it was the absence of sound that had awakened me. I'd never known it to be so quiet before, so eerie in the dim light. I wasn't sure if I'd slept an entire day but then concluded it was late afternoon.

I rolled onto my side and saw, on the floor by the window, a dented 350-ml can of Sapporo Black beer. Was it there when I laid out the futon? Did I not notice it? I didn't like the way my thumb seemed to fit the dent perfectly. The tab had been pulled and left standing up, the can was half-full, and there was a trace of saliva on the edge. Were there fingerprints too? Of course, if there were, how would I know whether they were mine or not?

I sniffed the saliva, backed away immediately, reflexively, from the sour-sweet metallic stink, losing my grip on the can. The dark liquid seeped out onto the worn tatami floor but not before soaking a corner of the futon. Like everything else in my life, they were now stained, beyond cleaning.

Picking up the can with thumb and forefinger, I took it over to the kitchen and poured the remainder of its contents down the drain. The smell was enough to trigger a nausea that came in waves and, unable to hold it in any longer, I heaved into the sink, again and again, the bile dripping from my nostrils. I felt like my body had been invaded, just like my unlocked house. I laid down on the mattress, too weak to sop up beer, and closed my eyes. That same unnerving silence. And just like that, my life seemed to enter into a period of unusual calm and quiet.

That night, the entire Kanto region was hit by a severe cold front, and for the next few days the temperature never made it above zero, leaving me no choice but to stay holed up in the house like a hibernating animal. It was as if I'd been cut off from the world.

I'd been unable to summon the courage to call my former workplace, but I did manage to get to a payphone—my line at home having been cut off—and call my uncle, who made his disappointment crystal clear. I said I'd been in an accident, which was why I hadn't been able to call the office, but when he asked about the accident, I found myself at a loss for words and hung up. Of course, I couldn't blame him for being disappointed. Although I had been indisposed, the fact was, I had determined to end my career as an office worker that Monday morning weeks before the so-called accident occurred. I'd already taken a step out of the real world.

With the exception of forays to stock up on basic food supplies, I spent my days huddled around a small heater, feeling strangely serene. When I'd started doing drugs a few years ago, I'd been trying to escape an inexplicable, pounding anxiety that plagued me day and night. When in August I felt the same anxiety returning, I'd decided to change my life. Since then, I'd lost my woman and my job, I'd been drugged and beaten up, and I was still in danger of violence. But for some reason, the anger and irritation started to fade, and from somewhere within me, I began to feel peace and tranquility. No longer was I desperate to find a respectable job. And no longer did I feel the need to give my spirits a chemical lift.

I had nothing to lose. It was as simple as that. I had a roof over my head for shelter and a heater to keep me warm. I was grateful for them both. All I wanted, at least until the pain in my chest eased, was to enjoy this period of convalescence. And even if I were to lose the heater and the roof, I took comfort in the newfound knowledge that society would provide me with a place to stay, like the hospital where I'd spent two weeks.

At some point, I started not to care if I died. This might not really make a lot of sense, but I thought it a kind of reaction to the extreme determination to live that I'd felt in the hospital. I had no woman, no job, and no desire to claim them back. My only needs were—like an animal's—food for survival each day. So if my life were to come to an abrupt end after I'd swallowed a mouthful of stir-fried pork and ginger from the convenience store in the festive shopping arcade, then that would be that. I wasn't afraid, and I'd have no regrets. That was the mind-set I had. My will to live, which had been fueled by my hatred for old man Koyama and my desire to kill him, slowly faded into the blur of everyday life, where it was being consumed with the passing of each moment, as transient as a mouthful of food or the warmth from a heater, in days of inconsequential incidents strung together.

In other words, I was spending my days in delirium. There were times when I wasn't sure what was real, what was part of an elaborate illusion. One example comes to mind of a time: I'd returned from the convenience store to find a footprint on the tatami floor that I was certain had not been there. Another example: I'd nodded off while watching a brain-dead TV show about celebrity scandals. When I woke up, I went into the kitchen for a glass of water and found cigarette butts in the sink that weren't my brand. Such strange incidents. But stranger was the fact that I didn't care one way or another. I just accepted them and turned my thoughts to how quiet life could be.

Now that I was so thoroughly tainted, I could take anything that was thrown at me. I thought back to the time when I'd been haunted by the words:

*To become tainted*
*Becoming tainted*
*To have become tainted*

as if they were an evil spell. Only now did I realize this was a state of idyllic happiness, where a festering filth had become ingrained in me. It was as if I was in limbo, where forces were passing freely through my body but the situation was perfectly normal, nonetheless. It is possible that these forces were actually a part of my body. Once I understood this, I could know relief. I could be cleared of guilt over who I am by simply accepting that I must live with the filth within me.

There was, however, one urge that rose within me like a sudden thirst: It was to see that sixteen-millimeter film that juxtaposed scenes of Tomoe having sex with grotesque shots of insects. The one I got halfway through before falling into a hypnotic trance. Yes, I wanted to see that film again. After all that'd happened to me since, I felt certain I'd see it in a completely different light—because it was as if I'd become a character in it. Having stepped away from a regular life—with its jobs and social units—I'd stepped over a boundary and into the realm of that film.

I was just a filthy halfway house for spirits. I accepted that, and I no longer had reason to feel anxious or terrible. I didn't need to worry about who left the half-full can of beer. I didn't care if it was the ape Takabatake or if it was the fool Sugimoto, who turned out to be less cunning than I thought and was probably dead for all I knew. I didn't care if it was a different self—a merciless demon—lurking inside me. I did wonder what the zodiacal animal for next year was. Even when you think you've been pushed over the edge, life goes on. I pondered these things, surprised about my cavalier attitude to everything. Or was this just a peaceful resignation brought about by the fact that I had no specific object to focus my newfound lust for life on? I was a hamster on a treadmill. I was a child abandoned by its mother, toying with spools of thread and scraps of paper.

So I'd stepped outside this world. Was there no way for me to get back in?

*We go back... Listen, this is the important part. We aren't moving forward toward the final destination of death. We go back. We go back to a different "now" … We just make a loop and slip inside a different "now."*

So I wasn't going to be in this state of being forever? Well, then, how about making some flies for fishing? Flies for fishing for smelt. It'd been a while. But when I went to the drawer for my materials, they were missing! And not just the materials—the twenty or so flies that I'd made were missing too.

Days and nights passed.

Then, suddenly in the middle of the night, I was scared awake by the phone ringing. Scared more than simply startled, because my phone had been disconnected. I picked up the receiver and said a sheepish, "Hello?" There was no response, and after a moment the line went dead. A few minutes later, the phone started ringing again. Again I picked up, and again no response. The same thing happened five or six more times, until I finally pulled the cord out of the jack.

The next evening, almost as soon as I plugged the cord back in, the phone started ringing. I picked up the receiver and held it to my ear, saying nothing.

Thirty seconds later, a deep voice said, "I know you're there." It sounded like someone in his forties or fifties.

I remained silent.

A long pause. Then, he spoke again, slowly. "I know you're there." Short pause. Then, "Hiroko, I know you're there."

I was caught completely by surprise. "What do you want?" I said, my voice raspy from lack of use. I cleared my throat and repeated, "What do you want?"

"Aah … Mister … Otsuki, I presume?" His voice dripped with hatred.

"Yes, that's me."

"I know Hiroko is there."

"No, she isn't."

"You don't know what you've done."

"Who are you?"

"Tsutami." It was Hiroko's husband.

"Put Hiroko on the phone."

"I'm telling you, she's not here."

"Shunichi Otsuki, right? I know all about you. You're a real piece of work, or so I hear. I don't know what she ever saw in you. Well, I don't care. She's yours. You can have her. I'm tired of her—so proud, so slow in the head. And ungrateful too. You can keep her. But what I won't let you keep is the thing she took from me when she left. I want that back."

## 17

## THE LEDGER

DURING THE BUBBLE economy, Hiroko had worked as a hostess in a club in Ginza. It was there that she met the president of a small construction firm, who, like others in the construction business at the time, had money coming out of his ears. So when Hiroko married this guy, she must have felt that she'd been slapped across the face with a bundle of cash.

She never gave much away about him, and I assumed that he was legitimate. But as he was casually threatening me on the phone, this guy Tsutami had all the manners of a yakuza, and I had the feeling an icicle was being shoved down my throat and into my gut.

"The thing she took … ? I don't know what you're talking about. I don't know where Hiroko is … and frankly I don't care," I said, and immediately I bit my lip, realizing I'd neglected to add the honorific san after her name. "I haven't seen her in a long time," I added, cursing myself for sounding unconvincing.

"I want the stock certificates and the ledger," Tsutami demanded in his deep voice. "You know what I'm talking about."

"I really don't," I replied, feeling the chill in my gut spread.

"She can keep the stocks. I'll call it palimony. They're only worth a few million yen. And she can keep the five or six hundred thousand yen she ran off with, too. But I want the ledger. It's of no value to you or her anyway."

"I'm sorry, I really have no idea what you're talking about. I'm going to hang up now," I said politely. But I didn't; I stayed on the line, pressing the phone to my ear as Tsutami went silent and hung up himself.

The quiet was deafening, and suddenly it occurred to me that the printing press next door wasn't clunking away as it usually was. I was probably too out of it to realize it earlier, but now that I thought about it, I hadn't heard it at all since I'd been back.

Two days later, on December 30th, I was on my way back from the convenience store, carrying a microwave dinner, when I was met by a man standing in front of my house. He was wearing a long, gray coat with the collar turned up, his hands in the pockets, and his face was buried in a black scarf, looking down at his feet. It was only when I stopped in front him that he looked up, fixing his dark eyes on my face. He was slim, of average height, with a long, hollow face and short hair, peppered with gray. He stood noticeably straight, exuding the air of someone used to getting what he wanted.

"The ledger," he said in the deep voice I'd heard on the phone.

"I still don't know what you're talking about," I blurted out. I didn't have a chance to say anything more, as two young men in double-breasted suits emerged out of nowhere, grabbed my arms from behind, and pulled me up until I was straining to stand on my toes, barely holding on to my dinner. Then, they dragged me off the street.

"The ledger," Tsutami mumbled again.

"I told you, I don't know," I answered, weakly.

The fracture in my collarbone hadn't completely healed and in my weakened state I didn't have the courage to put up a fight, so I thought to just get down on my knees and beg for forgiveness, if that's what it would take for them to leave me in one piece. Then, one of the guys knocked my dinner out of my hands and stepped on it. Blood rushed to my head.

"I told you I don't know, you bastard!" I shouted.

Tsutami stepped in close and locked eyes with me, grinning crookedly. "So what did you do? Team up with Koyama to get Hiroko to steal it?"

"You know Koyama?" I was completely surprised.

Tsutami snorted, his grin more crooked. "Koyama's an idiot. What does he think he's doing, snooping around in my business. After all I did for him too. So what's your story? What does he have on you?"

*What does he have on me?* My mind was empty. I replayed the memory of Tomoe running into my arms. Her sweet, citrus smell. I tried to think what Koyama could possibly have on me, dropping my eyes to the ground. The two men didn't like that; they gripped my arms more tightly and shook me. I looked back up into Tsutami's expressionless eyes. They were the eyes of dead fish, two infinitely deep chasms.

"I hear you've been doing weird stuff. Like dressing that young girl up in strange outfits and filming her. So what are you anyway? A gutless, jobless bum? Just like Koyama, the old pervert who can't hold his liquor? You two become buddies because you've got so much in common? Is that it? Or he's got dirt on you."

I was ready to spit in his face, but wasn't fast enough. He drove a fist into my gut, so hard that I tasted bile. I hung my head gasping for air. "I'm telling you I don't know. I really don't know." I sounded like I was pleading.

"What a useless coward," said Tsutami, as if he was talking to himself. "Perhaps it was a waste of time to come down here."

"Go ask Koyama yourself," I managed to say, hoarsely.

"Then tell me where we can find him."

"In Nezu."

"Come on now. He disappeared from there weeks ago."

"What?"

"Are you playing dumb with me or what?"

"No," I said as loudly as I could. "But what about Koyama? What's his deal?"

A hint of amusement seemed to cross Tsutami's eyes, the first sign of human emotion he'd shown. "You want to know about the old bastard? I'll tell you. He's scum. He lost a stack of money gambling in Kansai. Then, when he can't keep up with interest payments on the loan, he comes to me, crying for help. Of course, he went to his brother first, as he always does when he gets in trouble. This time, his brother said, forget it. It was the last straw. So the bastard comes begging to me. Being such a nice guy, I go talk to the boys in Kansai and convince the boss to reduce the debt. And I even help to pay it off. Ever since then, we've been putting the bastard to use whenever we need, or more specifically, we've been putting his brother's contacts to use. But we also broke our backs to accommodate the old bastard's perverse hobby. I guess it was a give-and-take relationship. Then, four years ago, his brother dies."

"His brother?"

"Yeah, Masamichi, the calligrapher."

I was totally confused. "I thought the Koyama I knew was the calligrapher."

"You mean the guy living in that house in Nezu? No, he's the younger brother, Takero. Once in a while he plays around with a brush and acts like his brother, but Takero is a total amateur. Masamichi, on the other hand, was a real artist, a man admired by many; he even got awarded some precious order. A man of character, who, until this business with the loan, always stood by his pathetic brother. He let him live in that house and gave him an allowance.

"Takero wanted to be like his brother, but he didn't have the talent. And he didn't have the discipline to turn his envy into motivation for anything else. He tried his hand at antiques, but he had no eye, no business sense, and no patience to learn. That's how he ended up always scrounging off Masamichi, how he ended up throwing money away on the tables, and how he ended up a sad old bastard. When Masamichi died of liver cancer four or five years ago, everything changed. Masamichi never had any kids, so his wife and Takero shared a pretty big inheritance—not to mention that mansion. Takero got rich. And he went completely off the rails."

Hmm, could that mannequin-like lady in a kimono be Masamichi's widow? I wondered. And this tough guy Tsutami was a weird guy; once he started talking, the words just kept flowing, like a stream. He was looking at me the whole time, but it was like he was talking to himself.

"… they never married. It's a common-law marriage these days, but in more traditional terms, he was sleeping with the maid. She took care of him when he got sick at the end, though. And she probably was the one who convinced him to write a will—people are easier to persuade when they're weak. Anyway, Masayo is over forty now and still very sexy. She and Takero have been lovers for a long time. In fact, when Masamichi died before he even reached seventy, I thought it seemed pretty fishy. I mean in this day and age. I figured Masayo and Takero were behind it …"

All this talk was making me dizzy. Nothing made sense anymore, the entire picture had been redrawn. First, Koyama says *because I'm a calligrapher* ... I buy this because of an out-of-date biographical encyclopedia in the library. Wouldn't have been hard to do a little more research and find out that Masamichi Koyama was dead, but did I bother? I'd gone through all this, to the brink of death, because of that one lazy mistake.

Ha! I thought I was so clever, bringing up the *bold architectural beauty* to Koyama. He'd looked perplexed for a moment, before regaining his composure and laughing it off. I completely misinterpreted his expression. I thought I made him seem foolish with my petty sarcasm. Turns out I was the real fool.

"Then," Tsutami was still talking, "the guy goes and opens a whorehouse. His brother would turn in his grave if he knew what was happening in his house ..." Tsutami's voice trailed off a bit, and a hint of caution flashed in his eyes, as if he'd caught himself saying too much.

*The drugs, the equipment, the heart attacks, the deaths ... Wrinkled old perverts, tying up women or begging to be tied up themselves ...* Words that I could no longer be sure if I'd really heard were surfacing from the depths of my memory and echoing in my brain. "That was pretty bad," I mumbled, glancing up to see Tsutami's reaction.

"Yeah, I guess," he said with feeble interest. His eyes fixed on mine so as not to miss a trick. I swear he didn't even blink.

"Just terrible," I continued, trying to keep the thread going. "All those deaths."

His eyes widened a little, but not a lot. In fact, I wouldn't have noticed anything at all if he hadn't been staring directly into my eyes. I waited for him to respond, but he said nothing.

I kept going. "It was you guys who took care of the mess when something like that happened, wasn't it?"

"Don't be stupid."

"You just said so yourself. A give-and-take relationship. Were you providing the girls for the brothel too? From, say, the Philippines?"

Tsutami drove his fist hard into my gut again, in the exact same spot as before. My stomach felt like it had been pierced with a stick, my legs collapsed from under me, and the two goons loosened their grip on me and let me slide to the ground. Then, curling into a ball, I shouted, "What they did to that Filipino girl was sick. I know you people think you can do whatever you like, but that was dumb, too. Her body's still buried there, right? How many others did you bury there? A police dog could sniff them out in a second …"

When, after a few moments, I looked up, Tsutami and his goons were gone. I dragged myself into my house and kicked off my dirty pants. I didn't like getting beat up, but, it occurred to me, I wasn't freaked out. I was also calm, trying to think clearly.

Was Tsutami telling me the truth? Supposedly I was taken in by a fake Koyama, but what if I was being played by Tsutami? No way of knowing whether the bastard who punched me in the stomach really was Hiroko's husband. The more I thought about it all, the foggier things became, until finally I couldn't be certain about anything at all. But if there was one thing that had the smell of truth, it was that Koyama had disappeared several weeks back. Even if everything else Tsutami said was a lie.

The next day was New Year's Eve. It was dark, and heavy clouds weighed down on me. The air felt like it might pour at any moment, and as I lay in my futon trying to ignore the dampness on my arms, I made up my mind. I would find out for myself what had happened to Koyama, Sugimoto, Hiroko, and Tomoe.

I left my place before noon and walked to the top of the hill by the Agriculture Faculty of the University of Tokyo. Although it was New Year's Eve, the streets didn't seem any more quiet or busy than on any other day. I made my way down the other side of the hill, keeping alert to avoid bumping into anyone I wanted to avoid. When I got to Koyama's mansion, I was surprised to find that a new, taller gate, complete with intercom, had been installed. But after all that'd happened to me here, I would have to be a complete idiot to push the buzzer. I'd get in another way.

I walked further down the hill to the back gate of Nezu Shrine. I walked across the premises and up the small path on Azalea Hill. Tomorrow, New Year's Day, this place would be teeming with the crowds. Not today. I stepped off the path at some point and made my way through the bushes to the stone wall that marked Koyama's property.

# 18
## House Abandoned

I scaled the wall and got through a thicket of trees, coming up against a bluish glass wall. This was the rear of the conservatory that Koyama had called his winter garden. I walked on around and peered inside. The place was a mess, panes of glass cracked and shattered. I stepped on a shard of glass accidentally, and it snapped with a sharp crack. I froze, preparing to make a run for it if someone showed up, but there wasn't a soul in sight.

I proceeded toward the entrance to the marble-floored inner garden, poking my head around the corner to survey the situation. Again, there was no one there; the silence was eerie. I made my way further in and stepped into the conservatory. The door was wide open.

What I noticed first was the smell—dusty and metallic—instead of the pungent odor of tropical plants. The ivy that had covered much of the conservatory wall was dry and dead, like old twine, and plants were knocked onto the floor, the pots in pieces amid dried dirt and leaves. Glass was everywhere, so it was impossible to make a move without stepping on the stuff. What the hell happened?

I couldn't be sure, but I suspected this was the room in which I'd been drugged and beaten for ten days. If so, this was where I'd imagined Sugimoto's rotting, bleeding decapitated head on the floor, next to mine. This was where I'd lain, tied up, unsure whether Sugimoto's endless chatter was coming from his mouth or bubbling up from my dwindling consciousness. I looked around for clues.

The whole place was such a mess that I couldn't find a trace of myself or my ordeal. The floor was spotted with large black stains that could have been blood, but then again could have been something entirely different. The sixteen-millimeter film projector was lying on the floor where someone had apparently thrown it against the glass wall, by a gaping hole. Maybe it still had the film in it?

No such luck.

But it was clear that *something* happened here, something terrible. What?

I stepped outdoors into the open air, flummoxed. Suddenly, my legs felt weak. I stumbled past the fountain, walking like I was on stilts, then continued on across the inner garden until I got to the glass door to the corridor leading to the main house. It was ajar, unnervingly, like an invitation.

I tried to think. I didn't know what to believe. I couldn't believe everything Tsutami had said about Koyama—or of Koyama's disappearance. Why should I?

Who I needed to find was Sugimoto, if he was still alive, so I could get some answers. Like to the questions why? and why me? Sugimoto was eccentric, but I found it difficult to believe that this ridiculous man with a shaved head was my enemy. Perhaps I was naïve. Sure, he could swindle money out of me without regret. Sure, he wouldn't think twice about punching me out. And sure, behind his playful sarcasm referring to me as Mr. Intellectual was a hatred that he wasn't fully aware of. But when he rambled on like a possessed man about how much he revered his sensei, I could detect nothing but sincerity in his eyes. He'd been living at the Koyama mansion for three years, and if, as Tsutami said, Masamichi Koyama, the calligrapher, had died four or five years ago, and Sugimoto had been living at the mansion for three years, then Takero was playing Sugimoto for a fool.

To think of this old Takero as a wolf in sheep's clothing—or a sheep in wolf's clothing—was mind-boggling. Everything that he'd said in his unnaturally composed tone, everything that had sounded so convincing at the time, was now suspect. He was a fraud. He'd craved the greatness of his brother because he couldn't achieve his own. He'd snatched his dying brother's identity and used it to steal respect from strangers. He'd needed someone like Sugimoto at his side to give him validation. Of course, he couldn't deceive the whole world, but it took no effort at all to fool an uneducated thug like Sugimoto, who didn't even read the papers. Just his living in that mansion and surrounding himself with calligraphy was probably all it took.

Dependency breeds contempt, and for a personality type like Takero to take the next step and murder his brother, as Tsutami alleged, was not implausible. If Takero also seduced his brother's wife, then collaborated with her to kill him, then this was a cruel man, although not quite the cold-blooded monster Sugimoto had described him as. But what use was Sugimoto's opinion anyway? Takero was just a petty, small-time criminal being used by another. But then again, I was being used, too. But for what?

I also wanted to see Hiroko, of course, although I wasn't sure if what I felt for her was longing or hatred. I was unable to forget the image of her—in the throes of sexual ecstasy with Takabatake—when I was struck by the agony of knowing that this was the woman who was everything I wanted. *I was waiting for you*, she'd said to me once. I could still hear her saying it, as if she were standing right behind me.

No matter how far she'd sunk, I was prepared to give things another try. If only I could reach out to her. Or if only she'd reach out to me.

I had no idea what the fuss over the ledger was all about.

I slipped through the glass door, then walked to the end of the corridor. I was no longer feeling hesitant. Actually, I was feeling quite bold and wasn't making any attempt to be quiet.

I'd been to the mansion only a few times, so I wasn't familiar with the layout of the place. I went from room to room, finding things covered in dust, as if no one had lived here in a long time. There were Japanese-style rooms of different sizes, a large parlor with leather couches and a piano, a dining room with a bay window. Some things had been left untouched. One Japanese-style room had an antique vase still standing, but other rooms seemed like they might have been looted. And needless to say, there was not a human being around.

Near the main front entrance, sandals were strewn across the floor. In the kitchen, the tap of an old-fashioned sink was dripping; in the large bathroom, the floor tiles were completely dry. I retraced my steps and suddenly became aware of several men standing around the fountain in the garden. I quickly hid behind the curtains, worrying about having left my shoes at the glass door. Would they notice? The men had their hands on the metal sculpture and were talking quietly.

"Don't be stupid!" a familiar deep voice suddenly came through loudly.

It was Tsutami, the collar of his long, gray coat turned up. He was looking up at the top of the sculpture and explaining something to the three men with him. Then, apparently on Tsutami's instructions, the men grasped the sculpture and appeared to try to lift it. To take it away? Or to knock it to the ground?

With all my attention focused on this going on, I nearly jumped out of my skin when someone touched my elbow. Managing to keep from screaming, barely, I swung around, and there in front of me was Tomoe! As if she'd appeared out of nowhere. For a split second, in my panic, I didn't recognize her with her hair cut short and dyed brown.

"You—" I began. But Tomoe stopped me from saying more, shaking her head violently. Then she gestured for me to follow her.

We passed the dining room and the parlor. Then, in a corner off the front entrance, she opened a small door that I'd never noticed before. It was a storage space, piled high with cardboard boxes and sundry. Since the room had no windows, we were immersed in complete darkness as soon as she pulled the door shut.

"You had your hair cut," I whispered.

She didn't say anything, although she might have nodded. I could hear her breathing heavily, her fear seeming almost palpable.

"Do you know that guy, Tsutami?"

Again, no verbal response, although a nod seemed probable.

"Is Koyama here? Or Sugimoto? Are you all alone?"

No answer.

"What happened? The conservatory is a complete mess."

"A complete mess," she repeated after me. "Everything is a mess."

I waited for her to say more. When she didn't, I asked sternly, "Where is everyone?"

"I don't know."

"How can you not know?"

"I was skiing with a friend in Yatsugatake. When I got back, everybody was gone."

"When did you get back?"

"Last night."

"What'd you do then?"

"I didn't know what to do ... I was looking around at the mess, and then those guys in the garden came bursting into the house with their shoes on and started rummaging through the house. I ran into the garden and hid behind the bushes. I don't think they saw me. After they left, when I came back inside, I saw that paintings, framed calligraphy, all sorts of things were gone."

"Did you call the police?" I asked, the slivers of light from the ventilation slats at the bottom of the door allowing me to see the contours of her face. Suddenly, I was aware of her sweet scent. She was close enough for me to touch her.

"I was so scared that I spent the night in this room. The phone rang a lot, but I just let it ring. Then, day came. I started feeling hungry, and I didn't know what to do. Then I heard footsteps ... so I decided to get out of here and call the police. I crept out, and that's when I saw you, Mr. Otsuki."

It was the first time she'd ever referred to me by name.

"I was so relieved ... and then I saw those men in the garden."

"Calm down. Everything will be all right."

She seemed to relax, and the thought occurred to me that she might let me put my arms around her. Yeah, but it'd also be such a cheap move in a moment like this, so instead I just said, "Let's stay here a little while longer. I don't know what they're up to, but I think they'll be done before long."

"Shouldn't we get out of here?"

"That's easier said than done . . ."

"I'm scared," she said, her voice cracking. "Please, let's get out of here. I don't want to be in this house."

"Where do want to go?"

"I don't care. Anywhere."

So, carefully, we stepped out of the storage space. The plan was to go through the dining room and kitchen and then out through the back door. But first, Tomoe went to the front door to retrieve her sneakers and grabbed a brand-new pair of basketball shoes for me. They were a little big, and I wondered if they belonged to Sugimoto, which I didn't like thinking about. We were out the door when a loud thud from the inner garden could be heard. We didn't stop to find out what it was.

I led the way through the thicket, with Tomoe trailing close behind. Soon we were at the spot where I'd gotten into the property. Placing my hands on the top of the wall, I hoisted myself over first, then helped Tomoe land on the other side.

The only option was to bring Tomoe back to my house, the prospect of which led me to feel pleased as well as guilty. We left Nezu Shrine by the front gate, then walked up the wide road to Nippon Medical School. Despite her heavy sweater, Tomoe hugged herself as if she was freezing.

# 19
## ESCAPE

WE WALKED UP the gentle hill to the intersection of Mukogaoka 1-chome at Hongo Street. It occurred to me that this was the same corner where I hailed a cab for Hiroko that midsummer evening that I ran into Sugimoto. Now, it was this dark afternoon on New Year's Eve.

Old man Koyama's voice came to my ears again. *We go back ...* And though I tried to drown it out of my mind, it remained crystal clear. *We go back to a different "now" ... We just make a loop and slip inside a different "now" ... Encapsulated in every "now" are infinite other "nows."*

Suddenly, it was as if I was seeing myself at an angle in front of me. It is that hot midsummer evening. I am drained after hours of lovemaking that have left me smelling of Hiroko. "Finally," I'm thinking, "I can put her in a cab." The car door has swung open and Hiroko has gotten into the backseat. The door shuts; Hiroko turns toward me. The setting sun beats down with heat and brightness, silhouetting her hair and face, obscuring her expression.

That face, I think to myself.

My heart was pierced, and I was brought to a standstill. On this midwinter day, I found myself turning in search of Hiroko's silhouette. Almost bumping into Tomoe, who was glaring at me, was what brought me back.

The expression on Hiroko's face as she got into the cab was a blur. But I could vividly recall her thin, fleeting smile as she glanced back toward me as the car pulled away. It was a plastic smile that she'd put back on for her role as the young wife in a household that could afford to keep a maid; she was out of the character she'd played when she was in bed with me. But I didn't dislike that artificial mask. In fact I found it strangely and irresistibly erotic.

Then, in my mind, her face slowly began to take on detail, began to take on the same expression of pity and contempt that she'd shot me as she left my house in Koishikawa the last time.

"What's happened to Hiroko?" I found myself blurting out.

"What?"

"Hiroko. Where is she now? She was staying with you. Hiroko Tsutami. It was last month. No, a couple of months ago."

"I don't know her," said Tomoe, although a little too quickly to sound convincing.

"No, I think you do. A slim, pretty woman—"

"I said I don't know her."

But it was only natural to assume she did. Hiroko had certainly suggested she knew Tomoe—"What a waste ... Such a pretty girl." But Tomoe wouldn't let on, and we continued in silence while a flurry of thoughts cluttered my mind and a strange sensation started to wrench my gut. I wasn't unfamiliar with irrational anxiety, the helplessness of a child abandoned by his parents, but this was different. It was solidifying into rock.

Then I understood. This rock was *fear*. Fear that comes from being fooled into thinking I'd treated Hiroko badly when I'd been trapped like a pitiful insect in a well-designed web. Fear that comes from realizing that all the while I'd made decisions rationally, the world had been operating according to a set of rules I never knew about. Fear that comes from seeing that I'd been so focused upon my sexual obsessions that I'd been blind to the hatred and contempt she was suppressing. But *why*? Why me? Why did they choose me? What did they have against me? What did they have to gain from using me like this?

Hiroko had absconded with a ledger when she left her husband and moved into Koyama's. Obviously, this all didn't just happen by sudden coincidence. Obviously, Hiroko had known Koyama long before the summer night that I first stepped foot in the mansion. She'd been sympathetic, warning me not to let the perverted old man talk me into doing anything, when in fact she had been manipulating me into doing the opposite. If so, how much of a coincidence was it when I ran into Sugimoto in his underwear later that evening? It had to be a coincidence! I'd been walking along with no destination in mind, or had I been lured, somehow pointed, in that direction?

Could my aimlessness have been a precisely crafted illusion planted in my brain? Or, on the other hand, could the total coincidence of running into Sugimoto be what got the entire conspiracy rolling?

After I finished the filming, they dropped me like a stone. Then, for the first time in my life, in my mid-thirties, I tried to make it as a regular-salary man, only to get sick of it after one month and make my way back to Koyama. Surely it would be ridiculous to think that Hiroko and the others had planned that—as if they could take the weakness of my resolve into precise account and predict the moment of my return. And what about the events after that? Could Hiroko have just happened to answer the phone when I rang—then bought herself time by muttering a series of resentments, all the while planning her next cunning move until she finally decided to invite me over? It was child's play for them—tricking someone who pretended to be a cold-hearted gigolo but was nothing more than a weak, sentimental idiot, happy to be drawn into their web. Behind my back, Hiroko must have been sticking her tongue out at me the entire time.

Thick, gray clouds covered the sky, raindrops falling sporadically, but it didn't seem like it was going to turn into a full-blown downpour, so we walked on—in silence, through residential Bunkyo ward, which was quieter than usual with people away for New Year's, then down the hill to Hakusan Street.

Tomoe stopped me with a touch of my arm. "Where are we going?" she asked.

"To my place, for now."

"And where is your place?"

"At the bottom of this hill," I answered, and started walking again, but Tomoe didn't budge. "It's only another ten minutes or so. It's near the botanical gardens."

"Is it safe there?"

"What do you mean?"

"I mean ..." she said, trailing off as she shot a glance to the top of the hill we'd just come down.

I began to feel the rock of fear in my stomach again. She did have a point. We'd gone to all this effort to escape Tsutami and his men, but now we were going to a place they knew. I thought of the half-empty beer can on the floor—I didn't know if Tsutami had anything to do with it, but my place wasn't entirely safe for sure.

Seeing my hesitation, Tomoe said in an uncharacteristically decisive tone, "Let's go to Jin's place."

"Jin? You mean … Takabatake?"

Takabatake. The guy who smashed a two-liter bottle on my back. The guy who made both Tomoe and Hiroko cry out in ecstasy by subjecting their bodies to the most degrading sexual acts, while I'd been forced to watch.

"Yes," said Tomoe. "His place. I think nobody's lived there in a while. I'm pretty sure Jin won't be there either."

I was shocked to hear her refer to that beast in such a friendly manner.

"I'm sure it'll be safe," she continued. "Let's go."

"No, I don't want to see that guy."

"But he's not there. He's gone."

"Gone where?"

"I don't know." Her voice was flat. Just like it when I'd asked her about Hiroko.

"Well, when did he leave?"

"I don't know."

I was at a loss. No way could I seek shelter at Satomi's apartment in Higashi-Nakano—certainly not with the baggage I was walking around with. And no way could I show my face at my relatives'. One option would have been a hotel. But on New Year's Eve, we'd never find a room anywhere.

In the end, we caught a cab and headed for Senzoku. I felt a little diminished being told what to do by a young girl, but I went along because my legs were starting to feel very heavy and walking was becoming a struggle. "Fuck it," I thought to myself as I plopped down in the warm cab. I took a breath and felt the tension subside, warmth spreading to the tips of my fingers and toes, then exhaled as my surroundings began to fade away, until they had disappeared completely, as if I was separated from the world by a layer of skin, as if nothing around me had anything to do with me at all.

"Do you want to go down Dangozaka and get on to Meiji Street via Dokanzaka? Or should we go through Yanaka?"

The voice of the driver was resonating in a different space from the one I was occupying. I closed my eyes and leaned my head back against the seat. "Either way is fine," I said.

The driver decided to turn into Kototoi Street at the bottom of Kikuzaka, and soon we found ourselves heading past Yanaka Cemetery toward Asakusa. As I felt the vibrations of the car, I tried to reel in my disparate thoughts. Everything since the first night in Koyama's conservatory had happened so fast. Then, this guy Tsutami suddenly shows up and tells me that Koyama, or rather the Koyama imposter, has disappeared, so I go to the mansion to find it completely abandoned, with everyone gone except for Tomoe, who's been left to fend for herself. Then Tsutami and his goons come along with the apparent intention of stealing the metal sculpture from the garden . . .

But why had Takero gone into hiding? And was Hiroko with him? Had Koyama and Hiroko's plans fallen apart? Or was the disappearance of Koyama, Hiroko, and—according to Tomoe, at least—Takabatake as well, just part of an elaborate script they'd written together? And what about Sugimoto's decapitated head?

When we got out of the cab at Takabatake's store, I realized I'd never actually seen the place with the shutters up. We walked over to try the wooden doors at the side of the place, which slid open with little effort on our part.

"Are you sure nobody's here?"

"I'm sure," Tomoe said with certainty.

We walked down the path to the inner garden. The windows of the main house were all shuttered, which made me think we'd wasted our time coming here, but we were able to force one open. Behind the shutters, the window looked as if it might fall apart, with its sagging wooden frame, but despite its appearance, it wouldn't budge. Finally, I picked up a concrete block sitting nearby and knocked it lightly against the glass. I was trying to not make a lot of noise, but the glass fell on the floor with a crash that sent a shiver down my spine—I could just see the neighbors calling the police. I stuck my hand through the hole, undid the latch, slid the window open, and hoisted myself up and into the house. I was immediately assaulted by an overpowering smell of mold.

The disorder at Koyama's mansion was nothing compared to the state of Takabatake's house. It had been two months since I'd made the film here, and it seemed the place hadn't been touched since. The room was littered with cardboard boxes, old slippers, folded chairs, magazines … I opened the adjacent window for Tomoe, who looked a little helpless standing there. I stretched my arms out and gently pulled her up and over. I imagined how this must have looked—me looking like some pervert forcing a girl into an abandoned house to have his way with her—when in truth it had been her idea to come here.

As soon as she was inside, Tomoe placed her hands over her mouth, astonished by the mess. Her hair brushed the tip of my nose, and for a moment the smell of mold was gone, erased by a sensual citrus.

We stepped into the room where I'd had drinks with Koyama and Takabatake several months ago, and suddenly a wave of fatigue dragged me to the floor.

"I'm exhausted," said Tomoe, slumping down next to me.

We were both overcome, in a daze.

"Umm…" I began, "what should we do now?"

There was no response.

"Tomoe?'

"I'm cold," she whispered.

That was when I realized that I was shivering too, huddled in just a shirt and suede jacket. I hadn't noticed before. Well, it was the end of December. I found a small electric heater in the next room, but it wouldn't turn on. Was the electricity off? I tried the lights, and was relieved to see they were working.

I went through the closets and found a few blankets. Unfortunately, they were a little damp and musty, but I draped them over Tomoe anyway as she sat and pulled them tightly around her.

"Are you hungry?" I asked. She shook her head.

I wandered off to the kitchen, thinking to make some tea. The water was still running and the gas was on as well, but the cupboards were mostly empty. I found a kettle and, rifling through the other cabinets, eventually located a couple of teabags. When the water had boiled, I brewed the tea in two Asian teacups—the kind without handles.

When the tea was ready, I found Tomoe, the blankets wrapped around her, curled up in a ball and apparently asleep, like a kitten. I approached quietly so as not to startle her, stooped down, and peered into her face. Her breathing seemed to stop, and it was several seconds before a long, slow breath finally slipped from between her lips, followed by a long pause, then she began to open her eyes, ever so slightly. I was right in front of her, but she didn't acknowledge me at all. She was still, her eyes exuding a glow that was difficult to describe. A cool gaze, perhaps? No, her eyes seemed neither cool nor warm. Nor did they look in any way cruel. They were simply without color, without life. Like lenses in an optical apparatus, unblinking, uncolored by thought or emotion. Eyes that radiated silence, that observed me with an uncommon objectivity—like I was nothing more than an insect. No, it was more like she herself had the eyes of an insect. I was face-to-face with a beautiful girl, yet staring into the compound eyes of a filthy fly. Could these eyes really belong to a human? Up until that moment, I'd thought they were beautiful and innocent. Had I really been such an idiot all along?

I believe this was the first time the real Tomoe showed herself to me. It awoke me from my daze and brought the rock back, rolling around in my stomach. My crotch began to shrivel, though it was not from the cold.

# 20
## NEW YEAR'S EVE

IT WAS THE first time I'd seen the real Tomoe, but no sooner had that awareness crossed my mind than her eyelids snapped shut, hiding her insect eyes behind them. I'd seen her with her eyes shut many times, and often I recalled teardrops trembling at the corners. Small, transparent pearls that seemed to represent everything about her—her personality, upbringing, loneliness, helplessness. There were no tears in her eyes at this moment, but with her eyes shut, I saw in front of me that same girl who was as transparent as a drop of water. A small, helpless animal soaked to the skin and shivering in the cold. An animal so small and gentle that you wanted to pick her up with your hands, to hold her close, warm her, protect her, and help her as she tried desperately to survive in this world.

But was this really who Tomoe is? Was this the reason why her eyes were so tightly shut—to keep that illusion? Why does anyone close her eyes, after all? To stop the tears from escaping and betraying heartbreak? To hide their eyes from what people might see in them? As soon as this thought came to me, a teardrop formed in her eyes, which I watched calmly.

For the first time, I was able to look at Tomoe with a clear mind. A pearl? A poor beautiful girl? A helpless little animal? Was that who she really was? Or was she more like a plastic doll that bats its long eyelashes when tilted back and releases tears when squeezed?

"I'm cold …" came her trembling voice again.

"Have some tea," I said in a voice that was cold.

She poked an arm out from under the blanket and rubbed her eyes with her fist. She then sat up and reached her hand toward me. I offered the teacup to her, but just as she was about to take it, I teasingly pulled it back a bit—the kind of thing a school kid would do. I watched the way Tomoe's five fingers hovered in the air before returning my gaze to her face, to where her wide-open eyes were staring straight into mine.

I observed her eyes carefully. At first they were the eyes of a poor beautiful girl, helpless eyes that seemed to plead for help. But as I continued to withhold the cup of tea from her, she seemed to read something in my eyes and her irises changed to a shade of color that exuded audacity. She frowned as she reached her hand out again; once again I pulled the cup back from her. Now she was irritated, her hand falling onto the blanket, her eyes saying: "What are you doing? What are you playing at? Don't tease me."

I kept my gaze focused on her eyes, and I thought I glimpsed hesitation as she considered playing along with me; she might even throw in a smile or two. But immediately her expression changed into distrust as she tried to read deeper into my eyes. Still, I held my gaze, and in the next moment the mist over her eyes lifted, she smiled and stuck her palm out face up. She gave me what one might call an innocent smile. But this innocent smile betrayed no emotion, reminding me again of a doll's.

"Tea, please?" the doll asked, sounding like a recording.

I quietly placed the cup on the palm of her hand, and she reached out her other hand to clasp it. I wanted to see those fly eyes once more, but all that remained on her face was innocence.

"Eyes like those—they're a little scary."

"What do you mean—'eyes like those'?" Tomoe asked calmly as her smile began to fade, replaced by a carefully controlled expression that suggested surprise at hearing these words from me.

I wanted to tear off that veil of calm and set free whatever was wriggling behind it. "Empty eyes ... Eyes with nothing in them ..."

"I don't know what to say ... Are my eyes like that?"

"They say that eyes are the windows to your heart. Are all girls' eyes like yours these days?"

"All my friends have normal eyes."

"And did your mother have those eyes?"

"Stop referring to them as 'those eyes.' I never knew my mother. She died when I was a baby."

"So I heard."

"And my father, too."

"So you're an orphan."

"That's right. An orphan."

"Poor thing." My words came out reflexively, artificially, and in response she smiled a smile that was no longer so innocent—it was more of a smirk—then suddenly pulled off her blanket and moved closer to me until she was right in my face, spilling tea in the process.

Tomoe sipped her tea without looking up, then spoke softly, "Mr. Otsuki."

"Yes?"

"You're wondering how you got yourself into this mess, aren't you?"

"Yeah, something like that."

"Well, I'm tired. I want to take a bath."

And with that, she placed her mostly untouched cup of tea into my hands, turned, and disappeared down the hallway.

From the crackly, distant speakers of that miserable shopping arcade in the area, I could make out the melody of "The Glow of the Fireflies." This winter day was coming to a close, and everything slipping into darkness. I slumped down on the floor and tried to think. I don't know how many minutes had passed, but after a while, I found myself mumbling *my mother died, and my father died, too.*

The sound of running water was coming from somewhere in the house. Was she really taking a bath? I was starting to feel cold. I poked around and found an old gas heater in the hallway. The rubber hose was stiff and cracked in places, which was worrisome, but when I plugged it in and turned the gas tap on, there was warmth.

I tried the television sitting in the corner and found that worked as well. It had been a long time since I'd last watched TV. Inside the whitish glow of the small screen, people were getting excited about unspectacular things, like the top-ten news stories of the year, events of the coming year, and a lot of singing and dancing. I'd forgotten it was New Year's Eve. Watching happy people on TV was nauseating, but for some reason it wasn't boring. I had no regrets about living life cut off from such idiocy and the idiots who waste away their lives watching it—for all I cared, they could drool in idle happiness until they died—but maybe that wasn't such a terrible way to live after all.

I wanted to ask the people on TV if they were enjoying themselves as much as they appeared to be. But when I watched as they
screamed stupid jokes at the top of their lungs, I noticed the sweat
soaking into their collars and I could see hints of exhaustion and irritation on their faces. The loud laughter of the celebrities was a desperate attempt to mask fear and anxiety. It was all an act, like everything
else in this world; it was the same wherever you went, and this was
how everything ended up.

"Hey!"

I jumped. Tomoe was behind me, wearing a very serious expression.

"Aren't you hungry?" she asked.

"Yeah, I suppose I am."

"Then I'll go buy something."

I pulled out cash I'd stuffed in my pocket and handed her several
thousand yen. Her hair was wet, and she was wearing baggy gray
sweats and a navy blue sweater. I didn't know where she found them,
and I didn't ask, although I wondered if they belonged to "Jin" and I
didn't like the thought of it.

Tomoe was gone for at least an hour before returning with a plastic
bag from a convenience store. "What took you so long?" I asked.

She didn't answer, choosing instead to frown. All she'd bought
were a few rice balls.

We ended up sitting side by side, eating the rice balls while
watching the New Year's Eve sing-off on television.

How did I get in this mess? Why was this happening … why was
this happening … *We have a few words of encouragement from a crew
of deep-sea fishermen … We also have a message from Prime Minister
Tomichi Murayama of the Socialist Party … Now we would like to go
back to our emcee Furutachi-san at the NHK Hall in Shibuya, Tokyo …*

Into this reverie entered the fragrance of Tomoe's shampoo. Why
on earth was I watching Furutachi-*san* on the tube when Tomoe
was right within my reach. I should just take her, like I'd done with
other women. So I made my move. I put my arm around her, then
touched her delicate chin, gently pulling her toward me. She didn't

resist. Gently, I brought her face closer to mine, and she appeared to close her eyes and pucker her lips slightly, making me sure she was giving herself to me. Then, suddenly, she pushed against my chest.

"Don't," she said.

Normally I would have made a joke of it and backed off, but this time I wasn't prepared to accept such an outcome. I pulled her back toward me and climbed on her to pin her down. It had been a while since I'd last touched a woman, and as I held down this sweet-smelling body wrestling in my arms, a savage excitement in me escalated beyond my control. Tomoe resisted with much greater strength than I'd imagined her thin frame could muster, and after a few seconds we were both breathing heavily. Then, she stopped resisting entirely. The hand she'd been pressing against my face went abruptly slack, and I took hold of her wrist and gently pulled it off my face. I now could see her face with those insect eyes.

"Why don't you at least tell me you like me?" she said.

"I like you," I said, feeling the savage excitement begin to fade.

"Liar."

"I'm not lying."

"I'm cold." Slowly she crawled out from under me, grasped the blanket, and wrapped herself in it. "Stay away from me," she said.

"After those things you did with Takabatake, you're—"

"What? So I have to sleep with you, too? You must be stupid."

"I wouldn't be able to get it up with you looking at me like that."

Tomoe brushed her hair back with her left hand. Her face was ghostly pale, making her look as if she were freezing. "One minute you're saying 'poor you' and then you do this."

"Tomoe, the orphan, huh?"

"That's right. Poor, poor Tomoe," she said, dripping with sarcasm.

"You—"

"... *are such a poor girl,*" said Tomoe, finishing my sentence. "My mother died of pneumonia. Died even before I finished breastfeeding. I was born in Hong Kong. But when my mother died, my father moved to London for work and took me with him. Then we moved to Italy. Yes ... that's right, it was Rome. Or was it London first, then

Rome? Rome first, then London. What does it matter? My father held some high position at a newspaper, an editor-in-chief or branch head or something. But he had a heart attack and died. Then my grandfather took me in and paid for my schooling." Tomoe paused for a moment, then staring straight into my bewildered face, she added, "It's all a lie."

Several images flashed through my mind like camera shots. A man walking toward me dragging a body by the ankle. I see the ankle, the leg, the buttocks, the back, and so on, until I see an entire human body face down against the ground. The guy dragging the body is Takabatake, wearing gray sweat pants. His filthy naked back is covered in spots and shards of glass, glistening. And the images are accompanied by sound. I felt like I'd been hit on the head with a hammer.

"Lie? What do you mean?"

"It's a lie. That's all there is to it."

"That means—"

"I memorized it all. I was told to. I was born in Hong Kong. My mother and father died. That's what I was told to say."

"Who . . ."

"You, Mr. Otsuki."

"No, I mean who told you to tell me that?"

"Sugimoto-*san* and the others."

As the horrible sound of a body being dragged around faded in my mind, another image took its place. The chronology wasn't clear, so I wasn't sure whether this image should have preceded the other or, if so, how far ahead, but it was the same body, lying on the ground sideways, the legs in long underwear covered in blood, twisted unnaturally. The head lying sideways against the ground, yet seeming to float until it was on a level with my face. My face and Sugimoto's, nose-to-nose, but his eyes weren't looking at me. No, they seemed to be fixed like beads on some terrifying thing behind my back. Then I realized that his head hadn't risen to meet me at all, but that I instead had collapsed onto the floor next to him. But why? And what was the sharp pain I could feel digging into my side, like a sharp kick or a punch? Everything seemed to be moving very, very slowly, in very,

very slow motion.

"So you aren't Koyama's granddaughter?"

Tomoe smiled in silence. A smile that was similar to, though in many ways different from the innocent smile she'd been wearing earlier. No, this was more of a malicious smile that knew it wasn't a real smile. A mask that resembled the real face so closely, yet emphasized the defining difference between the two—a lie bold enough to point at itself with pride and say, "Look at me—I'm a lie!"

"So who are you?"

"I'm Tomoe."

"But that's not your real name, is it?"

"Real name? What's a real name?"

"The name your parents gave you."

"But I don't know my parents," she said, her eyes and tone filled with the same audacity I'd seen earlier.

"And what about Koyama?"

"That old man? Always acting like he was the most important thing in the world. You've got to laugh. Do you remember the way he introduced me to you in his self-important tone? 'This is my granddaughter.' On that damn hot summer day, in the inner garden of the house. I was waiting for Sugimoto's cue to step out and say, 'I'm home, Grandpa!' The good girl who always abides by her curfew. It was like one of those comedy skits on TV. You were staring at my body with such lecherous, bloodshot eyes, like you were going to jump me at any moment. And then Grandpa said, 'Her name is Tomoe. She's a good girl. I'm sure she's pleased to make your acquaintance.' What a pretentious idiot."

"So you're not Tomoe."

I waited, but she said nothing.

"If you're not Tomoe, who are you?"

"You wanted to sleep with me, didn't you? Trying to act suave, but sounding like an idiot the whole time. Saying, *'poor girl,'* in your best *here-kitty-kitty* kind of voice. You should have just said you wanted to do me. I would have let you."

How could I have believed her when she'd said, her voice faint, that she was seventeen? Because it was clear, as I looked at her now, that there was no way this pale, dry-skinned woman with a fake in-nocent smile was in her teens. If anything, she was in her mid-twen-ties. But how could I never have noticed that before? How could I, having focused so much on that face through my sixteen-millimeter lens, never have noticed this?

"Don't patronize me, you little brat."

"Whoah, scary ..."

Enraged by her sarcasm, I grabbed her shoulders and shook her, watching her jostle in my arms like a plastic doll with its plastic grin frozen across its face. At that moment, another bright image flashed through my mind. Takabatake was raising a sword high above his head, then bringing it down with a scream of animal ferocity on bloody flesh on a countertop. He was raising the sword again and, let-ting out another wild cry, bringing the sword down again, and again, with a sickening thud, the body flinching each time, until finally, Sugimoto's head fell to the floor.

"Just twenty-five more minutes left of 1994!" came a voice from the sing-off, oozing enthusiasm.

# 21
## MARKS

"Is THIS HOW you did it?" asked Tomoe in a long drawn-out voice. "Is this ... how you did it?"

Her eyes glowed suggestively and were bleeding color around the edges. I hadn't noticed her bright red lipstick before. The corners of her lips were turned up in a plastic smile that slowly closed in on my face. A terrifying image crossed my mind: her mouth open wide to swallow my head whole. Then the corners of her lips turned up even more, and I realized with gut-wrenching horror that my hands, which had been shaking Tomoe by the shoulders, were now gripping her slim, pale neck. "Like this? Is this how you did it? Just like this?" she repeated feebly, her words trailing off into a pathetic gagging. A white light flashed: *That's right*. I strangled that woman—*just like this*—just the way I was strangling Tomoe now—eleven years ago, when I was twenty-three.

A bright circle of rouge floated above the woman's pale face, above the white bed sheets. It was like an entrance to a different world. Lips that had been caressing the body of a man moments before were now a perfectly round "O," twitching under my face, silently crying out. Every so often, she emitted a sound from the bottom of her throat, like air escaping from a tear in a bellows. Like the sound Tomoe was making now. Had the sudden memory of Sugimoto's head hitting the floor triggered this other image that had been hidden even deeper in my mind? Had that sudden memory triggered something within me that I should now find my hands wrapped around Tomoe's neck? Or was it the other way around? That the return of this nightmarish memory had been triggered by Tomoe's saying "Like this? Just like this?" One thing was clear: this woman under me, whose name I was uncertain of, knew about this incident in my past—this incident that I thought I had succeeded in repressing.

In fact, she must have known from the very beginning. During the few weeks of filming, she'd always been respectful, diffident, but all that was an act, too. If Sugimoto had dug up the dirt of my drug addiction, why wouldn't he have dug up stuff on me before my days at the Oriental Economic Research Institute. How stupid was I not to figure that out? Defeated, I loosened my grip on Tomoe's neck, which seemed to coincide with the voice of a male singer crooning on TV. But Tomoe didn't move—her head was tilted back like she was in a daze, and the gaze of her transparent eyes, now glowing deeply, did not waver. Without thinking, I began gently to stroke the smooth skin of her neck.

"You were kicked out of the university for that. Messed your life up, didn't you?" The tone of her raspy voice rose a pitch at the end of the sentence.

She was wrong. I wasn't kicked out of school because of that incident. I had already been expelled for not attending classes and not paying the tuition. And I hadn't been at the university that long before I was expelled—so *that* had nothing to do with it.

When things fall apart, it doesn't just suddenly happen. Things shift out of line 0.01 millimeters, or more like 0.001 millimeters, every day, until the tiny shifts accumulate and one day you've got a big problem. The cogs stop turning, and the wheel won't turn. You wonder what the matter is and apply a little pressure to see what will happen, and to your utter surprise, the entire wheel comes flying apart, breaking the entire contraption.

Ever since I was a child, I hated the system that the wheels of this world turned by. And the person who represented this system the most was my father. He was hardly ever home, but on the rare occasions he was, he would give me as much money as I begged for. I can't explain the connection, but the reason I worked so hard to get into the University of Tokyo was to get back at my father. But once I got in and moved into my own flat in Tokyo, getting back at him didn't seem so important. The classes were boring, my classmates were childish, and I lost interest. I skipped classes and hung out with a group of guys who'd gone to my high school. Most nights we were at this bar just off Yotsuya that was popular with delinquents like us. These guys were older than me, but I had this hefty allowance from my father, so I paid their tabs and they treated me as an equal.

I did so badly the first year at school, I didn't have enough credits to get moved up to the second year. The whole thing was starting to feel absurd, and I didn't have any patience for listening to timid, middle-aged men who'd done nothing else in their lives but stand at the podium and mumble on about one boring topic or another. Still, I had my pride, so for the final exam for Civil Law101, I intimidated a classmate I barely knew into letting me photocopy his class notes, and I crammed all night. When I went to campus the next morning, however, the classroom was empty. The exam had been given the day before; I had misread the schedule. After that I couldn't get myself to care. I suppose I thought in the back of my mind that if all else failed, I could always work for my father's company and that, until I got kicked out of university, I could spend my time doing whatever I wanted.

One night I walked into the usual Yotsuya hang-out to find the girlfriend of one of the guys drinking at the bar by herself. It was still fairly early, but she appeared to be quite drunk already.

"Are you here alone?" I asked.

"So what if I am alone?"

"It's just unusual."

"Leave me alone. I'll do what I want."

"You look like you could use the company."

"Shut up."

"Where is he?"

And then she started talking. "The bastard picked up some cheap rich girl in Shonan the other day and decided he wanted her, not me. She goes to Aoyama Gakuin University, family's got a vacation home in Hayama. The creep. Who does he think bought him his watch, his suit, and all his other stuff?"

After a few, we moved on to a bar in Kabukicho where she worked and where she got very drunk.

"He called me an old woman," she said, sobbing.

I got her back to her apartment in Akebonobashi that night, and she begged me to stay. Which I did. The woman was several years older than me, and though I wasn't a virgin, over the next several weeks she walked me step by step through a sex course that involved things that I never imagined people doing. I got hooked. My excitement completely blinded me to the coldness of the woman, as I let the experience get to my head. We started practically living together. I would pick her up after work at the back entrance of her bar, and I would cook her a snack when she got home like I was her partner, spend the night in shameless pursuit of sexual pleasure, and fall into a deep, swamp-like sleep. During the day, I would go to Shinjuku and kill time bowling, playing billiards, or hanging out at the video-game arcade, then in the evening I would go drinking with my buddies in Yotsuya, before going to Kabukicho to meet the woman at her bar.

The affair lasted a few months. This woman was similar to Satomi in that she was hungry for pleasure and liked to lavish attention on her man, but she didn't have the heart that Satomi did, although there was no way a naïve student living on an allowance from his father could have seen that. The woman turned cold on me, and after several weeks of her refusing to see me, I grew furious beyond control. In hindsight, I know that it wasn't a broken heart I was suffering from; it was simply a case of a male in his prime being robbed of his sexual outlet and thirsting for the sweet juice of the female.

In a bloody rage, I went to the woman's apartment one night and let myself in with a spare key I'd made without her knowing. When I opened the door, there she was—in a naked tangle with the guy who had left her. I completely lost it. I flew into the apartment without taking off my shoes and slammed my foot into the guy. I couldn't stop kicking him—I kicked him in the head, stomach, and legs, over and over again. And after the guy grabbed his clothes and ran out of the door naked, I grabbed the woman and began to strangle her as she screamed.

I was staring at a circle of rouge. A red-rimmed, circular entrance into a different world. Suddenly, I heard the sirens—apparently, a neighbor had called the police—and I came to my senses. I loosened my grip on the woman's neck, but by then she wasn't moving and her eyes were turned up so that all you could see were the whites of her eyes. I was in a daze, staring at the two red thumb-size marks on the pale throat of the woman under me. My crotch felt cold and wet, which made me think I had pissed in my pants, but then I realized it was come. I hadn't ejaculated, but I had been leaking come as I was strangling the woman. Ironically, we had played this sexual game many times. I sat down next to the colorless, motionless body, and, unable to think what else to do, I rubbed the marks on her neck until the police came storming into the apartment.

The woman was taken to a hospital, where she was revived. If the police had arrived any later, she would have been dead. The newspapers carried a small article with the headline, "Unemployed former University of Tokyo student to be prosecuted for assault." Luckily for the University of Tokyo, I had already been expelled that March—although I didn't learn this until later. If I had been a current University of Tokyo student, the press would've had a field day. I was given a relatively light sentence due to my "temporary insanity"—a two-year prison sentence with a three-year suspension.

After that, there were many twists and turns before I landed at the Oriental Economic Research Institute and many more after I left the place as well. Not experiences I choose to remember. The cogs moving my wheel had ground creakily to a stop. When I put my hand on the wheel, in the next moment pieces went flying in all directions. The entire device had broken down, and there was nothing I could do to fix it. Anything can happen in life. It's like to your right there is a hell roaring with flames, and to your left there is a hell roiling with waves waiting to suck you into a bottomless pit, and you are walking cautiously between them along a very narrow white path. I suppose that's just the way it is. I suppose that's life.

I had meant to say, "Who the hell are you people?" but the words got stuck in the back of my throat. I tried again, but the words only came out as a whisper. "Who the hell are you people?"

"What do you mean by 'you people'?" Her voice was much stronger and clearer than mine.

"Koyama, that old man, he isn't the real Masamichi Koyama, is he?"

"I don't know. And I don't care. I just do as I'm told."

"Told by Sugimoto?"

Tomoe didn't answer that. She leaned forward, dropping the

blanket that she had wrapped herself in. I removed my hands from Tomoe's neck, and found me—not her—collapsing to the floor. The tables were turning. Tomoe climbed on top of me and put her hands around my neck. All the fatigue that had been building since my hospitalization was now weighing down on me.

"Like this?" Tomoe whispered, leaning her face into mine.

*That's right, just like that.* The woman would mount me and slowly, very slowly twist the towel tied around my neck. I had never told anybody, but the truth is, when we were in bed it was always the woman whose hands were around my neck, not the other way around. She would choke me, then loosen her grip, choke me again, and repeat it many times, playing with my body like a toy. "You're getting really hard …" she would moan, pressing herself down on me, and I would somehow manage to press back, rock hard the entire time, until I finally ejaculated like a geyser. The day after those intense sessions I would have such a terrible headache that I wouldn't be able to get out of bed.

I couldn't hold anything against her for playing the same dangerous sex games with her ex-boyfriend before we were together, but what pushed me over the line was the thought that she was now doing it with him and comparing him with me and deciding that he was better than me, that I hadn't been good enough. That thought stuck to my brain like tar, and I couldn't peel it off. But Tomoe didn't know this. There was no way she could. But if there was no way she could, why was this unfathomable creature sitting on me and whispering *like this?*

"Like this?" Tomoe repeated, tightening the grip around my neck, as my heart beat faster, sending blood rushing to my head until it began to burn like it was going to explode. A burning red darkness spread out behind my tightly shut eyes. When Tomoe loosened her grip, blood drained from my head, leaving the back of my head feeling cold, and the hard, fast throbbing in my head settled down in the heart. Taking a deep breath, I opened my eyes—and was met with Tomoe's, right up close to mine. I saw in them not the blank eyes of an insect or plastic doll, but the eyes of a woman glowing with desire and excitement. I could see the glow grow intense, and in the next moment her hands, thin but as tough and supple as a whip, once again began to choke me. I couldn't breathe. A crimson darkness whirled through my head again, the darkness growing deeper and hotter. As it reached the point where I was certain that this time my head was going to burst, she loosened the grip around my neck again. "Like this?" *That's right, like this.* The thought flashed through my mind, but it remained just that, a thought, in my mind, which I was unable to voice, and then I didn't know where I was. Could I be back in bed with that woman in her apartment in Akebonobashi? Because I was feeling that same excitement—when I thought the world was full of unknown pleasures waiting to be discovered, and I started to think about school and did I have enough credits to move on to the next year and decided I would speak to the Student Affairs Department, but then found myself lost in the flesh of this woman and forgot entirely about school. *Like this?* The sound of Tomoe's faint laughter reached my ears, and I smelled her sweet breath float by. It was, I realized, the first time I had heard Tomoe laugh.

I was floating. I wasn't looking out through glass walls. I am in the inner garden, that strange, inorganic space, and I am floating above the fountain with the moonlight reflected in its rippling waters. I am floating face-up, the tip of the twisted top of the sculpture grazing my center of gravity, which I imagine to be between my back and hip, as if my body is balanced at this point on the sculpture. I am naked, exposing everything about myself in the moonlight. I am so tired. So very, very tired. Is it Sugimoto saying these words? Or is it me?

*I paint a single horizontal stroke on a white sheet of paper ...* It's Koyama, who always butts in whenever he pleases ... *Not bad, wouldn't you say? You can consider that my calligraphy as well. Tomoe's pale horizontal body floats in the darkness of the night ... On the other hand, I also paint a single black line on a white sheet of paper... The white and black are reversed, but the two are in truth two sides of the same thing* ... He's talking nonsense again. It's not Tomoe floating in the air. It's me.

*It is a grand receptacle. One that catches and embraces everything—*

*beauty, evil, purity, impurity ... But it isn't enough. That single horizontal stroke isn't enough. It is a receptacle that catches falling things, takes them in, purifies them, and ultimately saves them. It is a device that relieves sinking things of their own weight, allowing them to float back up to the surface. It is a sign that can represent anything and everything. But, in the end, to represent everything is the same as to represent nothing. Everything is the equivalent of nothing.*

*So what should one do? One needs to find something to cross that single horizontal stroke—a curved line to supplement the straight line. In other words, the sign has to couple with another sign. It has to copulate, to fertilize.*

The two of us are now floating. It is the New Year, the first dawn of the year approaching, light slowly edging into the night sky. We are naked, and I hold Tomoe's pale body firmly from under her, as we float through the thick darkness of the star-scattered night, and I feel a rush of happiness together with the firm conviction that we, the two of us, are going to melt into the sparkling star clouds. So that's what it is, this thick, hot, star cloud—

It is my semen. It is this dense mass of life that I have spouted. *Mr. Otsuki, it may still be something that only you can do. You do want Tomoe, don't you?* What I fear is that it was not Tomoe's laughter at all that I heard; it may have been the evil shudder that Koyama made as he laughed.

# 22

## I Wash My Hands

"DAMN BASTARD."

I swear I heard Tomoe say that before she walked away. Or at least I think I heard her. But then, it could have been a dream.

I'd been dragged slowly out of a heavy sleep by a phone ringing. For a moment, I didn't know where I was. But I felt like I really had to take this call, so I dragged my numb body and aching head into the freezing hallway and rummaged through the junk on the floor until I found the phone hidden under a pile of yellowed papers. I picked up the receiver, but it slipped from my hands and fell to the floor with a single, sharp ring that made me worry the line had gone dead. I quickly picked it up and said hello into the receiver, but my voice was so hoarse it was inaudible. I cleared my throat and this time managed a feeble hello. But there was no reply. My next hello was much clearer, but whoever was on other end remained silent. So I stayed silent, too. It had taken everything I had in me just to get to the phone and say those hellos. There was a hammering going on inside my skull, a hammering to the rhythm of my heart, draining away any will I could muster to speak.

Finally came the calm voice of an elderly lady: "Tomoe is there with you, is she not?"

"No, she isn't," I said brusquely. The pressing need to answer the phone had vanished, and now I didn't care about anything.

"Oh."

"Who is this?"

"I'm … from the Koyama household."

Ah, it was the woman in the kimono. Masayo. Who, according to Tsutami, was Masamichi Koyama's wife and Takero's lover. Who may have had a hand in Masamichi's death.

"Is this Masayo?" I asked, mentioned her name casually with the intention of irritating her.

"Where is Tomoe?" she responded flatly.

Where *is* Tomoe anyway? All I knew was that she wasn't in the room I'd fallen asleep in, and although it was possible that she was somewhere in the house, I was pretty certain that she wasn't here.

"She's not here. She was here last night. But she isn't here anymore. Choked." I found myself saying.

"You choked her?"

"No, she choked me."

"Really." Masayo sighed, but did not lose her composure.

I couldn't be sure if I was hearing what I expected to hear, but I got the feeling she was scoffing at me. I was sure her Noh mask-like face would never break character, but in her next sentence, her speech was far less formal:

"So, you sleep with that?"

I was taken aback but quickly mustered a reply. "How could I? She was strangling me!"

"Is that so?" she replied, her tone once again polite. "And after you took her all the way there."

"Why would I want to sleep with *that* anyway?"

"I got the impression you were infatuated with her."

"Infatuated? Come on. I felt sorry for her."

"She's not the type of girl you should be feeling sorry for, don't you think?"

"Besides, she made me bring her here. Where are you all anyway? Where are you calling from?"

No reply.

"And where is Koyama? That big house is empty. What's going on?"

"I see. I guess things didn't go according to plan."

"What do you mean by that?"

"Tomoe."

"What didn't go according to plan with Tomoe? And how can you call her Tomoe? That's not her name."

"She's Tomoe as well."

"*As well?*"

"She is Tomoe as well. I suppose you could say that she is *the* Tomoe. You could say that she is the *real* Tomoe," she declared over the sound of traffic in the background.

"Are you telling me that there are fake Tomoe?"

"No, there's only one. She is Tomoe."

"She told me she was pretending to be Tomoe. She told me she was pretending to be Koyama's granddaughter. She was doing as she was told."

"Koyama doesn't have grandchildren," said Masayo patronizingly.

"Yes, I know that … All right, let's talk about Koyama. That old bastard, is he the older brother or younger brother?"

"Who told you about that?"

"That's not important. Is he the older brother or the younger brother?"

There was a pause. She must have brought the receiver closer to her mouth because her voice was now much clearer: "What difference does it make? They're both worthless scum."

"But I want to know which worthless piece of scum he is. The renowned calligrapher piece of scum or the lazy failure piece of scum?"

"What do you think?"

"How should I know?"

"Listen to me. There is only one Tomoe. And it's been inverted."

"What?"

"An inverted *tomoe*. A *sakasatomoe*."

"What the hell is that?"

"A *tomoe* …You know what a *mitsudomoe* is, don't you? A symbol made from three joined *tomoe*."

"*Mitsudomoe* … ?"

"That's the real *tomoe*. The one and only. But it's been inverted."

I was at a complete loss. "Explain what you mean, please."

"An inverted *tomoe*. A *sakasatomoe*. It's all so funny."

Then, unbelievably, Masayo laughed out loud, as if what she'd said was really funny. It was a little spooky. I didn't say a word.

"The *sakasatomoe* starts spinning. In the middle of Tokyo. The whole thing sounds crazy, I know …"

"I don't know what you're talking about."

"Tomoe," she said once again, although this time her voice took on a fiery tone that was new, as if the Noh mask had been torn off.

"It's *tomoe*. Everything begins with *tomoe*, and everything ends with *tomoe*. Don't you understand? Well, I'm not going to have anything more to do with it. I'm frightened. I've been telling him to stop, but Koyama gets carried away. That piece of scum. Always so self-important."

"What did he get carried away with? And where is he now?"

"He kept raving on and on that he was going to make a *tomoe*. That he was going to make it spin. Then that woman appeared and egged him on."

"You mean Tomoe?"

"No, don't be stupid. I mean your precious, precious woman."

"You mean Hiroko? What did she try to make him do?"

"You are so naïve. You did exactly what we wanted you to do. Walked straight into our trap without a clue. I told them to leave you alone. But Hiroko is cruel. Compared to her, I'm like an innocent young girl."

"Masayo? Can I meet you? … Just once. Can we talk? I'm having trouble understanding what you're saying."

"You never will. People like you don't understand anything. But as I said, I'm frightened. I'm very frightened."

Then the line went dead.

I checked the entire house to make sure that Tomoe wasn't around, then I sat in a daze for a while, not knowing what to do. So it was New Year's Day. Well, Happy New Year! Best wishes! How nice and full of good cheer it all was as I sat with my aching head in my hands. What now?

From the moment I'd stepped foot into Koyama's house, everything I did was wrong, almost like I made the conscious decision to screw up. Each time, I was faced with the decision of whether to keep going or to back off. I chose to keep going, and every decision I made backfired on me. But what could I have done differently? Leaving the office job at the pharmaceutical company in Hachioji—I guess I had no regrets about that. Despite the benefits of health insurance and a monthly paycheck, my gut couldn't take it. There really was no other option, period.

The real question is, why did I call Koyama's house once I made that decision? There were other options. So what if Hiroko left me— it shouldn't have been difficult to find other women. I'd developed a certain finesse in that department. Was the reason I made the call because of Tomoe? Had the memory of filming her floating in the water tank been too irresistibly sweet?

Or could it be simply that I was bored? That everything started from boredom. That after all the horrors I'd been subjected to, beginning with Takabatake beating me up, I'd still been left bored. But who knew enough to tap this ghastly boredom of mine? Who coolly observed my ecstasy through slightly open eyes as we devoured each other? Who looked at me with contempt and pity as she got into the cab and dispatched me to Tomoe? And when I called Koyama's place, seeking a lifeline, who, like a ghost, answered the phone? It was *my precious, precious woman.*

Who, according to Masayo, had egged Koyama on ... but to do what? She'd arrived, ledger in hand, at Koyama's house, where she played hostess to important guests, where she'd put on that shameless sexual display with Takabatake.

But hold on a minute. Wasn't I doing it again? Believing exactly what I'd been told like a naïve lamb? Masayo said Hiroko was cruel, but that was one woman's opinion. Why did Masayo call in the first place? How did she know Tomoe was here? Did Tomoe tip off Masayo or Koyama? I was pretty predictable, after all. Tsutami threatens me, so being the gullible guy I am, I go straight to Koyama's place. Maybe they were waiting for me to return to the mansion but got fed up waiting. Maybe they dispatched Tsutami to scare me back into action. Either way, unsuspecting, I show up at the mansion, I find Tomoe hiding there, I allow her to pull me in deeper, so easily. The mousetrap was baited with a piece of delicious cheese. How could I resist the young girl with lonely, teary eyes that made me feel she'd follow me wherever I went? She was a small, helpless animal, a tiny little mouse, but all along I was the mouse. She was the cat, licking her lips, waiting, biding her time, before leaping on my neck and dragging me off to her lair with a smirk on her face.

I say, Let's go to my house, it's safe. Gently but firmly, she says,

No, let's go to Takabatake's place instead; nobody's lived there for a while. She doesn't say more. Once the feline has gotten me here, she goes out and fills in Masayo, Koyama, or whomever before coming back to spend the rest of the evening toying around with her prey. *Like this? Just like this?* Her teeth are into her prey, her claws sunk in. She knocks it around, letting it bleed, pretends to drop her guard to give her prey hope, lets it escape a little, then slams her paw down and pulls the prey back, plunging it into the depths of desperation. I'm bruised and bleeding, I'm curled up in a ball trying to bear the pain. Masayo calls to check if the plan has played out. *Plan?* Plan for what?

No way was I going to let Masayo put more things in my mind. For all I knew, the entire phone call was scripted. How could she call Hiroko cruel? Hiroko could, like me, be a victim. Maybe her cries only sounded like ecstasy, maybe Takabatake was raping her. But what was she doing now? The last time I saw her, she was lying motionless, as if dead, not responding to pain or pleasure, her voice silent from all the screaming. That raging bull could have snapped her stick-thin body in two. Was *my precious, precious woman* safe? Sugimoto's head sure wasn't.

Thoughts cast into the abyss came flying back at me, before falling away again, going around and around, an endless loop, keeping me in a constant state of confusion. I turned the television on again— nothing but people wishing each other a happy New Year. I turned it off. I was exhausted, but somewhere inside me I could feel a flame of vengeance igniting. Masayo's phone call could have been a pack of lies, but when she said she was frightened, she didn't sound like she was faking it. Something was spooking her. Maybe it was time to attack. But how?

I pulled a thin and moldy blanket from the closet, crawled under it, and tried to sleep. But I couldn't. Fragments from my summer experiences kept whirling out, one by one, from a circle of glistening ruby red lips—a Japanese sword, rolls of yen notes, fishing flies, words *it's fine*, an undershirt, a squashed plastic lunchbox—only to be sucked back into the dark, infinite abyss. Eventually, I slipped into a sleep of disturbing dreams. By the time I awoke, it was late afternoon. My head ached, and I felt like throwing up. I stumbled into the kitchen and gulped down some water. I looked for something to eat. I washed my hands, slowly and thoroughly. Dusk began to fall.

Is this boredom—this heavy weight I feel deep inside me? Over the past thirty-four years I'd been drawn to trouble, as if by some dark power reeking of blood. But could this dark power be really a simple thing compared to the grandiosity of love or hate? Could this power just be boredom? Was that what I'd been trying all my life to stave off? If so, why stop now? Why not go all the way? Time to stop running. Follow the maze wherever it leads. Come out on the other side, even if nothing's there.

# 23
## LADY TOMOE

FOR DAYS, I holed up in a recently renovated five-square meter room on the third floor of a Sanya flophouse I found as the New Year festivities wound down.

At Takabatake's house, the phone rang and kept ringing, in the middle of the night, creeping me out with fear of what they planned to do to me this time. I didn't pick up the phone. I snuck out of the house, and this is where I ended up. I needed time. Time to clear my head and pull myself out of this thick, muddy fatigue, time to regain my footing, time to prepare to attack. At first I wandered aimlessly through the flophouse district, not sure where to go. When I saw the sign for this place, I went in without a second thought. I paid a week's rent in advance and settled down in the room given me, trying to tolerate the weight of my own body, which felt crushing.

I say New Year's festivities, but there was nothing festive about New Year's in Sanya. It was just a time when the streets were more empty than usual. Things closed down for New Year's Day, but on the 2nd and 3rd, construction in Greater Tokyo resumed, and contractors came around to recruit day laborers. But for most of the Sanya guys, who seemed to have no family, the first three days of the year were spent in a flophouse like mine were, staring at a small TV. The place I'd stumbled on was, however, upscale as far as these places go; I had my own room. Most guys shared a room with three or four strangers.

Sometimes I turned my old TV on—reception was lousy—and stared blankly at the images. I was more occupied with the thoughts in my head, although it's hard to describe what they were about. In a word, I guess they were about curves. About what a curve was. For example, the silhouette of the female body had these curves. The gentle line running from the shoulders to the back and along the back to the hips. They were curves. Koyama said that wasn't enough.

He said that Tomoe's body was actually a single, straight line. A sign that was everything and nothing. *One needs to find another stroke to complement that single horizontal line—a curved line to complement the straight line ... the sign has to couple with another sign. To copulate, to fertilize ... And Mr. Otsuki, it may be something that only you can do.* But my attempt to couple with Tomoe had failed miserably.

I was caught in this nonsense because I couldn't break free from the allure of Tomoe's single horizontal line. But when she said point black, "It's all a lie," everything changed. The chains were broken. Or more precisely, what I thought were chains were the chains of my own illusions, and they were gone.

I was freed. But when Tomoe's plastic-doll eyes turned a sinister glow as her fingers closed tighter around my neck, was a whole new chain being wrapped around me? The fake Tomoe, the inverted Tomoe ... What the old woman called *sakasatomoe*. What the hell was *sakasatomoe*?

Women ... women from my past ... Out of the blue, one calls in October. Would I be interested in managing a bar her boss owns? It's a genuine offer, but I have to move to Osaka. I'd just started the job at the pharmaceutical company, so I brush the offer aside. Looking back now, I think: a loss, a missed opportunity to get out of Tokyo and start again. If I'd done that, I wouldn't be in this mess, worrying about crazy signs and curves. I wouldn't have to be here, trying to figure out their *plan*, trying to plan my attack.

By January 5th, activity at the Sanya food stalls and drinking stands had picked up in the evening, but the days are sleepy. I left the flophouse in the late afternoon and trudged through the heavy, cold air, crossed the train tracks, and found myself in front of a small building that had the curious sign "Street Corner Library." With time to kill, I stepped inside, wandered around, and came to a stop in front of a shelf lined with encyclopedias.

None had an entry for *sakasatomoe*, an inverted *tomoe*. I tried a range of dictionaries. No luck. I was flipping through a heavy reference book, when I thought to try *tomoe*. And this is what I found:

**Tomoe.** A pattern with a spherical base connected to a curving tail-like shape. One theory is that this spiral-like shape gradually evolved from the hieroglyphic for a snake. In Japan, the shape is associated with the *tomo* or leather guard that archers wear on their left wrist to absorb impact when shooting an arrow. The design combining three *tomoe* in a circular pattern is called a *mitsudomoe*. A wide range of designs and crests has been created by combining the mitsudomoe with patterns of swords, clouds, and other objects. The *tomoe* design was used not only in China and Korea but also in regions across Central Asia, Scythia, and Greece.

The word "spiral" immediately caught my attention. Tomoe was a curve after all. Not a horizontal line but originally a spiral. So why was there a need for a curve to "complement" something that was already a curve? Or was she was in fact a straight horizontal line, making her a fake Tomoe?

Tomoe's body was in the center of the circle; the three parts of the *mitsudomoe* were fighting over her ... A struggle among Koyama, Takabatake, and me. No, not me, probably Tsutami instead of me, that thin, graying man with his back as straight as a pole. Koyama, Takabatake, Tsutami. Three of them. With one, you have only a lonely dot. With two, you have conflict, but you get a straight line. One straight, horizontal line. Add another, you allow the line to start to move. Pressure is applied from the side, the line bends, the line begins to spiral. *Mitsudomoe.*

Then who was Tomoe, the fake Tomoe? The *sakasatomoe.*

My eyes returned to the book. At the bottom of the same page was this:

**Tomoe Gozen (Lady Gozen).** Date of birth and death unknown. Lived from the late Heian to Early Kamakura periods. Daughter of Nakahara Kaneto, mistress of Kiso Yoshinaka. Appears in *The Tale of the Heike,* in which she was described as follows: "Tomoe was especially beautiful, with pale skin, long hair, and charming features." Tomoe Gozen was known as a brave warrior who fought battles under Yoshinaka but returned to Shinano (present-day Nagano Prefecture) after Yoshinaka's death on the battlefield on New Year's Day, 1184. According to the story of the Genpei Wars, Tomoe was summoned to Kamakura by the first Kamakura Shogun Minamoto no Yoritomo but narrowly escaped execution due to the mercy of Wada Yoshimori. She married Yoshimori and gave him a son Asahina Saburo Yoshihide, who grew up to become a legendary warrior. When both Yoshimori and Yoshihide were killed in battle against the Hojo, Tomoe went to Ishiguro in Ecchu-no-kuni, became a nun, and lived until the age of ninety-one. One of the stories in the Noh Shuramono Warrior Play is "Tomoe."

I moved to a corner of the reading room, and after a quick glance around to be sure I would not be seen, I ripped out the page—which also included entries for Tomoega (*Spirama Retorta*), Tomoe-style copperware, and Tomoeso (St. John's Wort)—and stuck it in my pocket. Then, I placed the volume back on the shelf, strolled out of the building, and walked quickly away.

After a while, I stopped to reread the entry on Tomoe. And that was when, with a jolt, I saw this:

**Tomoega (Spirama Retorta).** Common name of insects of the *Noctuidae* Family, *Spirama* Genus. A relatively large moth with *tomoe*-like spiral patterns on its front wings. Has a wingspan of about 5.5 to 7 centimeters and is distributed throughout the Southeast Asian tropics. The male is generally a plain, dark color, and the female has greenish-brown striations on the upper surface of its forewings and is red on its reverse. There are two species in Japan: the *Osugurotomoe or Spirama Retorta* and *Hagurumatomoe or Spirama Helicina*. Breeds three times a year. The moths born in the summer have large *tomoe*-shaped spiral designs on the upper surface of their wings, which are blackish-brown on the male and reddish-brown on the female, with wavy lines spread across them. The nocturnal larvae look like measuring worms and eat the leaves of silk trees …

*Spirama Retorta. Spirama* as in spiral. Apparently, all moths with spiral designs on their wings are classified as *Spirama*.

Darkness was falling fast. I knew if I rushed back to the flophouse that I would just hole myself up in my dungeon-like room, so instead I took the long way back. I passed by the Minami-Senju shopping arcade and headed toward Namida Bridge. Cars had turned their headlights on. If I kept walking straight, would I come out in Asakusa? Or would I end up at the banks of Sumida River? I veered right, then zigzagged from one side street to another. Was this path I was tracing a curve or a spiral?

Out of the blue, I could hear Koyama's voice in my head:

*… when suddenly a human shadow cut across my path on the right. I quickened my pace, approaching it, but there was nobody there. So I continued on my way, a bit perplexed, when suddenly the shadow cut across my path again. I ran over toward it, but again there was nobody there … After some time, I realized the figure always appeared on my right. Never on the left. And every time I quickened my pace after it, the street curved to the left. Strange.*

It was our first meeting, when Koyama droned on about his experience in a small town in Italy. I didn't know why he was telling me this, but apparently it had stuck with me. *Always appearing on my right. Never on the left.* I thought they were mindless disconnected ramblings, but was there an invisible thread connecting them? Curves, spirals, and turning around.

*Shakti, the female deity, that keeps spiraling downward … to lower levels of existence …*

*We go back. We just make a loop and slip inside a different "now" …*

*I wasn't walking forward to a completely different destination.*
*Neither was I making a circle back to where I started. I had gone*
*around and entered a "now," but a different "now." I'd slipped*
*right into a different me …*

My heart began beating faster. I took one right turn after the other, spiraling toward my right, always keeping an eye on the area before me and to my right. But as I made my way through Taito-ward's narrow streets lined with characterless buildings, I found no mysterious man walking in front of me. In fact, the only other person I saw was a middle-aged woman pedaling toward me with her groceries in her basket and her bike light on.

Once I got back to my room at the flophouse, I locked the door and lay down on the floor without turning on the light. I told myself again that I would find Koyama. I would find him and make him tell me who he was and what was going on. But how was I going to find someone who had managed to evade Tsutami?

The next day, I purchased a small flashlight and a large camping knife from Ame-yokocho in Ueno. I wanted to be able to protect myself if the need arose, but whether or not I actually used the knife, having it would make me feel safe. It came in a leather sheath that you attached to your belt, but since the thing ended up hanging below my jacket, I bought a longish, black windbreaker to wear over it. It had the added benefit of providing warmth.

The second thing I did was to call Tsutami from a payphone at a department store. "This is Kinoshita calling from Sumitomo Securities," I said, using the code Hiroko and I had made up. "May I speak to Mr. Tsutami, please?"

A female voice asked me to wait. Which I did, for so long I was ready to hang up, when Tsutami's booming voice came on. "Where are you? Put Hiroko on the phone," he demanded. "I know she's with you."

That was all I needed to know, that he hadn't found Hiroko. I could have easily hung up at this point but thought: why not try to find out more. So I snorted.

"Where are you? You calling from abroad?"

That was a surprise. "Mr. Tsutami," I said, "I'm looking for Koyama."

"He isn't with you?"

"Nobody's with me. Especially not that bastard."

Tsutami was quiet for a while, then in his booming, emotionless voice went on, "We don't know where he is. Masayo and that girl Tomoe have disappeared, too."

"The whole family, huh?"

"Family?" said Tsutami in an amused tone. "They were no family."

"You know that Tomoe girl? She isn't Koyama's granddaughter?"

"I don't know."

"Do you still want the ledger?"

"Don't try to play cute with me. It's of no use to you—you wouldn't be able to make head nor tail of it anyway."

"Actually, I do know a little about accounting. But if I didn't, somebody else would."

"You're bluffing. You're in way over your head. If you keep this up, you're going to find yourself in the hospital ... if you're lucky—"

"Well then," I said, cutting him off, "I'll talk to you later." From now on, things were going to be done on my terms.

Around midnight, I put on my windbreaker and slipped on the pair of basketball shoes Tomoe had gotten me from Koyama's place. I was just about to step out of the flophouse when the reception window slid open and a woman in her fifties with a large grin and goggle eyes stuck her head out. "You're going out at this time of night?"

I forced myself to be polite, telling her that I was going to meet a friend.

"What time will you be back?"

"I don't know."

"Well, I'll leave the front door unlocked, but I'm turning the light off."

"Okay."

"You never know these days. It isn't as safe as it used to be."

"Okay."

"The end of last year, there was a big fight at the corner. This drunk was waving a knife around …"

    I left her rambling and started off toward Takabatake's place, my armpits already sweaty and the heavy knife in its sheath bumping against my hip.

# 24
## BRIDGE

WHEN I TRIED the window that I had broken the last time, it slid open with ease, and once I was inside, I switched on my flashlight and looked around. Nothing seemed to have been moved. The two teacups from New Year's Eve were still in the kitchen sink, so I assumed no one else had been here. Except that the electricity had been completely shut off.

After going through the house, I slid open the glass doors and stepped out into the garden and made straight for the fountain. I had no idea why Tsutami was so intent on ripping the statue from the fountain in Koyama's garden, but not surprisingly, the statue was gone from this fountain as well.

I looked down at the base the sculpture used to stand on. I had a hunch what the design engraved in it was going to be, and I was right. A *mitsudome*—three *tomoe* coming together like three snakes eating each other alive.

I found myself replaying the dream of myself floating naked, face-up, balanced on the tip of the two-meter tall spiraling sculpture, my arms tightly holding the naked pale body of Tomoe lying face down on top of me. And for some time—less than a minute or more than several, I couldn't be sure—I stood shivering in a daze in the cold night breeze, trying to recapture the feeling of that soft pale flesh.

The sound of paper scuttling behind me brought me back down to earth. Or to put it more accurately, it was the eerie silence that followed the sound of the paper being stopped in its motion, coming up against something where there was nothing before. I turned around. Several meters away were two men dressed from head to toe in black. I glanced around, desperate for an escape, and saw a third man in black, his face obscured by a hood, stepping from the house into the garden and walking toward me. Close behind him was a big black cat, which dashed to keep up with the man and rubbed its head against his leg. It struck me that I hadn't seen the cat in months.

"I knew you'd be back," said Takabatake in his high-pitched, hoarse voice.

I took a moment before replying; I didn't want my voice to tremble. "Well, I just had to see you again," I said, trying to sound calm and confident.

"Is that right? Well, you look like you've recovered nicely."

As he intended, the comment struck a deep chord with me and I was ready to lash out. But I restrained myself.

"Well, let's go then," he said, as if we'd already made plans together.

"Go where?"

Takabatake ignored my question, as he came toward me. I braced myself for contact, but he walked past me, so close that we almost brushed faces. At the fountain, he placed both hands on the *mitsudomoe*, bent down slightly, and dug his feet into the ground. Taking a deep breath, he leaned forward and exerted pressure. For a few seconds nothing happened, but gradually the *tomoe* pattern began to move clockwise—at the same time that a clunking mechanical sound seemed to come from the conservatory ten meters away.

"Idiots. They couldn't figure out the one in this garden either," muttered Takabatake before heading into the conservatory, paying me no attention. The two men in black stepped forward and urged me in the same direction. I glanced at them to see if I could make out their faces, wondering if they had been part of the crew that helped set up the water tank for the filming. I could only guess that one was in his twenties, the other was in his forties. Neither said anything; they were like highly trained dogs, nudging me into the conservatory like herding sheep. For a second, I fingered the handle of my knife but decided I'd have no chance.

Once in the conservatory, I shone my flashlight around. The place was wrecked just like the conservatory in Nezu, with shards of glass, paper, and other kinds of junk strewn across the floor. It had never had as much greenery as the Nezu conservatory, but there had been a few palms, cacti, and other potted plants. Not anymore. Takabatake strode over to the center of the thirty-square-meter room, under the dome, and got down on his knees. Then he hooked his fingertips into a seam in the marble flooring and began to pull, his shoulders and upper arms bulging as he slowly unearthed a panel that was about fifty centimeters square. Apparently, when Takabatake turned the *mitsudome* in the garden, it had unlocked this panel, and that had made the clunking sound. The panel was the cover for a hole, which Takabatake slipped down into. Peering down the hole, I saw Takabatake's hooded head bobbing as he descended a ladder propped at a ninety-degree angle. I shone my flashlight down there to get a better look.

"Switch that thing off," Takabatake said, squinting at me.

But I didn't, and Takabatake didn't bother to tell me again.

From the gestures of the men around me, it seemed it was now my turn to go down into the hole. It was my last chance to make a run for it, but from the look of their stance, my chances weren't that good. Besides, I'd come this far for a reason; running off with my tail between my legs would leave me none the wiser.

The ladder must have been three meters tall. And when I got to the bottom, I found myself in a space such as you'd expect under a manhole. It was like being in a vertical coffin. The space was lit by a single bulb, which revealed condensation everywhere on the concrete walls and on one side a low, narrow, dark tunnel. Following Takabatake, I ducked down and entered the tunnel. The flashlight, which I kept trained on Takabatake's back, came in handy now. If I wasn't careful, I'd bump my head on the ceiling of the tunnel. Before long, we emerged into a chamber with a larger tunnel stretching out in both directions.

"Don't fall in," said Takabatake in a scornful tone.

I wasn't sure what he was talking about, but from the overpowering pungent smell and the dark stream flowing alongside us, I guessed this was the sewer. In fact, the stench was so bad I had to struggle to keep from throwing up. Feeling a bump from my two escorts in black, I shuffled sideways along the wall as Takabatake was doing. A little way ahead, I could make out the silhouette of two boats. Takabatake clambered into one of them and fiddled with the engine. He didn't invite me on board, he expected me to get in, which I did, rocking the boat in the process. I sat at the opposite end, facing Takabatake.

"You better not tip this boat over," said Takabatake. "I don't care if you fall in. Just don't drag me down into the shit with you."

The engine let out a soft purr that grew louder until it was a roar echoing against the tunnel walls. Then one of the men untied a rope and off Takabatake and I went speeding downstream. The canal was so narrow that there was only a tiny gap between the boat and the walls on either side. When I turned back, the two men were in the second boat following us. The tunnel was fitted with intermittent lights, and in this half-darkness, I kept my eyes on the back of Takabatake's hood and felt the occasional icy drip of condensation. When a drop fell onto my neck, I nearly jumped.

We came to a ninety-degree right turn, and I wasn't sure there was space enough to make it. But Takabatake, who seemed to know the drill, slowed down, switched off the engine, pulled out an oar from under his feet, and slowly maneuvered us around the bend by pushing against the walls. Once we were around the corner, he started the engine up again and off we went.

"Where does this go?" I asked, yelling over the sound of the engine and hearing the echo through the tunnel. If it was loud enough for Takabatake to hear, he chose not to respond and his hood didn't move in the slightest. I leaned forward, shining my flashlight in the direction in which we were headed, but all I could see was another right turn in the distance.

As the air grew danker, I began to have difficulty breathing, the stench got worse, and claustrophobia descended on me. I felt like screaming, but then the tunnel came to an end, we turned a gentle curve, and a cool breeze lightened the stench. In front of us, I could make out a bluish light that grew gradually brighter, and soon we emerged in the open—under the night sky.

We were now in a canal that was wider than the sewer, but not much more. It was flanked by three-meter-high concrete banks lined with streetlights, with the backdrop of a night sky lit by the hazy glow of the city. My cheeks stung from the piercing cold. As we passed under a bridge and I saw the headlights of cars driving by, I felt relief to be back in the real world.

Now I could make out Takabatake's profile, which remained expressionless as he steered the boat, staring straight ahead. The canal made a gentle right turn into a river, and even as the waves knocked against the boat, Takabatake continued without hesitation. We passed a well-maintained park lined with the cardboard structures of the homeless to our right and a highway teeming with cars to our left.

"This is the Sumida River, right?" I shouted a little too loudly, as if we were still in the tunnel. No reaction from Takabatake, but I didn't need one. I was sure I was right. We passed under the Kototoi Bridge and the railway bridge of the Tobu Isezaki line, and soon we were approaching the Matsuya department store. I looked back to see the other boat following right behind us, and when I looked forward again, we were approaching the Azuma Bridge, near the Asahi Beer building with its stupid turd-shaped sculpture, followed soon after by the Komagata Bridge. We weren't going particularly fast, but we never once slowed down.

I think next was the Umaya Bridge, and after that the Kuramae Bridge. Or was it the other way around? At any rate, we passed under the two bridges, then the Sobu-line railway bridge, then just before the Ryogoku Bridge, Takabatake turned right into the Kanda River.

Even though it was past midnight, there were a lot of cars crossing the Asakusa Bridge. A little further on, surrounded once again by darkness and quiet, Takabatake slowed down and pulled up on the left bank. Takabatake hopped off and tied the rope to a post. With his chin, he gestured for me to get out. I stood up slowly, careful not to lose my balance, and got out. I switched on my flashlight to look around. Takabatake approached me, snatched it out of my hand, and hurled it into the river. All I could do was watch, stunned, as the flashlight spun in the air, drawing circles of light, before landing in the middle of the river with a modest splash.

At almost exactly the same moment, the second boat arrived and the two men swiftly tied up the boat. I turned toward Takabatake, who was already making his way down an alley that led away from the riverbank, and thought again about escape: I could run along the river for a hundred meters, then climb up the bridge and disappear.

Yes, I could do it. The men might not even chase me. But for reasons I couldn't explain, perhaps having to do with recklessness and regret, I took a deep breath, glared at my guard dogs, and entered the alley that Takabatake had gone into.

Twenty meters later, the alley approached a well-lit street. But before we got close, Takabatake stopped, pulled an object out of his pocket, and started to feel the wall on the right. A door opened. From beneath his dark hood, he nodded at me, then stepped indoors. I guess I was to follow. I lingered at the entrance to a small closet-like space. On the right there was a flight of stairs on which Takabatake's thick legs and muddy shoes could be seen, turned as if waiting for me.

"Don't worry, I'm coming," I shouted.

"Then come!"

"What—no elevator?"

Again, no reply. Takabatake just kept climbing the stairs, his feet beating out a steady tattoo. As I took my first step, the two men entered the space, and there was the clunky sound of the door being locked.

# 25
## The Last Tomoe

I PRACTICALLY HAD to jog up the stairs to keep up with Takabatake. We climbed three, four, five flights of stairs. At the landing of the sixth floor there was a dim lamp, but beyond it I was staring up into a black hole. I stopped for a moment but was immediately jarred back into motion—like a puppet with a sound sensor—by the scraping of metal against metal above and the rising footsteps of the two men below.

The stairs grew steeper and narrower and more cluttered with junk—stacks of magazines, crushed cardboard boxes, office chairs missing their backrests. A flashlight would've come in handy now. At what I mistook to be a landing, I tripped and kept myself from falling only by grabbing on to a stack of paper. After that, I got down on an all fours and crawled up the stairs. I looked up again, this time seeing a white square of light a few meters above me. The trail of junk came to an end, and after another five or six steps, I arrived at a rusty metal door with light leaking through the side. Takabatake's pushing the door open must have been the scraping I'd heard earlier. Turning my body sideways, I slipped through the crack and entered a space that appeared to be at the bottom of a small hole. A ladder stretched straight up, and moisture was running down the walls.

It was another vertical coffin. I placed my hands on the first rung, which was so cold I thought that my skin would stick to it, and started climbing. When I got to the hole, I pulled myself up, finding—with less than total surprise—that I was at the center of a glass conservatory, one exactly the same as at Koyama's in Nezu and Takabatake's in Nihon-zutsumi. The only difference was that it was completely empty. Bright fluorescent lights beamed down on this dusty space. I slowly walked over to the exit and opened the glass door. The moment I stepped outside, a strong river breeze blew in my face and rustled my hair.

I was on the roof of the building. The first thing that caught my eye was the by-now-familiar circular fountain and the metal sculpture rising from the center. Everything was positioned at the same distance and angle from the conservatory as the other two gardens. I half expected my mind to be racing with questions, but instead it was calm and clear.

The fluorescent lights were the conservatory's only illumination, but they lit up the area quite well. Once my eyes got accustomed, I could see that the roof was the size of two tennis courts set end to end and the conservatory and fountain faced each other in the center of that space. I wondered if the sculpture had been brought here from one of the other gardens.

Out of the corner of my eye, I sensed movement. It was Takabatake, who'd been hidden in the shadows, leaning against the iron fence and pointing at me, his fingers in the shape of a gun. He pulled the trigger. Then, removing his hood, he raised his arms over his head, grabbed the top of the fence, and, like a caged gorilla, shook it violently, cackling. The fence's creaking and Takabatake's screeches filled the air before the freezing winter breeze ripped the sound away.

A human shadow appeared slowly from the other side of the fountain. Dressed in a long coat, looking as if he'd aged ten years in the last couple of months, it was Koyama.

"Mr. Otsuki, it's been a while. It looks like you've recovered nicely."

His self-important way of speaking hadn't changed, and it somehow accentuated his new emaciated look. My blood boiled to hear him mouth the same words as Takabatake had earlier, in a way that suggested that neither of them had anything to do with it.

"What? I can't hear you." I said.

Koyama opened his mouth to reply, hesitated, and closed it.

"So what happened to you, Mr. Koyama? Your voice sounds old and hoarse. Is it because of the wind? I can't hear a thing you're saying. You don't look very well."

Koyama dropped his gaze to my feet and shuddered with laughter, which was soon replaced with a hacking cough. He didn't seem to have his walking stick.

"You're in pretty bad shape, old man. You got to get yourself together."

Koyama staggered to the fountain and sat down on the edge.

"I must be stupid. Coming again. I guess I just don't learn," I said, trying at conversation.

Koyama raised his head and, ignoring my sarcasm, spoke in a firm and clear voice: "No, no. I'm really glad you came."

Even with his head held high, Koyama's shoulders were stooped and his back slouched. His dark tweed coat was unbuttoned, and he was wearing just a white shirt underneath. His long gray hair was a mess, as always, and it looked greasy, like it hadn't been washed in a while. He smelled, emitting the unmistakable odor of the homeless.

"Are you sure you mean that?" I said. "I promised myself I'd kill you the next time I laid eyes on you."

"You can kill me if you want. I feel empty inside. And I've done most of the things I wanted to do in this world anyway."

"Is that so? Well, fortunate for you."

"I suppose it is. So I guess I'm going to die right here. That wouldn't be so bad. But whether that guy will let you do the dirty deed is another matter," said Koyama, glancing at Takabatake.

"In fact," he continued, "it's possible he'll push you aside and try to kill me himself. I can't tell what he's thinking anymore. After all I did for him, he doesn't have the least bit of gratitude. After all the beautiful women I arranged for him to sleep with. The man is a monster—he loves the smell of blood, and once he gets a whiff of it he loses control. You wouldn't believe the number of times I've had to clean up after him. I don't know why he's so unhappy or why he holds such deep-seated resentment. It's possible that he hates all people," Koyama said, stressing the last sentence and addressing it directly at Takabatake, who gave not a hint of a response. "He's basically a wild animal. A wild animal with a sharp mind when it comes to causing trouble."

"You're the one who's been using me," Takabatake suddenly said, still facing the fence. "You want me to run through the list of all the things I've done for you?"

"Well, you know, it's a give-and-take relationship," said Koyama.

Ah, that phrase again.

Turning to me, Koyama spoke very deliberately. "If you try to kill me. And that guy smells blood. He'll intervene immediately and wring my neck himself. He wouldn't hesitate for a second."

"And I'd be next?"

"That's hard to say. That would be a matter between the two of you."

"Where's Hiroko?"

"She's somewhere, waiting for me. She should be packed by now. We're planning to take a trip. Actually, it'll be a long trip—out of the country. I don't know when we'll be back."

"If you ever do."

"No, no, we'll definitely be back. I want to die in this country. Although there is, of course, the question of how long this country will *last*. You saw what it was like at that party. That is the kind of people running this place, and they're running it like they own it."

"Shouldn't you be more concerned about how long *you* last? To-night could be your last night in this world."

"Perhaps I should."

"Hiroko would be devastated."

"No, I doubt she would be. Do you know? She really cared about you, Mr. Otsuki. At least until a certain point in time. I say that to protect Hiroko's honor. You're a stupid man to let such a fine woman go. She worried about your welfare. If she hadn't begged Takabatake to stop, you'd be dead."

Maggots wriggling from the eyes of the severed head on the floor … images, so horrific, so vivid, as if they were here …

"Hiroko cried and pleaded with Takabatake to stop. Somehow, she must have moved his heart of stone, because at the last second he showed you an ounce of mercy—enough to leave you alive."

"I should be thanking you."

"If you're going to thank anyone, you should thank Hiroko. That woman probably still cares about you. At least that's what I think. If I die here today, I wonder what she'll do? She might go back to you."

The hostility in me suddenly subsided, and something resembling hope entered in its place. But Koyama could be playing with my mind. I wasn't going to let him.

"I don't want her back. So that's not going to happen."

"Is that right? Well, I suppose that might be for the best. She comes with baggage, if you know what I mean."

"Baggage? You wouldn't be talking about a ledger, would you? Tsutami's ledger?"

Koyama didn't answer.

"What's the big deal about the ledger anyway?"

"Let's just say that many of our guests at that party you were present at would soon find themselves in jail if that ledger were to get into the wrong hands."

"So you're planning to skip the country with it."

"We're thinking of going to Rome. I know a lot of people there. After that, we may go to another European country."

I couldn't tell if he was being serious. Coming from the mouth of this filthy, pathetic old man, talk of a trip to Rome sounded like gibberish. It could be all in his mind.

"You taking him with you?" I said, pointing my chin in Takabatake's direction.

"You must be kidding. I'm sure he has plans of his own. Plans that have nothing to do with me."

Casually, I unzipped my windbreaker, turning to the side so that Koyama wouldn't see me unfastening the leather sheath. Takabatake was occupied, looking down onto the streets below. The two men in black were nowhere in sight. Grasping the handle of the knife, I slowly pulled it out of the sheath.

"Where's Tomoe?" I asked, my hand on the knife under my jacket.

"Tomoe?" Koyama muttered, then suddenly stood up straight, his eyes intense. "Well, let me tell you about Tomoe. After all, that's why I had you brought here. And that was the reason you came all this way, isn't it?

"I had no real reason ... other than to catch up with you," I said. In my heart, I knew he wasn't totally wrong.

"Tomoe is a written *kanji*," Koyama continued. "Her exposed body lying face-up, eyes closed, floating in the air. It's a gentle, horizontal line. That's what I told you, I'm sure you remember."

"Because you're a calligrapher, right? I've had enough of your tedious monologues. Your brother was the calligrapher. And he's been dead for a long time."

"That's not important."

"Why don't you just give it up? I know who you are."

"It sounds like someone's been putting ideas into your head. Was it Tsutami?"

"You've had your fun, *Takero* Koyama. Let's stop this nonsense."

"Listen to me. The Tomoe character made you lose your mind. Or perhaps you didn't exactly lose your mind, but at least the precautionary mechanism inside you malfunctioned, and you were pulled in like a moth to a light trap and sucked into the turbulence. Isn't that what happened? I mean, why else would you be here now? You want to kill me? You could be here for that one reason. But I suspect that what you really want is to know who Tomoe was … *what* Tomoe is … And what your purpose was … There must be desire still stirring inside you. Tell me, did you sleep with that girl?"

I didn't answer.

"It doesn't matter. It's the same whether you slept with her or not. Tomoe's body … it doesn't matter anymore. But you still *want* something. Isn't that right? I know you want it badly. There's a burning inside of you that can't be satisfied by mere sex. But you don't know what it is that you want."

A strong gust of wind flipped up the bottom of Koyama's coat and sent my upper body swaying backwards. Or did I just imagine it?

"I'll tell you what you want. You want to bend that single character and drag it inside the curved line. Levitation. Tomoe's body floating silently in the air. Beautiful but powerless. With that one horizontal line, you can't move time. The curved line has to cross the straight line, and for that you need something to bend it and give it spiral movement. That's what you want."

Koyama took a half step toward me. Or at least I thought he did because he suddenly loomed larger than before. I had to resist the urge to back away.

"How about Tomoe, that girl who … ?"

"That girl? Who cares about *that* girl?"

"Where is she now?"

"I don't know. She's probably back at the nightclub in Koiwa— or was it in Kinshicho?—where Sugimoto found her. That slut has nothing to do with your desire. Do you still not understand? I'm talking about *tomoe*—*tomoe*, the *kanji*."

Koyama stuck out the index finger on his right hand and slowly drew the *kanji* for *tomoe* in the air.

"*Tomoe ... tomoe ...*" the gaunt old man repeated slowly, his expressionless eyes staring deep into mine.

"Observe. This *kanji* for *tomoe*. It in itself is a spiral. A movement. Try writing *tomoe* with a brush. It signifies the movement of the brush starting at the center and moving in a counter-clockwise arc. In other words, it is the movement of the universe. Or put another way, the universe is *tomoe*. Everything in this universe, every existence, exists within *tomoe*. You, me, everyone—we are all born within *tomoe*, and we spend our tiny existence repeating meaningless things here and there, until we die within *tomoe*. We are born at the center of *tomoe*, we experience the short vector of the spiral, then we spiral outward and disappear. That is life. The time in your life is not a rotating circle, nor is it a straight line extending in one direction. It is a spiral. *Tomoe*. We are within a *tomoe*, and at the same time, there is a *tomoe* in each of us. There is a *tomoe* deep within you, and deep within me, and that is why you yourself are a *tomoe* and I am a *tomoe*.

"This in itself is nothing exceptional. It's simply the law of the universe, and all we have to do is live by it, leading a quiet life, trying not to do too much, and trying to keep within our bounds. We need to let the flow of the spiral carry our bodies around and around, and although there may be a few accidents and mistakes along the way and although you may stray at times and experience anxiety and pain as a result, you have to endure and slowly keep spiraling outward. Until the moment when the energy of the spiral runs out and each of our 'selves' ceases to exist... There will be differences between the speed of the movement, the length of the trajectories, and the brightness of the glow. Steep spirals, gentle spirals ... But the differences are tiny. It doesn't matter which you take. You asked whether I was Masamichi Koyama or Takero Koyama. The question is pointless. Who cares which I am? What does it matter?"

Koyama raised two fingers slightly to stop me from interrupting, then he lowered his voice and said, "Listen to me."

It didn't seem that he'd lowered his voice as a means to get me to pay closer attention. It seemed that he was running out of energy. In fact, his voice was becoming very hoarse, and it was getting difficult to understand what he was saying.

"Listen," he continued. "It's fine. It goes to show how little our lives really mean. We have to accept that fact ... graciously, without making a fuss about it ... If we can accept the spiral, if we can give ourselves to it, it will become much easier to endure life, disease, aging, and death. In the end, it makes no difference whether you become successful, whether you are awarded an honor, or whether you spend all your time gambling in a hand-to-mouth existence ... It's like a dream. Before you know it, ten, twenty, thirty years have passed ..." Koyama's voice seemed to be regaining strength.

"But the thing is ... the reason that we are able to accept it, that we resign ourselves to our fate, is because the *kanji* for *tomoe* is basically a good spiral. A good spiral ... Perhaps *good* isn't the right way to put it. It's a *natural* spiral. A spiral in harmony with the order of nature. The way that a *tomoe* spirals to the left is in harmony with the movement of the sun. The momentum of the brush as you draw the *kanji* for *tomoe* makes the spiral keep going around and around to the left. It spirals to the left and eventually it's thrown out toward that other, dark, faraway world that exists outside our own. To do that is to synchronize with the movement of the greater universe. That is when our minds and bodies will go from order to chaos, from consciousness to unconsciousness, and will gradually be freed. The world's entropy will steadily increase. However ... however, I ... I thought *why not go against this?* If infinite leftward spirals, from the macrocosmos to the microcosmos, from the gigantic to the minute, are turning in synchrony, what would happen if I threw one other spiral into the world—a spiral turning in the opposite direction? What if I reversed the rotation of *tomoe?*"

"*Sakasatomoe,*" I said.

"Well, well. You surprise me time and time again. So you *are* familiar with that word. Who told you about it? Hiroko? Masayo? Ah, I imagine it was Masayo. What else did she tell you?"

"A lot of things."

"A lot of things ... I somehow doubt that ... Anyway, I don't care. I thought that woman was tougher. Wouldn't have expected her to break like that ... But it doesn't matter. I'm sure you couldn't understand any of it anyway."

I didn't say anything.

"But I imagine that things are finally getting a little clearer now, aren't they, Mr. Otsuki? Yes, *sakasatomoe*, you could call it that. A *tomoe* that keeps spiraling to the right. Normally, no such thing should exist. A circle that puts a crack in the order of this world and reverses time. A fake *tomoe*. If the *tomoe* spiral is the protector of good and stability in this world, the *sakasatomoe* is the bearer of evil and misfortune. It completely defies providence. It is contradiction itself. The embodiment of impossibility. A monster. How can you draw the character for tomoe by tracing a rightward spiral? It is a spiral that defies the laws of nature. It is a spiral that must not exist."

Staring up at the starless sky, Koyama, raising his voice, concluded, "And very soon, it will be complete."

KOYAMA PAUSED, then repeated *very soon* in a quiet voice that made him seem drained. He took a breath and seemed about to continue but instead let out a long wheeze, dropped his head and shoulders, and let a string of saliva dangle from his lower lip. Then he clutched his left shoulder and slowly crouched.

Distracted by Koyama, I did not immediately notice Takabatake's approach. When I turned, he was mere steps away, and the moment our eyes met, he charged. I tried to leap out of his way, but I was slow, my reflexes freezing momentarily at the sight of an ugly gash that stretched from his temple to his chin. He got his arms around my middle and sent me crashing down onto my back along the side of the fountain. I thought he was going to come crashing down with me, but he kept his balance. I got back to my feet and braced myself for his next attack. Takabatake widened his stance and bent forward slightly, but instead of charging, he remained still, like a dark obelisk. My side was in pain.

"What happened to your face?" I said.

The mass of rock shook back to life, furious. I crouched, preparing to drive my shoulder and upper arm into his face when he came into range, but instead he adjusted the angle of his charge—tilting his head, his arms going for my waist, which sent me smashing into the fence. It bowed under the weight of my body, and I worried it might fall apart and I'd end up flying in the open air. Quickly, Takabatake closed in on me, drilling punch after punch into my chest and stomach until, unable to breathe, I let go of the fence and began flailing punches at his head. A couple of my punches made contact, but compared to his, mine must have felt like a child's. Trying to stop his blows, I threw my arms around his back with the aim of pushing him into the fence. But it was like moving a tree with its roots deep in the ground. Letting out a snicker, he grabbed my throat with one hand and pummeled me with the other.

Frantically, I kicked at his shins until his grip around my throat eased. But as soon as his grip eased, he threw me down onto my back again. I got back into a sitting position, winded, without strength, trying to catch my breath. I could see that Takabatake, towering over me, wasn't going to let up. I stuck my hand under my jacket, grabbed hold of the knife, and removed it from its sheath. Then I waited.

"Get up," he said. "Let's have some more fun."

I leapt up, whipped out my knife, and tried to slash him. Takabatake was quick to dodge the knife, and I succeeded only in nicking his anorak.

"I see you've brought a toy with you," he said.

It was the first time in my life I'd ever tried to hurt anyone with a knife, and I'd missed, but I might also have missed my sole opportunity to get him. I should have waited until he was closer. And I should have lunged at him and stabbed him, rather than trying to slash him. Too late now. I swung the knife again, again without success, and Takabatake seemed to be almost playing with me, feinting this way and that. Finally, in one swift movement, he grabbed my wrist, twisted my arm up behind my back, and removed the knife from my grasp with ease. Then he pressed the blade against my cheek.

"What was that you said about my face?" he said quietly. "How about I give you a face that'll make everyone look away?"

A sharp pain was followed by a warm trickle of blood that ran down onto my lips and chin. Takabatake's stinking breath was right in my face, and then he stuck out his thick tongue and licked the blood up from my cheek.

"You little bastard. Keeping your toy a secret. But I don't need toys like this," he said, tossing the knife behind his head, sending it jangling to the ground. This was what this man did—snatched things from you and tossed them away. Still pinning my arm to my back, he dragged me back to the frayed, rusty fence and forced my head down, scraping my face like he was grating cheese. I screamed and tried to push him away, but there was nothing I could do.

"You like that?" said Takabatake, pleased with himself. "I think I'll just finish by smashing your face, burning off your fingerprints, and feeding you to the fish."

He shoved my face back into the rusty fence as I struggled to get his leathery hands off me. His fingers dug into me like the talons of a hawk. I began to panic, terrified of losing an eye. I grappled with him for twenty or thirty seconds, or maybe it was just a few seconds—I couldn't tell—until suddenly, Takabatake's grip weakened and he let go. I crumbled to the floor in a heap, my face in my hands.

Takabatake was lying on the ground in front of me, squirming like a caterpillar with a pin through its middle. Thick, black liquid was pumping out of his side, from which something resembling a stick protruded.

I wiped away the blood that was trickling into my eyes and tried to focus. I caught sight of a man with a rounded back staggering toward the conservatory, his gray hair blowing wildly in the wind. Koyama. I looked back at Takabatake. That stick-like object sticking out of his side wasn't a stick. It was my knife.

I crawled over to where he lay and cautiously peered into his face. It was too dark for me to see his expression; all I could hear was his heavy breathing. A painful, animal panting accompanied by an agonizing groan—a complete contrast from his sexual grunts. I grabbed hold of the handle of the knife and twisted it, causing Takabatake to let out a loud moan. I was pathetic, not having been able to do the deed with my knife myself. I sat slumped, legs crossed, hanging my head.

Once I'd gotten my breath back, I got up. I was about to start in Koyama's direction, when my ankle was yanked from behind and I fell flat on my face. I turned toward Takabatake, whose eyes were illuminated by the light of the conservatory. They were a combination of absolute fury and desperation, striking fear deep in my heart. Trembling, I tried to break free, but Takabatake's grip on my ankle was iron. If I tried to drag myself away, I was dragging him along. I kicked him, over and over again. Still, he wouldn't let go. I kicked his arm, I stomped on his wrist; finally his grip loosened enough for me to pull my leg away, although my shoe came off in his hand.

Takabatake lay completely still, one arm stretched forward, his face flat to the ground. I backed away, watching the pool of blood spread around him until I was a good twenty meters away. Only then did I feel it was safe to turn my back to him.

I could see old man Koyama inside the conservatory, with the two men in black helping him down the hole in the floor. I wasn't about to let him get away, but before I got near the glass door, a wave of dizziness overtook me. I crouched down, closed my eyes, tried to fight the nausea. When I opened my eyes again, they were gone and the conservatory was empty. Or was it? I squinted, and in the blur thought I saw a woman peeking out at me. In the next second the lights went off, immersing me in darkness. It had only been a glimpse. Was it Hiroko? Or was she an illusion?

I was wearing only one shoe, but it was too creepy to go back for the other. I tried the door to the conservatory, but couldn't get it to budge. I thought about breaking the glass, but was it possible to break glass so thick? They probably locked the hatch, too. To unlock the entrance to the sewers, Takabatake had done something fancy with the fountain in Nihon-zutsumi. What exactly had he done? What had he turned? And in which direction? I tried to calm down. Calm down and think. Think of another way out of here.

Taking a few steps back from the conservatory, I surveyed the roof. There, where I'd been scuffling with Takabatake, was a break in the fence. To my surprise, I discovered a narrow emergency ladder that led down the exterior of the building. I paused, walked to Takabatake's motionless body, and grabbed my other shoe. I wondered if he was still alive. Not that it mattered. Even if he was, he wouldn't be for long with all that blood leaking out. Takabatake wasn't my problem.

I slipped the shoe on, tied the laces, and, trying not to look down at the tiny cars parked on the street below, slowly climbed down the unsteady ladder. To my disappointment, it terminated at the landing for the top floor, and the metal door there was locked. At least there was a window near the edge of the landing. I took off my leather jacket, wrapped it around my fist a couple of times, then leaned out as far as I could and slammed my fist into the glass once, twice, three times. Nothing happened. My choices were limited, so I gave it another try, throwing as much weight as I could behind it. This did the trick. A crack snaked across the pane of glass. I punched the window again and again. Shards of glass went flying into the building, until the hole was big enough to get through. I cleared the edges of the frame, hoping no one had seen me from below and called the police, then pulled myself up and in.

Except for a hazy glow, the place was dark. Once my eyes adjusted, I found myself in a big empty room, full of dust and mold. Perhaps it had been an office at one time. I fumbled my way around, the floorboards creaking, linoleum crumbling. You had to wonder if the building was scheduled for demolition. The source of the glow, I discovered, was a sign for an exit at the end of a hallway. An emergency exit. Exactly what I needed.

Under the sign, which had this low buzz, was a metal door without a knob or a handle. But in the dim light of the sign, I realized I was standing in front of an elevator door. I pressed the DOWN button, not expecting anything. Immediately, the machinery kicked in! The elevator chugged its way slowly upward, taking forever. But it got to where I was standing, and when the doors opened, a bright light streamed out. I couldn't believe it.

The elevator even made its way back down without a hitch. On the first floor, the doors opened up into a narrow hall, and even after the elevator doors closed, I could just about make out my surroundings under the light that filtered in from the small, fogged windows near the ceiling. The main entrance had its shutters down, but nothing I did—including almost ripping my fingernails off in the process—could get them to budge.

Stuck again. How was I going to get out? There was a staircase next to the elevator that went to the second floor, but the last thing I wanted to do was to go up after using so much effort to come down. Then I remembered a button in the elevator for the basement level, so back into the elevator and down I went.

The elevator doors opened into a dimly lit hallway. No windows or doors that I could see. I followed the path of the hallway, which eventually made a ninety-degree turn to the right, taking me beneath a wide horizontal window that was slightly open, hinged so that the window could be pushed outward. So yet again I pulled myself up, feeling that this sort of thing was becoming an unfortunate habit, leaned my body into the rusty frame, pushed my head, then shoulders, then my arms, through the gap. Finally, I tumbled out into a patch of mud.

Breathing more easily, I surveyed my surroundings. I was in a narrow space between a wall and a one-and-a-half-meter fence. Without a pause, I climbed over the fence and onto the street.

I had no idea where I was until I heard the sound of lapping water, then I knew I was on a street just parallel to the riverbank where Takabatake had moored the boat. At the river, I could just about make out the shape of a boat speeding off in the opposite direction from where we'd come. I wasn't sure if there were two, three, or four people in it, but I was sure that the man with hair fluttering in the wind was Koyama.

The other boat was still moored, the key still in the ignition. I wondered if it had been left there by accident or on purpose, but I didn't have time to ponder. I got into the boat, turned the key, and off I went. Suddenly, I was seized with regret: why didn't I pull my knife out of Takabatake and bring it with me? It was covered with my bloody fingerprints.

# 27
## The Chase

ALTHOUGH IT WAS the middle of the night, the sky glowed, like an ee-rie background painted onto a dream to foreshadow the end to come.

I stared at the sky in awe and got the strange sense that this re-ally was a dream. The wound on my cheek stung, my chest and gut ached where Takabatake had whacked me, and waves of gut-wrenching nausea ebbed and flowed. These sensations were painfully real, but I felt oddly disconnected from them, as if by a thin layer of film. But it wasn't like any random thin layer of film; it was more on the order of my consciousness having been sucked up into the glowing sky, and I was looking down on the world below, gazing indifferently on some other self, speeding along the river in pursuit of a boat.

I passed under a bridge, the echo of the roar of the engine deafen-ing. Emerging on the other side of the bridge, I could hear Koyama's boat, but nothing else. No voices, no laughter, nothing. There were no cars in sight, no people in sight. There was nothing besides the sinister, crimson sky.

The surface of the river was dark and calm, so even as Koyama's boat sped ahead, I could always see traces of its wake. We approached another bridge, a highway crossing the Kanda River before snaking off into the distance. I expected Koyama's boat to go straight under it, but instead it slowed down and made a wide right arc of a turn be-fore the bridge. Wanting to maintain a distance, I slowed down too, watching as Koyama's boat turned into a tributary, which you could easily miss if you weren't looking for it. I followed but miscalculated, going too fast, barely managing to keep from crashing into the bank by reversing the engine. Unfortunately, that caused the engine to stall. By the time I got it going again, I was far behind Koyama's boat but close enough to see it make another right turn.

It'd apparently gone into a tunnel so tiny I doubted my boat would fit. But if Koyama's boat fit, then surely mine would. I slowed the engine almost to a stop and let the foamy current carry me in.

The water was so shallow that the propeller scraped the bottom. No damage, though, it seemed, so once my eyes got used to the dark, I increased my speed.

The tunnel snaked in sharp and gentle turns, so much that I again questioned whether all this was real. Nonetheless, I faithfully followed in the wake of the boat ahead, which glistened under dim fluorescent lights. I could hear the sound of an engine in the distance, although I couldn't now be sure if it was from Koyama's boat or the echo from mine. This opened the door to further doubt: was I following in the wake of Koyama's boat? or was I pushing ripples my own boat had created? The dream quality of the moment returned, bringing on that sense of disembodiment, as if I was standing elsewhere, coolly observing the unfolding of my dream. I was no longer sure where I was.

My "task," Koyama had said early on, required someone who had "some knowledge of Tokyo." A lot of good that knowledge of Tokyo was when I was stuck in a dark underground tunnel. "To the right," he'd said. "It always keeps spiraling to the right."

*My task* … What was it that I had been doing since August? Going back and forth between Nezu and Nihon-zutsumi, drawing a straight line between the two. But that wasn't enough. What did I need to do? The straight line needed a curve. What curve? Tomoe's or Hiroko's smooth, fragrant skin? The gentle line descending along the pale, silky skin of their backs. Those were curves all right. Tomoe's floating body was, however, just a horizontal line. It needed a curve to complement it, to make it whole. What kind of curve could I possibly draw? And then it came to me—something I'd known all along—where we were heading. There was only one place it could be. To the house in Nezu. To the first Tomoe. To the place where I'd first met her. The first Tomoe. I had been moving clockwise in a circle—from Nezu to Nihon-zutsumi, from Nihon-zutsumi to Asakusa, from Asakusa to Nezu. By moving to all these points, the *mitsudomoe* would finally be complete at dusk—at *ōmagatoki*, "the time of evil encounters." Then the three tomoe would combine and begin spinning in the opposite direction. The *sakasatomoe* would be complete.

I continued ahead, careful not to go too fast or knock into the wall when navigating the sharp turns, while I daydreamed about a flask. That small flask hat, which was emitting a dim glow and vibrating quietly, contained everything in this world. I had failed. Failed to get my hands on that beautiful flask. And worse, I failed even in locating it. Had everything been a waste of time and energy? Had everything been for nothing?

While maneuvering the boat through a section of the tunnel, the wake from Koyama's boat, which I'd hoped I was following, got swallowed up by gushing water from a pipe high up near the ceiling of the tunnel. I was at a loss for which direction to follow. I wasn't too concerned, though, because if the canal was winding its way from Asakusa to Nezu, then I was directly beneath Shinobazu Pond, near the temple dedicated to the Benzaiten goddess. I pictured the pond, carp swimming among the lotus, waterfowl frolicking. I may have lost track of the wake, but I was pretty sure that I hadn't missed any turns, so all I had to do was continue forward.

I had no idea how much time passed. Every so often, a fluorescent light would come into view, on the left wall, then the right, then the left, then the right… each light would get closer, then I'd pass it and the light would fade away; I'd be bathed in light, then plunged into darkness. I don't know how many times that pattern of darkness and light repeated, but it had the effect of making me extremely drowsy. When I encountered a different kind of light, the tunnel became a little wider, and I came to a platform that a boat was tied. It had to be Koyama's.

I cut the engine, and after the echoing subsided, my ears, which had gotten accustomed to the confined sounds of the engine, suddenly felt as if the silence was pressing in on them. It took a few seconds to get used to the quiet. I picked up an oar from the bottom of the boat and paddled to the side of the canal. I placed a foot on the narrow ledge and, as I was about to bring my other foot over, the boat moved and I very nearly fell in the water. I regained my balance, even as my body was trembling from the vibrations of the engine.

On land now, the first thing I did was to unzip and take a long, satisfying piss. Wiping my hands on my pants, I looked around. There were three stone steps, leading to what appeared to be an entrance to—or exit from—the tunnel. Whichever, it looked very familiar. Before getting on the boat with Takabatake last night—no, this was the same night—I passed through one exactly like it. But when I went through this one, I knew that I wouldn't be coming out at Takabatake's store in Nihon-zutsumi. I'd be coming out in Koyama's mansion in Nezu. I'd made a complete circle back to where I'd started. Of this, I was certain.

As I proceeded through this passageway, I kept my head down. If this was going to Takabatake's place, it would have terminated at a ladder leading to ground level. But here, I emerged into a fairly large space bathed in white light. Again, there was a terrible stench; it was also freezing cold. By a window sat a huge glass tank—the very same tank that I'd used when making the film for Koyama. It was filled to the brim with a grayish liquid that was fairly clear near the surface, cloudy toward the middle, and sludge-black at the bottom.

I felt completely disoriented. Like time wasn't running as it should. I stepped toward the tank, my body feeling sluggish, as if I were wading through sewage. The glass was dripping with condensation, with an assortment of bright, colorful objects stuck to it, red, yellow, and blue. They were fishing flies! Fishing flies I'd made! I peered into the tank, but the water was too cloudy to see anything. I tapped on the glass a couple of times, not expecting anything to happen, but suddenly there was motion and something floated into view. It was… a head! A human head! It was swollen, bloated, like a balloon, the face contorted, unidentifiable as male or female. But when I noticed the shaved head, I knew it belonged to a male. A male named Sugimoto.

I reflexively wanted to leap back, but my feet were rooted to the spot. I couldn't stop staring into the tank. At the bottom, bobbing around, were body parts—hands, fingers, feet, and parts unrecognizable. There were other heads. One with its eyes closed as if in prayer. Another with its eyes wide open, surprised. One with long hair flowing like seaweed. One with a gold earring dangling from a torn earlobe. One with the flesh around its mouth ripped away, exposing its teeth, cheekbones, and jaw. One that was shriveled like a dried persimmon. And one swollen to the size of a watermelon, slowly turning in the water.

I backed away, and, happening to look down, I discovered that the floor was littered with my gleaming fishing flies, which I squashed underfoot, reminding me of the murder of my beloved morning glories back in August, under the heat of the midsummer sun, to the accompaniment of the song of the cicadas.

I might have been screaming in horror, I couldn't be sure. But I felt very strange. When I looked back into the tank, I could see none of the human flotsam. All had disappeared! Had it all been an illusion? My mind whirled. Frantically, I looked around the room. There was a ladder; I decided to climb it. There was, after all, no alternative. As I climbed, hand over hand, foot over foot, I told myself I was going to go to Osaka to start a new life there. I'd become the manager of a bar or I'd become a waiter—that'd be fine, too. I was going to turn over a new leaf—no more messing around with women, just hard, proper work. Then that old bastard Koyama ruined the picture.

"I hope you enjoy it," he'd said nonchalantly.

I'd had him pegged as nothing more than a cheap imitator of greatness, nothing more than a wannabe show-off. But I'd been too quick to judge. He had, after all, in his own way, dedicated his life to living according to his own sense of time. He was not to be taken lightly. I tried to divert attention from my growing fear by mumbling these things to myself, but I couldn't stop trembling. A cold sweat dribbled down my neck. A new, perhaps ridiculous thought burst into my mind. Could Koyama have seen his younger self in me? No, surely not. Could he have dragged me into this mess for that ridiculous reason?

*The sensei says he has the feeling he's known you for a long time...*

*Just a gutless, jobless bum. Just like Koyama ...*

Koyama's concept of time. It was fine with me. He could continue to do whatever he pleased with his time. But what about my time? What was this strange flow of time I was feeling now? Was it more than sluggishness? And could it be possible for me to be born again? To start a new life?

I kept climbing up through the narrow cavern. My feet slipped a number of times, but each time I managed to hang on and stop myself from falling.

"And very soon *it* will be complete. Very soon." Koyama again.

"And very soon it will be complete. Very soon." Koyama again.

I wasn't sure how far I'd climbed, but it felt like an eternity before I finally reached the top. There was a hook-shaped handle sticking out above my head. I grabbed it and turned it to the right until I heard a click, then I pushed on it, but it wouldn't budge. I repositioned my feet to get a firmer stance, then I pressed the palms of my hands against the ceiling. Slowly, the heavy panel began to rise, but I lost my grip and the panel came crashing down. I stepped a couple of rungs higher on the ladder and tried again, this time putting my head and shoulders into it. Again, the panel rose, bit by bit, until eventually the balance shifted, the panel grew light, and it fell away, flopping over onto the other side. I stood still, catching my breath again. Then I used all my remaining strength to pull myself up and out of the hole.

I was immediately assaulted by a blindingly bright light. When I got out of its glare, I could see that it was coming from a large circular lamp a few meters away. There was a whirring noise. A large piece of white cloth was draped on a wall, with a blurry tinge of colored lights near the top. I knew where I was: I was back in the conservatory in Nezu. Except this time, the place wasn't a mess. There was no hole in the wall, and it was just as neat and elegant as it had been during my first visit in August. The room was filled with the sickly sweet smell of tropical plants, and I could see now that the whirring noise was coming from a sixteen-millimeter projector in perfect condition.

Was I alone? Was somebody hiding behind the projector?

I faced the screen, touching it with one finger. This caused a ripple to spread across the entire piece of cloth. I observed my shadow pointing its finger, which was connected to me, and I observed images coming into focus on the screen, though I was too close to tell what they were. I took a step back. Something was writhing ... an insect, writhing. No, it was a close-up of a hornworm with a blue vein that ran the length of its body. I couldn't stop staring, I'm not sure for how long, until the hornworm began to swell and pulse around its middle. And before I could understand what was going on, the hornworm erupted and out burst some white thing. The camera zoomed in, bringing the thing into sharp focus, and the screen filled with the image of a tiny maggot's head. The mouth was large and ferocious, with sharp teeth that were still chomping on bits of the worm. Then the image on the screen faded into a bright red and yellow mosaic.

Tomoe's closed eyes slowly surfaced through a whirlpool of color, followed by her nose, her cheeks, and her lips as ripples radiated outward—making me realize that I was staring at the surface of water. A single crimson maple leaf sticks above one eye. She opens her eyes, very slowly, so that it feels like years pass between the first flicker of an eyelash and an eye opening completely. Now, with both eyes wide open, the camera focuses closer and closer on her gaze, a close-up, an extreme close-up, until her brown iris fills the entire screen. But her eye sees nothing, focuses on nothing, remaining as empty as the screen behind it.

Then the eye begins to close again, like the eclipse of the moon, until eventually it is shut. She leans back, breathing heavily, letting out near-silent cries of joy. A man holds her from behind—it's not Takabatake, it's me! I drink in the sweet scent of her perspiration, of her breath. I grit my teeth as she squeezes and massages my manhood with the muscles of her sex, and she brushes her long hair away from her face, the ends of it falling as far as the middle of her back. Between her moans of pleasure, she breathes heavily, and she looks as if she might collapse if it weren't for the support of my hand. She's drenched in sweat, from her face to her breasts, to her back, where her jet-black hair lays, pasted to her porcelain skin. Both eyes are closed, her long lashes trembling, and every now and then, I see tears before they trickle down her face. Her eyes slowly open, revealing the compound eyes of an insect—and the next thing I know I'm being grasped from behind.

I struggle with all the strength I can muster, but I can't move. My side where Takabatake beat me throbs with pain, which grows greater until I lose all will to fight back. Then she ... Tomoe ... clutches my body with her razor-like pincers and tears into my head with her teeth. I let out a silent cry, like Tomoe had earlier; now in her insect eyes, there is no expression, nothing. Again, I try to cry out, uncertain if in pain or pleasure. No, it is neither. It is laughter. That's right, I'm laughing. Of course I am. Because that's all I can do. Laugh out loud. Because nothing could ever be funnier than this.

Heavy clouds part in the sky above me, making way for the moonlight—a striking, cold light that penetrates and bursts each cell in my body. Then the light disappears as suddenly as it had appeared and I am immersed again in darkness. The flask. That delicate flask is quivering. Shaking. Dancing. I am laughing as my female praying mantis of a lover tears through my head, while I watch on the other side of the screen with indifference. The self watching me is spinning around and around very, very slowly in the freezing coldness of time eternal. Thin cracks are spreading on the flask, cracks reaching out, connecting, weaving themselves into a spider's web before fracturing into a million tiny pieces. And I continue to spin to the right, spiraling, spiraling, endlessly, endlessly. Further and further from all the world's tomoe. Further and further into darkness.

HISAKI MATSUURA was born in 1954. He is a professor of French literature at the University of Tokyo, with a doctorate from the University of Paris III. He first made his name as a poet before going on to become a prizewinning critic and author. His debut as a novelist came relatively late; his first collection of stories, *The Jest of Things*, was published in 1996.

DAVID JAMES KARASHIMA has a BA in International Relations from Tufts University, and an MA in Writing from Middlesex University in the UK. He has published translations of works by authors such as Hitomi Kanehara, Takeshi Kitano, and Taichi Yamada.

MICHAL AJVAZ, *The Golden Age.*
*The Other City.*

PIERRE ALBERT-BIROT, *Grabinoulor.*

YUZ ALESHKOVSKY, *Kangaroo.*

FELIPE ALFAU, *Chromos.*
*Locos.*

IVAN ÂNGELO, *The Celebration.*
*The Tower of Glass.*

ANTÓNIO LOBO ANTUNES,
*Knowledge of Hell.*
*The Splendor of Portugal.*

ALAIN MRIAS-MISSON, *Theatre of Incest.*

JOHN ASHBERY AND JAMES SCHUYLER,
*A Nest of Ninnies.*

ROBERT ASHLEY, *Perfect Lives.*

GABRIELA AVIGUR-ROTEM,
*Heatwave and Crazy Birds.*

DJUNA BARNES, *Ladies Almanack.*
*Ryder.*

JOHN BARTH, *Letters.*
*Sabbatical.*

DONALD BARTHELME, *The King.*
*Paradise.*

SVETISLAV BASARA, *Chinese Letter.*

MIQUEL BAUÇÀ, *The Siege in the Room.*

RENÉ BELLETTO, *Dying.*

MAREK BIEŃCZYK, *Transparency.*

ANDREI BITOV, *Pushkin House.*

ANDREJ BLATNIK, *You Do Understand.*

LOUIS PAUL BOON, *Chapel Road.*
*My Little War.*
*Summer in Termuren.*

ROGER BOYLAN, *Killoyle.*

IGNÁCIO DE LOYOLA BRANDÃO,
*Anonymous Celebrity.*
*Zero.*

BONNIE BREMSER, *Troia: Mexican*
*Memoirs.*

CHRISTINE BROOKE-ROSE,
*Amalgamemnon.*

BRIGID BROPHY, *In Transit.*

GERALD L. BRUNS,
*Modern Poetry and the Idea of Language.*

GABRIELLE BURTON, *Heartbreak Hotel.*

MICHEL BUTOR, *Degrees,*
*Mobile.*

G. CABRERA INFANTE,
*Infante's Inferno.*
*Three Trapped Tigers.*

JULIETA CAMPMPOS,
*The Fear of Losing Eurydice.*

ANNE CARSON, *Eros the Bittersweet.*

ORLY CASTEL-BLOOM, *Dolly City.*

LOUIS-FERDINAND CÉLINE,
*Castle to Castle.*
*Conversations with Professor Y,*
*London Bridge,*
*Normance,*
*North,*
*Rigadoon.*

MARIE CHAIX,
*The Laurels of Lake Constance.*

HUGO CHARTERIS, *The Tide Is Right.*

ERIC CHEVILLARD, *Demolishing Nisard.*

MARC CHOLODENKO, *Mordechai*
*Schamz.*

JOSHUA COHEN, *Witz.*

EMILY HOLMES COLEMAN,
*The Shutter of Snow.*

ROBERT COOVER, *A Night at the Movies.*

STANLEY CRAWFORD, *Log of the S.S,*
*The Mrs Unguentine,*
*Some Instructions to My Wife.*

RENÉ CREVEL, PUTTING *My Foot in It.*

RALPH CUSACK, *Cadenza.*

NICHOLAS DELBANCO,
*The Count of Concord,*
*Sherbrookes.*

NIGEL DENNIS, *Cards of Identity.*

PETER DIMOCK,
*A Short Rhetoric for Leaving the Family.*

ARIEL DORFMFMAN, *Konfidenz.*

## ⬚ SELECTED DALKEY ARCHIVE TITLES

COLEMAN DOWELL, *Island People,*
*Too Much Flesh and Jabez.*

ARKADII DRAGOMOSHCHENKO,
*Dust.*

RIKKI DUCORNET,
*The Complete Butcher's Tales,*
*The Fountains of Neptune,*
*The Jade Cabinet,*
*Phosphor in Dreamland.*

WILLIAM EASTLAKE, *The Bamboo Bed,*
*Castle Keep,*
*Lyric of the Circle Heart.*

JEAN ECHENOZ, *Chopin's Move.*

STANLEY ELKIN, *A Bad Man,*
*Criers and Kibitzers, Kibitzers and Criers,*
*The Dick Gibson Show,*
*The Franchiser,*
*The Living End,*
*Mrs. Ted Bliss.*

FRANÇOIS EMMMMANUEL,
*Invitation to a Voyage.*

SALVADOR ESPRIU,
*Ariadne in the Grotesque Labyrinth.*

LESLIE A. FIEDLER,
*Love and Death in the American Novel.*

JUAN FILLOY, *Op Oloop.*

ANDY FITCH, *Pop Poetics.*

GUSTAVE FLAUBERT,
*Bouvard and Pécuchet.*

KASS FLEISHER, *Talking out of School.*

FORD MADOX FORD,
*The March of Literature.*

JON FOSSE, *Aliss at the Fire,*
*Melancholy.*

MAX FRISCH, *I'm Not Stiller,*
*Man in the Holocene.*

CARLOS FUENTES, *Christopher Unborn,*
*Distant Relations,*
*Terra Nostra,*
*Where the Air Is Clear.*

TAKEHIKO FUKUNAGA,
*Flowers of Grass.*

WILLIAM GADDIS, *J R, The Recognitions.*

JANICE GALLOWAY, *Foreign Parts,*
*The Trick Is to Keep Breathing.*

WILLIAM H H. GASS,
*Cartesian Sonata and Other Novellas,*
*Finding a Form,*
*A Temple of Texts,*
*The Tunnel,*
*Willie Masters' Lonesome Wife.*

GÉRARD GAVARRY, *Hoppla! 1 2 3.*

ETIENNE GILSON,
*The Arts of the Beautiful, Forms*
*and Substances in the Arts.*

C. S S. GISCOMBE, *Giscome Road,*
*Here.*

DOUGLAS GLOVER,
*Bad News of the Heart.*

WITOLD GOMBROWICZ,
*A Kind of Testament.*

PAULO EMÍLIO SALES GOMES,
*P's Three Women.*

GEORGI GOSPODINOV, *Natural Novel.*

JUAN GOYTISOLO, *Count Julian,*
*Juan the Landless,*
*Makbara,*
*Marks of Identity.*

HENRY GREEN, *Back,*
*Blindness,*
*Concluding,*
*Doting,*
*Nothing.*

JACK GREEN, *Fire the Bastards!*

JIRˇIˊ GRUSˇA, *The Questionnaire.*

MELA HARTWIG,
*Am I a Redundant Human Being?*

JOHN HAWKES, *The Passion Artist,*
*Whistlejacket.*

ELIZABETH HEIGHWAY, ED.,
*Contemporary Georgian Fiction.*

ALEKSANDAR HEMON, ED.,
*Best European Fiction.*

---

**FOR A FULL LIST OF PUBLICATIONS, VISIT:** www.dalkeyarchive.com

**FOR A FULL LIST OF PUBLICATIONS, VISIT:** www.dalkeyarchive.com

ABDELWAHAB MEDDEB, *Talismano.*

GERHARD MEIER, *Isle of the Dead.*

HERMAN MELVILLE, *The Confidence-Man.*

AMANDA MICHALOPOULOU, *I'd Like.*

STEVEN MILLHAUSER,
*The Barnum Museum,*
*In the Penny Arcade.*

RALPH J. MILLS, JR., *Essays on Poetry.*

MOMUS, *The Book of Jokes.*

CHRISTINE MONTALBETTI,
*The Origin of Man,*
*Western.*

OLIVE MOORE, *Spleen.*

NICHOLAS MOSLEY, *Accident,*
*Assassins,*
*Catastrophe Practice,*
*Experience and Religion,*
*A Garden of Trees,*
*Hopeful Monsters,*
*Imago Bird,*
*Impossible Object,*
*Inventing God,*
*Judith,*
*Look at the Dark,*
*Natalie Natalia,*
*Serpent,*
*Time at War.*

WARREN MOTTE, *Fables of the Novel: French*
*Fiction since 1990,*
*Fiction Now: The French Novel in the 21st*
*Century,*
*Oulipo: A Primer of Potential Literature.*

GERALD MURNANE, *Barley Patch,*
*Inland.*

YVES NAVARRE,
*Our Share of Time,*
*Sweet Tooth.*

DOROTHY NELSON, *In Night's City,*
*Tar and Feathers.*

ESHKOL NEVO, *Homesick.*

WILFRIDO D D. NOLLEDO,
*But for the Lovers.*

FLANN O'BRIEN, *At Swim-Two-Birds,*
*The Best of Myles,*
*The Dalkey Archive,*
*The Hard Life,*
*The Poor Mouth,*
*The Third Policeman.*

CLAUDE OLLIER, *The Mise-en-Scène,*
*Wert and the Life Without End.*

GIOVANNI ORELLI, *Walaschek's Dream.*

PATRIK OUŘEDNÍK, *Europeana,*
*The Opportune Moment, 1855.*

BORIS PAHOR, *Necropolis.*

FERNANDO DEL PASO,
*News from the Empire,*
*Palinuro of Mexico.*

ROBERT PINGET, *The Inquisitory,*
*Mahu or The Material,*
*Trio.*

MANUEL PUIG, *Betrayed by Rita Hayworth,*
*The Buenos Aires Affair,*
*Heartbreak Tango.*

RAYMYMOND QUENEAU, *The Last Days,*
*Odile,*
*Pierrot Mon Ami,*
*Saint Glinglin.*

ANN QUIN, *Berg,*
*Passages,*
*Three,*
*Tripticks.*

ISHMAEL REED, *The Free-Lance Pallbearers,*
*The Last Days of Louisiana Red,*
*Ishmael Reed: The Plays,*
*Juice!,*
*Reckless Eyeballing,*
*The Terrible Threes,*
*The Terrible Twos,*
*Yellow Back Radio Broke-Down.*

JASIA REICHARDT,
*15 Journeys Warsaw to London.*

NOËLLE REVAZ,
*With the Animals.*

JOÃO UBALDO RIBEIRO,
*House of the Fortunate Buddhas.*

---

JEAN RICARDOU, *Place Name*s.

RAINER MARIA RILKE,
*The Notebooks of Malte Laurids Brigge.*

JULIÁN RÍOS, *The House of Ulysses,*
*Larva: A Midsummer Night's Babel,*
*Poundemonium,*
*Procession of Shadows.*

AUGUSTO ROA BASTOS, *I the Supreme.*

DANIËL ROBBERECHTS,
*Arriving in Avignon.*

JEAN ROLIN,
*The Explosion of the Radiator Hose.*

OLIVIER ROLIN, *Hotel Crystal.*

ALIX CLEO ROUBAUD, *Alix's Journal.*

JACQUES ROUBAUD,
*The Form of a City Changes Faster, Alas,*
*Than the Human Heart,*
*The Great Fire of London,*
*Hortense in Exile,*
*Hortense Is Abducted,*
*The Loop,*
*Mathematics, The Plurality of Worlds of Lewis,*
*The Princess Hoppy,*
*Some Thing Black.*

RAYMYMOND ROUSSEL,
*Impressions of Africa.*

VEDRANA RUDAN, *Night.*

STIG SÆTERBAKKEN, *Siamese, Self Control.*

LYDIE SALVAYRE, *The Company of Ghosts,*
*The Lecture,*
*The Power of Flies.*

LUIS RAFAEL SÁNCHEZ,
*Macho Camacho's Beat.*

SEVERO SARDUY, *Cobra & Maitreya.*

NATHALIE SARRAUTE,
*Do You Hear Them?,*
*Martereau,*
*The Planetarium.*

ARNO SCHMIDT, *Collected Novellas,*
*Collected Stories,*
*Nobodaddy's Children,*
*Two Novels.*

ASAF SCHURR, *Motti.*

GAIL SCOTT, *My Paris.*

DAMION SEARLS, *What We Were Doing and*
*Where We Were Going.*

JUNE AKERS SEESE,
*Is This What Other Women Feel Too?,*
*What Waiting Really Means.*

BERNARD SHARE, *Inish, Transit.*

VIKTOR SHKLOVSKY, *Bowstring,*
*Knight's Move,*
*A Sentimental Journey: Memoirs 1917–1922,*
*Energy of Delusion: A Book on Plot,*
*Literature and Cinematography,*
*Theory of Prose,*
*Third Factory,*
*Zoo, or Letters Not about Love.*

PIERRE SINIAC, *The Collaborators.*

KJERSTI A. SKOMSVOLD, *T*
*he Faster I Walk, the Smaller I Am.*

JOSEF SˇKVORECKYˊ,
*The Engineer of Human Souls.*

GILBERT SORRENTINO,
*Aberration of Starlight,*
*Blue Pastoral,*
*Crystal Vision,*
*Imaginative Qualities of Actual Things,*
*Mulligan Stew,*
*Pack of Lies,*
*Red the Fiend,*
*The Sky Changes,*
*Something Said,*
*Splendide-Hôtel,*
*Steelwork,*
*Under the Shadow.*

W. M. SPACKMAN, *The Complete Fiction.*

ANDRZEJ STASIUK, *Dukla,*
*Fado.*

GERTRUDE STEIN, *The Making of Americans,*
*A Novel of Thank You.*

LARS SVENDSEN, *A Philosophy of Evil.*

PIOTR SZEWC, *Annihilation.*

GONÇALO M. TAVARES, *Jerusalem,*
*Joseph Walser's Machine,*
*Learning to Pray in the Age of Technique.*

## ⊑ SELECTED DALKEY ARCHIVE TITLES

LUCIAN DAN TEODOROVICI,
*Our Circus Presents . . .*

NIKANOR TERATOLOGEN,
*Assisted Living.*

STEFAN THEMERSON,
*Hobson's Island,*
*The Mystery of the Sardine,*
*Tom Harris.*

TAEKO TOMIOKA, *Building Waves.*

JOHN TOOMEY, *Sleepwalker.*

JEAN-PHILIPPPPE TOUSSAINT,
*The Bathroom,*
*Camera,*
*Monsieur,*
*Reticence,*
*Running Away,*
*Self-Portrait Abroad,*
*Television,*
*The Truth about Marie.*

DUMITRU TSEPENEAG,
*Hotel Europa,*
*The Necessary Marriage,*
*Pigeon Post,*
*Vain Art of the Fugue.*

ESTHER TUSQUETS,
*Stranded.*

DUBRAVKA UGRESIC,
*Lend Me Your Character,*
*Thank You for Not Reading.*

TOR ULVEN, *Replacement.*

MATI UNT,
*Brecht at Night,*
*Diary of a Blood Donor,*
*Things in the Night.*

ÁLVARO URIBE AND OLIVIA SEARS, EDS.,
*Best of Contemporary Mexican Fiction.*

ELOY URROZ, *Friction,*
*The Obstacles.*

LUISA VALENZUELA,
*Dark Desires and the Others,*
*He Who Searches.*

PAUL VERHAEGHEN,
*Omega Minor.*

AGLAJA VETERANYI,
*Why the Child Is Cooking in the Polenta.*

BORIS VIAN, *Heartsnatcher.*

LLORENÇ VILLALONGA, *The Dolls' Room.*

TOOMAS VINT, *An Unending Landscape.*

ORNELA VORPSI,
*The Country Where No One Ever Dies.*

AUSTRYN WAINHOUSE,
*Hedyphagetica.*

CURTIS WHITE,
*America's Magic Mountain,*
*The Idea of Home,*
*Memories of My Father Watching TV,*
*Requiem.*

DIANE WILLIAMS,
*Excitability: Selected Stories, Romancer Erector.*

DOUGLAS WOOLF,
*Wall to Wall,*
*Ya! & John-Juan.*

JAY WRIGHT,
*Polynomials and Pollen,*
*The Presentable Art of Reading Absence.*

PHILIP WYLIE, *Generation of Vipers.*

MARGUERITE YOUNG,
*Angel in the Forest,*
*Miss MacIntosh, My Darling.*

REYOUNG, *Unbabbling.*

VLADO Z ABOT, *The Succubus.*

ZORAN Z IVKOVIC´, *Hidden Camera.*

LOUIS ZUKOFSKY, *Collected Fiction.*

VITOMIL ZUPAN, *Minuet for Guitar.*

SCOTT ZWIREN, *God Head.*

**FOR A FULL LIST OF PUBLICATIONS, VISIT:** www.dalkeyarchive.com